PRAISE FOR THE NOVELS
OF CATHERINE RITCH GUESS

To be in the presence of Catherine Ritch Guess is to be baptized by the fire of creative energy in its purest form. Ideas flow from her brain like water cascading down a mountain; her readers' greatest challenge is taking time to savor one novel before hungrily devouring the next!

====================

Within the pages of *In the Bleak Midwinter*, Catherine Ritch Guess pays a fine tribute to John Wesley's 300th birthday in her heart-warming story of a choral teacher who has lost her zeal and a town in need of CPR . Baby Bobby and his poor but loving parents provide a compelling parallel to the Holy Family, and the peek into the world of NASCAR that this winter fairy tale provides is just plain fun!

====================

Though built on a premise of pain, *In the Garden* weaves a story of love so uplifting that the outcome becomes almost insignificant.

====================

We're not used to seeing characters like Shane Sievers in the pages of inspirational fiction. Catherine Ritch Guess is realistic in her portrayals, honest in her emotions, and unapologetic in her effort to present a story that is at once provocative and enriching. *Love Lifted Me* will stir your heart.

====================

-- Jayne Jaudon Ferrer, Author of *A New Mother's Prayers*, *A Mother of Sons,* and *Dancing with my Daughter*

Electricity fills the air when this woman speaks. The reason? She's knowledgeable, a consummate author, superb musician and inspiring speaker. But the REASON she speaks with power is that she shows the compassion of the Lord to all - every age, color, educational level, skilled and unskilled. She never fails to bring every listener to a higher level. Seize the opportunity to be in the presence of this woman of God.

--Chaplain (Colonel) Larry A. Walker, Ret.

Catherine Ritch Guess's trademark autograph fashions the final "s" of her name into a winsome question mark. There are, however, no questions in the minds of her many readers —and listeners — about the impact her work has made in their lives.

--John Shivers, Freelance writer and editor, Calhoun, GA

The first volume of the "Eagle's Wings" trilogy, *Love Lifted Me* by Catherine Ritch Guess is a deftly written romance between a minister and an unfortunate, downtrodden man, compassionate yet beset with internal and external demons to such a degree that he once attempted suicide while high on cocaine. A captivating story about the potential for redemption and the journey toward spiritual wholeness, Love Lifted Me is a most satisfying and romantic read.

--*Midwest Book Review*, Oregon, WI

Catherine's lightning quick wit and musical talent are astonishing enough, but combined with her never ending source of positive energy the woman is a ball of fire that's sure to inspire.

--Harriet Coffey, Radio Personality, Charlotte, NC

Catherine Guess is one of the most talented individuals I have ever met. Working with her is incredibly rewarding. She is not only brilliantly talented but also possesses a servant's heart, a rare combination indeed. At the heart of Catherine's abilities is her love and commitment to family, to friends and to God. Everything she does is done with a passion for excellence. In a world filled with mediocrity, Catherine is like a window that is thrown open wide, allowing the light of creativity and energy to enter a dark and forsaken room.

--Angel Christ, Christian Recording Artist, Jamestown, NC

OLD RUGGED CROSS

OLD RUGGED CROSS

Catherine Ritch Guess

CRM BOOKS

To

LaVonne Decker
the "real" angel of
OldRugged Cross

and

Sharon Powell
the woman behind
the artist

Books by
Catherine Ritch Guess

LOVE LIFTED ME
HIGHER GROUND
IN THE GARDEN
IN THE BLEAK MIDWINTER

Acknowledgments

To Roger Powell, whose talented hands and sand sculptures inspired this story within the first five minutes after I met him. And to Jerry DeCeglio, whose artistic genius and creative ability turned Roger's work of art into a compelling cover. Thanks, guys, for teaming up with me to create a terrific work of what I call "synartgy!"

To the Honorable Mayor John P. Stozich for making sure that I stayed dry and that every hair stayed in place while I was in Findlay; to Travis Simons and the Hancock Park District, and the entire town of Findlay, Ohio, for welcoming me with open arms and sharing the heritage of their lovely community through stories, love and support

To the following establishments of Findlay, Ohio, whose owners so graciously opened their doors and allowed me to write on their premises: John and Belinda Nesler (and Emmy) of Rose Gate Cottage Bed & Breakfast; all the brothers of Dietsch Brothers Fine Chocolates and Ice Cream; Nancy Wilch, Kay Kose, Vicki Powell and Renee Chaskel of the Swan House Tea Room & Shoppe; and lastly, to Greg Miller of Miller's Luncheonette for allowing his restaurant to become my Findlay hang-out, and to Karen Eier, Kathy Chamberlain and Shelley Crawford, Miller's wonderful waitresses who took such good care of me

To Beth Hendricks of *The Courier* and Marya Morgan of K-LOVE FM for use of their real names and their professional insight and comments

To Larry Whiteleather for his encouragement and the use of his poem *Cross in the Sand,* and for his helpful insight and inspiration on *Let Us Break Bread Together*, the second volume of the Sandman Series

To Pat Brenek, who taught me everything I needed to know about packing sand; Jacob, Joshua and Zach - my "three musketeers"; Norma Hindman, my "Golden Girl"; and Nick Powell, Roger's son, who became my personal photographer and right hand man while I was in Findlay

To Saint Michael the Archangel Parish for providing the perfect inspirational setting for Holy Thursday, and to Father Adam for his patience in answering all my questions

To Jerry, Lance, Mike and Randy of Sandman Trucking Company in Toledo, Ohio, for getting my Sandman Series off to a great start

To Joanne Nesbit and Marion Scher of the University of Michigan for their time, tours, information and personal encouragement for all three volumes of the Sandman Series (*and more novel ideas!*)

To Reverend Mike Whitson and the congregation of First Baptist Church in Indian Trail, NC, for your prayers and visits during my bout with a life-threatening illness. When I was finally able to be out again, I visited your church. That Sunday's final hymn, *There's Room at the Cross for You*, was the message from God that I was well on my way to recovery and back to a world of ministry through writing and composing. I went home and poured out 22 pages of this book on that afternoon. You were truly God's instrument at that point in my life.

And to Danny Funderburke and his parents, Bill and Betty, for bringing me a copy of his latest CD so that I could be surrounded by music during my recuperation and time of writing this book

To each and every one of you, *THANKS!*, and I look forward to working with you on the next two volumes of the Sandman Series.

~ CR? ~

Chapter 1
Early evening, Palm Sunday

"I'm outta here," announced Maggie, grabbing the attention of all the young women in the room.

Her dark, slightly wavy hair that usually hung halfway down her back was pulled up in a ponytail, and sticking out the back opening of a ball cap. The only thing that resembled the way her co-workers were accustomed to seeing her was the huge smile on her face, which was part - the biggest part - of the dress code for her job as an exotic dancer at Northern Exposure. Her scant black outfit, that showed off every curve of her body, had been exchanged for loose-fitting jeans and an oversized dark-blue sweatshirt bearing the name of her alma mater in big maize-colored letters – University of Michigan.

Having called attention to herself both audibly and visually, Maggie continued, "I'm off for a week of sun and sand, and I'm gonna find me a *man!*"

"I heard that," Ebony called out. Her jovial, supportive attitude made her the favorite among the girls. She was a friend to all of them; the first one they talked to when things weren't going as they should, and also the first one they ran to with a new joke. Even though her skin was a different color, she was the one most like a sister to all the employees.

"Yeah, me, too," yelled Sabrina. This was the young woman who looked her role in this place. She knew the business so well that she could have been brought up in it. Rumors had it that her mother was actually the "power" behind the establishment of Northern Exposure, and was a madam for several "houses" in large cities around the country.

"Don't you get enough men with all the ones coming in here all day and night?" came the cynical voice of Kara, the young woman who held the track record for seniority in the club.

"Those guys aren't real men. They're basically sad little teenagers who never grew up, or can't let loose of their mama," Candice, another pessimist, offered.

"You know, most of the guys who come in here have some type of problem. They're lonely, they don't have any friends, they lack self-esteem, and frankly, they don't have anywhere else they can go," defended Valerie, another veteran of the establishment, who held a graduate degree in psychology.

"Yeah, they come in here because we at least have to *act* like we care about them," Sabrina agreed.

"It's really sad," Maggie said, suddenly grieved. "They really *don't* have anywhere to go, do they?"

"Most of the ones that are married act like they never get any attention at home," explained Kara.

"Huh, I wouldn't give 'em any attention, either, if they spent their time gawking at other women. And I'm talking about *paying* for it!" bolted Candice.

The comments had made all the girls take a realistic look at the clientele of their workplace. This was not their typical conversation, and it left most of them feeling an odd pity for the customers rather than their usual apathy.

Sabrina spoke up, bluntly. "Everyone who comes through this door is a sucker with money. And you know what my daddy taught me? It's a sin to let a sucker keep his money."

"What was your daddy, a used car salesman?" Ebony joked.

All the other girls got a big chuckle.

"Well, all I can tell you is that when I go looking for a man, he certainly isn't going to be one of the guys who comes in here. If he'd pay to look at me, he'd pay to go somewhere else and look at other women," reasoned Kara.

"And if they'd pay to look, they'd pay to do something else," Candice added.

Maggie shook her head, wishing she had not opened this can of worms before she left. "I'm gonna leave you girls to settle the problems of this place," she said, throwing on a heavy fur-hooded coat that would protect her in any blizzard or blustering wind on her way from Ann Arbor, Michigan, to the final destination of Fort Lauderdale. "But as for me, I'm going to find a *real* man, one who can take care of me for the rest of my life."

"I heard that," called Ebony, flashing a smile that showed all her teeth while repeating her standard quote.

"You hear everything," laughed Kara, gathering up her things to leave for the day.

"All I can say is that you'd better be careful what you ask for," warned Candice, still unconvinced that her co-worker was making the right decision.

"Here, Maggie, before you leave, we have a little present for you," Valerie announced. "I could make a speech and offer you lots of tidbits of advice, but we all know you've got quite a trip in front of you. And we certainly wouldn't want to rob you of any precious time with that man of yours," she added, handing the soon-to-be vacationer a huge pink bag with lavender tissue

3

paper jutting out all around the sides in perfect triangular shapes.

Maggie took the large gift bag. "Little, huh?" she asked, joking as she pulled out a cotton throw blanket. It was deep blue, with her name embroidered on it in bold maize letters. "Oh, look," she exclaimed. "It's the colors of U-M."

"Yeah, it's kind of a late graduation present, too. We all know how much you loved the university," stated Sabrina. There was a hint of sadness in her voice that she had never been allowed the privilege of a college education.

"We thought you could use it to wrap up in beside that man you find," suggested Kara.

"Whew," gasped Ebony, fanning and pretending to have hot flashes.

"We know. You heard that, too," teased Candice.

"Thanks, girls, I'll put it to good use ... hopefully *very* soon after I get there," replied the recipient of the gift, sincerely touched by the thoughtfulness of her co-workers.

Maggie looked around the room, wishing she'd never have to darken the doors of this "exclusive" strip joint again. It was filled with gorgeous women whose looks should have hinted at the fact that they had no cares in the world. Yet their expressions showed that they all secretly wished they were in her shoes right now and on their way to find their own escape from this place.

"I almost forgot," Sabrina cut in. "Here's a chair that matches the blanket. You don't have to open it, but it's blue and has maize trim. There's a cup holder on one arm, and a place for your book on the other arm. We know how you love to read."

"There's even an umbrella to keep the sun out of your eyes while you're reading," added Candice, for the first time showing a real enthusiasm.

"You don't have to open it now. We know you've got a long trip in front of you," offered Valerie. "Take care of yourself and we'll see you in another week."

"Yeah, when we hear all about that man of yours!" Kara encouraged.

Maggie nodded. "Thanks again, girls. I love you. You've been my family these past four years." She folded the blanket and carefully placed it back in the bag, put the canvas carrier containing the chair under her arm and headed toward the door.

Ebony followed her to the door and grabbed her arm. "I fixed you a basket of snacks to hold you while you're driving," she said, giving Maggie a hug. "You be careful and take care of yourself. You know, there are some crazy people out there in this world. There's no telling what kind of a big, old dirty mess you can get yourself into if you're not careful."

"I heard that," Maggie smiled, the other women joining her as she playfully mimicked Ebony. "You're a real jewel."

"Yeah," smirked Candice. "Put her together with a hundred others and you could have yourself a crown."

"Hey, that sounds like a fun idea. Maybe I'll run into some kind of king or something, and I can come back with a crown of my own," laughed Maggie.

"Dream on, Maggie girl. You'd better get goin' before you get such a big head that you turn into a pumpkin," shooed Kara.

As Maggie, feeling like Cinderella going to the ball, headed toward her carriage - a dulled silver Honda - already packed and ready to go, she thought of how fabulous it would have been to make this trip in a new car. She had toyed with the idea of getting a new car when she finished her graduate degree in December, but finding a man to settle down with for the rest of her life seemed higher on her personal priority list than a new vehicle. Thus, she opted to save her pennies for a vacation to Florida.

Wanting to make an unforgettable impression on that perfect man when he came along, she pulled down the mirror on her sun visor and did a last once-over of her appearance. She checked to make sure every hair was in place and that her lip-stick was just right. *Who's to say I won't find him on the road on the way there?* she teased, feeling her anxiousness as she re-adjusted the ball cap.

The flawless quality of her olive skin shone with a rich luster even without a tan. She could hardly wait to see the glow on her face after a week in the sun and the sand. Her father's dark Italian features, mixed with those of her tall fair-skinned, blue-eyed mother, gave her a rare mystical look, accentuating her Patrician silhouette, that naturally caught people's attention. Combined with the hints of deep auburn that typically appeared in her hair after exposure to the sun, highlighting it like spun silk, her entire presence took on a radiance that was beautiful to behold, making it hard for people to take their eyes off Maggie.

A good thing in my line of business, she facetiously mumbled, but mentally thanking her parents for creating such a fine specimen of rare beauty, as she prepared to head out on her adventure. *I hope it comes in handy later this week.*

After checking the cooler and picnic basket to make sure everything was easily accessible, she popped the car into reverse and wheeled out of the parking lot en route to a perfectly planned vacation. *Nothing can stop me from accomplishing my mission now!*

Maggie had purposefully decided to drive as far as pos-sible before her head began to nod and her lids got heavy, then she would pull off for the night and get an early start the next morning. It was Sunday now, and if she made good time tonight and all day tomorrow, she could be sitting in her chair on the sand and enjoying the water by sometime Tuesday. *And who knows? If I'm lucky, I could even be wrapped up in my new blanket by that night!*

With that thought, she pushed the gas pedal a little harder.

Traffic was much worse than Maggie anticipated. It appeared that everyone else had made the same decision to "get out of Dodge" for Easter vacation. She had not expected to get stuck on a Sunday evening heading south on I-75.

Must be all the Canadians who headed out this morning. There can't be this many people leaving Michigan at this time of day.

Her thoughts, for the moment, turned from the traffic dilemma to how her last six years of studying Public Policy at the University of Michigan would come in handy during the course of the next week as she cast out her line for that "perfect man." All the communication skills would definitely be to her advantage. *And the experience of living a dual identity will keep my work a secret forever.*

She visualized a picture-perfect home with beautiful children and a playful dog. A home that was full of love and joy, and well lived-in, like the one she had known as a child while growing up with her parents in the Little Italy section of Cleveland, Ohio. Remembrances of visits from her paternal grandparents, the first recollection of them she had allowed herself to have in a number of years, danced through her head.

Wishing she could go back and change the way she had reacted toward her grandmother during the last few years of the elder's life, Maggie felt an overwhelming sea of guilt rise in her, like bile making its way to her throat from her stomach. Except this was a feeling that began in her toes and crept all the way up to the top curve of her head.

She slammed on brakes as red lights screamed at her from the car just ahead. All of a sudden, there was an ocean of red lights. It looked like Christmas trees on the highway instead of travelers on an Easter vacation. Sitting behind a luxury sedan, she spied a bumper sticker whose words caught her attention. Not only was it unusual for a luxury sedan to sport a bumper sticker, but the words "Real men love Jesus" jumped out at her – *not* what she would have expected from the driver of such an expensive vehicle.

Maggie recalled Candice's statement about real men. Any other time, the words on the bumper sticker would not have gotten more than a casual glance, but now they had her mind slowly turning. And on top of that, she again thought of her grandmother, who would have had a heyday with those words.

Everyone in Maggie's family loved Jesus. *Everyone . . . including me*, she reflected, the dark and shameful guilt of working at Northern Exposure creeping up inside her again.

This is not *the way I intend to spend my vacation.*

Maggie forced her thoughts to return to images of sitting on a stretch of sand, beside the water's edge, in her new blue canvas chair with its pockets for her drinks and steamy romance novel, basking in the sun and allowing her already dark skin to catch enough rays to heighten her tan. In her mind, she imagined the warmth of the blanket the girls had given her in which to wrap up at night on the beach beside her man – *that perfect man I'm going to meet before this week is finished.*

After nearly two hours of stop-and-go traffic, and having gone less than sixty miles, Maggie begrudgingly decided to stop for the evening. The slowness of the cars after a day at work, on top of the rush of the past couple of days in trying to get ready for her mission, had her eyes fighting to stay open. Finally, opting not to waste precious time on the highway, she found a cheap motel, reasoning that if she were going to sleep, it should be in a bed. She'd wake up early and get a fresh start when she could make better time.

Tomorrow's a new day. I can wake up looking like Sleeping Beauty, and be ready for that man when I find him.

She closed her eyes and unconsciously whispered, "Real men love Jesus," as she fell prey to the Sandman.

Chapter 2
Late evening, Palm Sunday

Joshua Redford lay with his eyes wide open, gazing out the window of his bedroom. The moon, approaching fullness, stared down at him as he stared back at the sister stars. Anxiousness fluttered in his stomach, not from fear or worry, but from the excitement of sharing his gift of art with the town of Findlay, Ohio, and its neighboring cities and communities, during the course of the next week.

All the arrangements had been made and the media had been contacted. Before Easter Sunday arrived, thousands of people were expected to visit Riverside Park to see his seventy-five ton sand sculpture of Christ.

Feeling God's presence all around him through the elements of nature, the landscape artist thought of all the shrubs and trees that stood on the south side of his house waiting for this Easter project to be over and transplanting season to begin. Their buds should turn to blossoms at exactly the same time as the sculpture was completed.

He smiled, thinking of how this all began three years ago, while lying in the same bed. The artist had felt God's presence all around him that night, also. For several years prior to that, Joshua carried out a tradition that had started in Findlay decades before by a man who carved snow sculptures for the town. It was a way the older man had been able to utilize his unique talent, pursue a hobby, and bring not only families, but the entire town together through their pride in his work.

After the man's death, Joshua began to use his artistic mind to continue the sculptures, turning Riverside Park into an entire village of snow creatures. As his array of scenes grew, so did the crowds that came to see his work.

However, three years ago, Mother Nature had not provided him with the one tool he needed to carry on his anxiously awaited project – *snow*. The artist's mind had to expand beyond ideas for his village to ideas of how to provide Findlay the family gathering time to which they had become so accustomed. He went to bed that night praying for an idea from God – an idea that would allow him an outlet for his talent, *and a gift for the town.*

Joshua lay there, letting his mind slowly replay the entire scenario from three years ago, as he anticipated another *truly* meaningful Holy Week – in more than one sense of the word.

Chapter 3
Three years prior, Two weeks before Easter

He had listened to the weather reports all week, hoping against hope that the announcers were going to be wrong with their predictions. But sadly, he accepted the realization that the weather was much too warm for snow. There was a large chance for precipitation, but given the unseasonably high temperatures Findlay was having, he might as well forget about the white flakes. *So much for living in the land of the Great Lakes!*

Joshua was a very successful landscape artist, not the typical grown-up "little boy" longing to build a snowman in the front yard. But he *was* interested in the snowman part, for he had done snow sculptures for more than a decade during the week before Christmas, and people had flocked into their small town from as far away as Indiana and Virginia to see his impressive work.

His work was not the issue, but rather, the unity of family and community that his efforts brought. People would take an entire evening and come to see the fruits of his many hours of labor. In the process of getting to Riverside Park, families and friends would be in the car together - talking, laughing, and strengthening their relationships. Many of them brought snacks to share, many went out to eat before or after. Most of them drove by the real-life snow village he created, but some of the more adventurous ones parked their cars and got out to walk among the icy creatures.

The man who spent his time doing this monumental sculpture knew that his underlying talent was as much in the art of appealing to people, giving them a special time together, as it was in his artistic expression. Joshua loved feeling that in some small way, God was using him for a unique purpose.

Now he was feeling terribly distraught over the number of persons who were going to come here expecting their usual family outing, and there would be nothing. He looked at his wife, Lynn, his expression one of total despair.

"There's got to be an answer here," Joshua said languidly. "I can't let all those people be disappointed."

Lynn didn't have any idea how important this task was to her husband until that very moment. She had seen it as a hobby for a little boy who never grew up, but now she realized the magnitude of his venture. Suddenly her heart reached out to him.

"Why don't you pray about it? If it's that important to you, I'm sure God will give you an answer," she had offered, placing her hand on Joshua's forearm as a sign of her support.

"I *have* been praying . . . all day as I listened to the weather reports, and tonight as I sat here wondering what will happen when all the usual spectators come to see nothing." He paused for a minute. "Perhaps I need to give it to God completely and quit worrying about it."

"I think that's exactly what you need to do," his comforting wife said with a nod of her head. "I'm sure that by the time next week rolls around, you will have a divine plan."

CRSO

"Lynn." Joshua sat up in the bed. "Lynn," he repeated, shaking her gently. "Wake up! I know what it is I'm supposed to do."

"Huh?" she asked groggily, wondering if she was caught up in some dream.

"Wake up, honey. God gave me my answer."

"That's nice, dear," Lynn mumbled, still sure she was dreaming.

Joshua shook his wife with a little more veraciousness. "Lynn, listen to me. I know what I'm supposed to do. God has given me an answer," he repeated, determined to get her attention.

Lynn rolled over and looked at her husband, realizing she was not in a dream. "What, dear?" she asked, shaking her head slightly to wake herself enough to listen to his pronouncement.

"I'm going to make a sand sculpture of Christ on the cross. It will be done in time for Good Friday, and maybe one of the churches would like to use it for the setting of their Tenebrae service on that day," he burst with pride.

"Joshua," Lynn stopped him, making sure that he wasn't the one dreaming now. "Where do you propose to do this sculpture?"

"Right here in Findlay."

Now his wife was sure he had gotten caught up in a dream. Lynn sat straight up in the bed, looking at him with a dumbfounded expression. "And just *where* are you going to find enough sand to make a sculpture of Jesus and the cross?"

"I'm going to have it brought down from Toledo."

This time it was Lynn who was shaking her husband's

arm. "Joshua, do you have *any* idea how much sand it will take to do that?"

"Yes," he answered, still bubbling with his idea, *or vision*, as he saw it. "Approximately seventy-five tons."

"Seventy-five tons!" she shrieked. "Where on earth could you even put that much sand here in Findlay?"

"The park would be the perfect spot. Then after Easter, when it blows from here to there, they can use it to make a better play area for the children. All children love to play in the sand."

"*Obviously*," Lynn said simply, shaking her head and falling back on the pillow. "Only some children never grow up," she muttered as she turned back toward the wall.

She closed her eyes and wished she *had* been trapped in a dream as Joshua sat up, lost in his own dream of how to make the vision in his head happen.

☙❧

By the time Lynn got up the next morning, Joshua was already downstairs, wide awake and chipper as he finished his third cup of coffee. He had spent the morning on the phone making the necessary arrangements to see his dream come true.

His wife looked at him, glaring wide-eyed, still trying to determine whether she imagined their midnight conversation, or whether it had been a reality. The ring of the phone swiftly gave her an answer.

"Good morning, Joshua. This is Lawrence Anderson. I got your message. What exactly is it that you want to do?"

"Hi, Mayor. Thanks for returning my call." He winked excitedly at Lynn as she fell onto a barstool. "For Holy Week, I'd like to do a sand sculpture in Riverside Park of Christ on the cross," Joshua said with determination, but not offering any more information until he got a reading of the mayor's response.

"You want to do *what*?"

Joshua could tell by the inflection of that last word that he'd better give a little more of the details. He wasn't sure whether the word came from the mayor not hearing clearly, or not believing what he heard.

"There's already sand in the volleyball court beside McManness Street," Joshua began. "We can have more sand hauled in, dumped there, and when the sculpture erodes after a couple of weeks, we can get some of the local businesses to haul it to schools or churches that need it for their children.

"The sculpture will be next to the street, so people can see it as they pass by. I propose it will give Findlay a sense of community, and make Easter more than just another day. This could become an annual event, bringing our town a sense of ownership. Who would ever think of coming to Findlay, Ohio, to see a sand sculpture?"

He could hear Mayor Anderson mulling over the idea even though there were no words coming through the phone.

"How much sand are we talking about, Joshua?"

"Seventy- five tons."

"Seventy-five *tons*?"

"Yes, Mayor."

"That will be quite a large sculpture."

"Yes, sir, it will. Larger than life."

There were a few more seconds of silence. Then with a positive energy in his voice, the mayor gave his official decision. "There is some red tape involved here, and I probably should call a meeting first, but I like this idea. And as for the message, you mentioned something about one of the local churches using the site for their Tenebrae, or Good Friday, service. I'll pass that on to my church. Sounds like something we'd be interested in."

He became silent for a few more seconds, thinking

through the details from his end, before concluding, "Tell you what, Joshua. You take care of Christ. I'll take care of all the bureaucracy."

"Thank you, sir." The artist felt the elation going off inside his body like fireworks.

"Thank *you*, Redford. I'll be anxious to see this work of art."

Man taking care of Christ. Now that's *a far stretch*, Joshua chuckled to himself. But somehow, Mayor Anderson's order gave him a sense of importance. Not of human importance, but of a supreme recognition. Not a recognition of superiority, but of being on a mission. A recognition of being chosen for a divine purpose.

Joshua immediately dialed the number of the sand company. His dream was going to become a reality.

But, then, was there any doubt? After all, look where the dream came from, he mused, looking at the stare of utter surprise on Lynn's face.

∞

"I've been thinking, Joshua," Lynn said, clearing the dinner dishes from the table. "Seventy-five tons is a lot of sand. Maybe half of that would be sufficient."

"I don't know," he replied. "That's the number I heard in my head last night when I had the vision."

"This *is* your project, dear, but I simply cannot envision anything that huge in a town the size of Findlay."

Joshua looked at Lynn, who was quietly returning his stare. "I'll tell you what. I'll think about it tonight and see how I feel in the morning."

"Okay," she agreed. "That sounds reasonable."

"But after that, you're right. This is *my* sculpture. Mine and God's," he stated. "He's the One who gave me the vision, and I want to make that vision a reality, with every detail done to the utmost perfection . . . according to His plan."

C3&C

"Good morning, honey," Joshua greeted his wife with a kiss the next morning, pouring her a cup of freshly brewed coffee.

"Hmmm," she sighed, breathing in the rich aroma of the Kona blend. "You really know how to get a girl up and going in the morning." Lynn walked toward the kitchen table. Seeing the newspaper already unfolded and spread across the table, she realized that Joshua had been awake for a while. "What has you up so early this morning?" she asked.

"You do," he replied. "I thought long and hard concerning your statement last night about the amount of sand. You may be right. I'm going to call the sand and gravel company after breakfast and tell them to cut back on the order. Instead of seventy-five tons, I'll only order thirty-eight. They're going to deliver it tomorrow morning, so as long as I call by lunch today, I'll be okay."

After they finished the luxury of a relaxed breakfast together, Joshua's reward of being self-employed and having his wife as the secretary, he called the dispatcher for the sand company.

"What do you mean you can't do that?" Lynn heard Joshua ask from the other room. "I was told that if any changes needed to be made to the order, I could call up until noon on the day before the delivery. This is Thursday, and you're not bringing it until tomorrow."

There was a pause as Lynn began to listen closer to the phone conversation.

"Oh . . . I see." She heard a light sigh coming from her husband. "Well, then. I guess there's nothing else you can do." Obviously things were not going in her husband's favor. "No problem. I'm not going to worry about it. Thank you, anyway."

Joshua walked back into the kitchen from his study.

"What was *that* all about?" Lynn asked, concerned, but trying not to seem nosy.

"God decided that I needed the seventy-five tons of sand."

"*What*?" she questioned, straining her neck to look into Joshua's eyes, sure that she must have misunderstood him. Before he had time to answer her, she bolted on. "Don't tell me the dispatcher got the same vision you did."

"No, nothing like that. But they loaded the trucks early and went ahead and sent them today. They're on their way here from Toledo as we speak. All five of them."

"*Five*? What on earth are you going to do with five trucks of sand?" Lynn gasped.

"I'm going to build a big King," he smiled. "The dispatcher was going to call me in a few minutes so that I could meet the trucks when they arrive. I guess I'd better get ready."

"And I'd better call the newspaper. They want to do a story. I'll leave it up to them to contact the other media sources that wanted to be there." Lynn kissed her husband on the cheek. "And don't you dare leave without me. If God went to this much trouble to make sure you got the seventy-five tons of sand, I'm going to be there to witness this grand and glorious event."

Joshua packed a cooler full of drinks and some sandwiches to carry him through the day, poured several buckets of water for washing his hands, and grabbed his coat on the way out the door. He found it most unusual that he needed no tools for this job, merely the two hands God had given him.

While he put the last of the items in his landscaping truck, Lynn ran out the door, throwing on her coat as she ran across the front yard to the garage.

"The *Courier* is sending someone down to the scene in a few minutes, and they are going to call the radio station and the news reporters that wanted to cover the story. I also called a couple of friends to start a phone chain of the folks who wanted to watch this project," she announced, jumping in the passenger side of the truck.

"As small as this town is," Joshua laughed, "everyone in the whole place will be there by the time the sand trucks arrive. You know the old saying, 'telephone, telegraph, tell a woman!'"

"Very funny. And you know what they say about the Three Wise Men. If they had been three women, they would have arrived on time, they would have made up the bed, and they would have brought useful gifts."

"Okay, now we're even," he sneered. Joshua reached over and squeezed his wife's hand.

Lynn knew her husband well enough to decipher his gesture as a signal that he was thinking through the task that lay ahead of him. It seemed so strange to her that before he began any landscaping job, he sketched out the final result. But for this, he had no sketch, no notes, no anything. Just the vision in his head. *And God!* she reminded herself.

With everything that had happened in the past few days, there was no doubt in her mind that this truly was a message delivered from God. Lynn felt goose bumps rise on her arms and down her spine as she swelled with pride knowing she was the wife of the awesome creature sitting across the seat from her – a creature specially chosen by God for this purpose.

Both of them were amazed at the crowd that had already gathered by the time they arrived at the park. Joshua drove past them to get as close as possible to the sculpture site. When he opened the door and stepped out of the truck, the artist was most humbled that people began to clap and cheer.

And as touched as he was by their reaction, he was even more humbled by the fact that he sensed they, too, knew the *real* Artist of this sculpture. Otherwise, they would not have taken the time to come out in support of his project. *God's project!* he reminded himself.

Chapter 4
Approaching midnight, Palm Sunday

Joshua turned off the recollection and glanced at the clock. He knew he'd better stop daydreaming – *nightdreaming!* he laughed silently – and get some sleep if he was going to be ready for the upcoming week. When he had walked out of the morning's worship service, going from the triumphal celebration of Palm Sunday to the quiet, reflective state of Holy Week, he felt sufficiently inspired for the genuine calling of his work for the next six days. Now he simply needed the necessary rest to accompany that inspiration.

He glanced over at his petite wife with her short brown hair shaping her face on the pillow. The moon's glow shone on her features, allowing him to get a good look at Lynn. She was still the most beautiful creature in the world in his eyes.

The artist knew that without the support of this woman, whom God had seen fit to place in his life, the task before him would be insurmountable. She was more than his helpmate; she was the power behind the man. He breathed a silent thank-you for being blessed with a godly woman.

There was only one more item on his agenda before tomorrow. *Oh, Lord*, he prayed as he closed his eyes, *let the work of my hands be blessed in Your sight, and let this sculpture touch at least one person in a very special way this week. May those who visit the park come to know you better through the talent you have bestowed upon me.*

Amen, he whispered as he opened his eyes and glanced out at the moon one last time.

"Amen," he heard quietly from Lynn as she lay there, seemingly in her own dream.

Chapter 5
Pre-dawn, Holy Monday

Maggie awoke before sunup, the weariness from the evening before gone. She jumped into the shower, letting the cold water revive her completely, preparing her for a full day's journey.

As she dried her hair, she took a long, hard look at herself in the mirror. The fineness of her mother's blonde hair, combined with the coarseness of that of her father's, had blessed her with wiry, dark hair that looked good pulled back away from her face, showing off her eyes and full lips. When she put it up on her head, Maggie left wisps on each side that added to the mystical look created by her amazingly large eyes. Her long, slender neck only helped to accentuate her face.

She looked on the counter at the glasses she had worn ever since the start of her job at the club. Cheap clear-glass imitations that she had picked up at the discount store to give her a studious appearance.

For her classes, she had worn little or no make-up,

donned the unbecoming glasses and pulled her hair back in a harsh manner, letting the uncontrollable wisps look wind-blown rather than naturally feathered. Maggie was careful not to wear clothes that clung to her body, hoping to divert attention away from her perfectly formed shape lest she should be recognized by anyone who visited the club.

On campus, she had come across as the intelligent female who had no thoughts of anything besides earning a degree and working herself up some corporate ladder. At night, she took on an entirely different appearance as her natural beauty appealed to the men who visited the club, either as regulars or passersby from the nearby interstate. She had a wardrobe of skimpy outfits that clung to her with every move of her body and that showed off her long, slender legs. Her lengthy, dark eyelashes, perfectly curved brow and bright-red lips made it easy for her to give the impression that she had just walked out of a make-up artist's studio. To look at her, she could have easily passed as a beautiful ballerina. *Or an exotic dancer.*

Maggie Matelli – the Great Contortion Artist – earning a degree by day and easy bucks by night.

A part of her wanted to dwell on how she had wound up in that situation, but another coaxed her to get dressed and get on the road to finding that man – the one who was going to rescue her from that degrading existence she had carefully and secretly held onto through her dual identity over the past four years.

She slowly picked up the glasses from the counter and put them on. Looking in the mirror at the image she had created for herself since landing her "exclusive" job, she bit down hard, pressing her lips together, and took on an expression of decisive determination. Maggie took off the glasses and placed them in the white plastic garbage can. *Sorry, but I don't need you anymore. I'm going to be the beautiful person that God created.*

The young woman stopped and again stared at herself in

the mirror, this time oddly, as if looking at a stranger that she was supposed to recognize. *Since when have you remembered anything about "God," Maggie Matelli?*

Not wanting to lose sight of her mission, she quickly threw her toiletries back into her overnight bag and carried her few things out to the car. Maggie noticed that the lobby was open for continental breakfast.

Good timing, she noted, making her way toward the black coffee and donuts. Approaching the cheap motel's buffet, Maggie's stomach began urging her to give it more than stale sweet rolls. Not usually a breakfast person, she obstinately acquiesced, reasoning that a good meal to start the day would be more of a timesaver in the long run, for then she could eat her sandwiches and snacks the remainder of the day and lose no time in her quest for "the perfect man."

She grabbed two large Styrofoam cups and filled both with coffee - one to knock the morning chill from her body, and one to keep her awake for the next hour or so until she found an exit with a hometown diner. *Hopefully, a diner that has a dose of personality to go* with *the breakfast . . . at no extra charge!*

Maggie noted the sky as she pulled out of the motel. *Not a cloud in sight. Clear blue. Ah, my new blue hat and purse will match it perfectly when I get to that sunny beach.*

Florida, here we come. The sojourner honked the horn in celebration as she pulled onto I-75 South.

She looked at the beautiful countryside, full of open land for miles and miles, just beginning to show signs of life under the morning sky. Trees that were starting to bud would be fully clothed in colorful blossoms when she returned. Where she was going, it was already spring. Here, the warmer season was still around the corner, but would come slower, allowing the Mid-Westerners a chance to enjoy the changing temperatures before the hot weather set in for the next several months.

Canadian geese flocked over the highway, changing their course and their leader as they headed north, completely in the opposite direction from which she was headed. A state patrolman buzzed by on the other side of the interstate. Even the cows in the fields watched as he sped down the highway in rapid pursuit of someone.

Maggie smiled, full of joyful anticipation at her upcoming week of a hunting expedition. *If I didn't know better, I'd think I was going the wrong direction.*

Chapter 6
Morning, Holy Monday

Perfect, thought Maggie, noticing an exit sign for a small town that looked like she could refuel both the car and her stomach and quickly get back on the road. She veered onto the exit ramp for Findlay, Ohio, and made a right turn. *There's got to be a family-owned roadside grill somewhere on this road. Maybe where I can get a whole stack of hotcakes. After all, this is vacation. NO salads or fruit bowls on this trip.*

Before she had gone even a mile, she had to slam on brakes to keep from smashing into the back of a dump truck. As soon as she came to a passing break, she edged over to the left to check the traffic. To her dismay, there was more than one truck. Maggie swerved back into her lane.

Great! This is all I need. I had sworn that nothing was going to keep me from my sun and sand and finding my man. Watch it be my luck that I have to follow them for twenty miles.

Maggie made up her mind that if they had not turned off, or she had not found a place to eat, within the next three miles, she'd make a u-turn and head back for the interstate. As she rounded a curve in the road, she was able to count five dump trucks full of sand in front of her.

Somebody's gonna have a big *sandbox!* she laughed to herself.

She shook her head, falling back into her fit of frustration. *I should have stuck to Ebony's snacks and fast food*, Maggie thought, aggravated that the slow trucks in front of her were eating into her vacation time. *And valuable time with my man*, she continued to muse.

The urge to blow her horn was biting at her, but Maggie decided it would do no good. Her four-cylinder Honda was no match for one full dump truck, much less five. She didn't want to take a chance on making the drivers mad. That could delay her even more.

Then she noticed the left turn signal begin to blink on the truck in front of her.

It's about time, she mumbled aloud.

She looked in the direction the trucks had turned as she passed. There sat a news van with the antenna stuck way up in the air, and several groups of people standing around watching all the activity. Maggie could see the reporters circled around someone, but whoever it was had become buried behind the cameraman and the crowd.

Hmmm, maybe they're giving their park a face lift, she decided, seeing a sign that read Riverside Park up ahead. *That's nice*, she reasoned, trying to make her delay not seem like such a horrific waste of time.

After driving several more blocks, Maggie came to Main Street. *Surely there's a small restaurant this way.* She made a right turn and closely scanned the businesses that lined the sidewalks. Up ahead on the left, she caught sight of an old neon sign that said in big red letters, "E-A-T."

Her attention was immediately drawn to the place, for it

was reminiscent of the pictures she had seen from her grand-parents' early years. The letters sprawled across the windowed front of the restaurant read, "Miller's Luncheonette."

Luncheonette? Did I enter some sort of time warp back at that turn?

She had never actually seen, much less eaten in, an establishment that looked like a picturesque antique place found in the travel magazines. *Perfect!* Maggie thought as she whipped the Honda into a parallel parking space near the front door and walked in, hoping the inside atmosphere matched that of the outside.

She looked for a table against the wall, but saw nothing available, so she slithered into a seat at a table stuck in the middle of the restaurant. *Boy, is this different,* she smiled, glad that she could enjoy the quiet solitude before she found the man of her life.

"You're new here. Need a menu?" the waitress asked.

"Yes, thank you," Maggie answered, amused that this was such a small dive that the waitress knew all the regulars.

But then, so do you, Maggie, she brooded, thinking of her own workplace.

"We get lots of visitors this time of year," the waitress stated as she handed the guest a menu, offering no explanation for the reason of the visitors. "Most people order one of our two specials, or the French Toast," she added, pointing to a dry-erase board that hung over the counter. "What brings you here?" shot the question as she walked back to the grill to pick up an order.

"I'm passing through on my way to Florida. I thought it might be fun to look for an eligible bachelor while soaking up the sun and the sand down there for a week."

Maggie's answer seemed lost in the activity and she wondered whether the waitress even cared or was simply making small talk. She turned her attention to the board announcing the breakfast specials. It appeared to be the only thing that had changed since the opening of the joint. *And heaven only knows when* that *was!* Maggie surmised.

Seeing that grease was a part of everything on the menu and the board, Maggie wondered if she should be concerned about her cholesterol level. *Ah, what the heck. I'll break my earlier promise of no fruit and have some for dinner.* Smiling to herself, she reasoned, *It might be vacation, but I still have to look good for work when I get home.*

The waitress shuffled back by the newcomer on her way to refill coffee cups around the room. As she passed, she leaned over to offer a word of advice. "We got some nice young men here in Findlay. You ought to stick around this week. It'll be interesting."

Maggie glanced around at the walls that proudly displayed yellowed newspaper articles about Miller's Luncheonette and its founders. Shelves above the counter held a line of plates that had been used over the years at the restaurant and old antique car models.

There was a comfortable feel to this place. Maggie continued to do a mental survey of this find she had made, while trying not to call attention to herself as a "foreigner."

The guest noticed two white-haired women enter from the back, walking through the kitchen, and speaking to everyone they passed. Maggie was impressed with their spryness as they livened up the place with their grins and words of wisdom.

As the ladies sat down at the table next to the wall that had cleared, she noted that they should be called the Golden Girls. They had reached those precious "golden years," as her grandmother used to call them, where you finally get to reap your rewards of raising children and overseeing grandchildren, and you can "live it up" again with your friends.

Live it up? She wondered what her grandmother could

have possibly done to live it up. That was a short-lived thought, for she forced her mind to forget about it before her new day got off to a depressing start.

The waitress, whose nametag Maggie now noticed as reading "Joni," came back for her order. Wanting to try a farmer's omelet, she settled instead for a Number One - the special with bacon, two eggs and home fries - thinking it would be faster, getting her to the "perfect man" that much sooner.

"White or rye?" Joni asked.

"Huh?" Maggie responded, caught off guard.

"White or rye toast?" the waitress repeated.

"Oh, sorry. I don't usually do breakfast out," she explained. "I'll have rye."

With pen and pad in hand, Joni turned around and yelled the order back to the kitchen, where the owner of the diner was manning the grill.

One of the two Golden Girls leaned over to the vacationer. "You're new here, aren't you, dearie?"

Before Maggie had a chance to answer, Joni called back over her shoulder, "She's just passing through. On her way to Florida to find a man. And sit in the sand and sun for a week. Told her she ought to stay here. That we got a few good eligible men right here in Findlay."

So much for getting in and out quietly, Maggie thought, as every eye in the place turned to her, then back to their plates and their own conversations. *Maybe this makes me a regular now*, she resolved, trying not to feel any embarrassment that the entire town would know her business within a few hours. *Oh well, at least I know she was listening to me when I told her why I was here.*

The Golden Girl who had spoken to her smiled, not a grandmotherly smile, but one of those huge flashes of teeth that gives the effect of a bubbling smile coming all the way up from one's toes. "Do you like ice cream?"

"Yes, actually I do," Maggie answered, wondering whether to clue the kindly woman into the fact that frozen dairy desserts were one of her weaknesses.

"Then you must stay in town long enough to go to Dietsch Brothers. They've got the best chocolates and ice cream in the world. And I do mean, *in the world*," she added emphatically. "The father started the business here in the thirties, and his sons took it over since then. The original building's still down on Main Cross." Leaning in toward the visitor, she loudly whispered, "Be sure to order a banana split to go. You get twice as much ice cream that way."

Maggie wanted to laugh aloud, but opted to smile and nod, not sure what to say. This place was too much. No one here knew her, but they were all insistent that she stay. Little did they know how important her destination really was. For it was more than just a vacation, or the routine of daily business. Maggie Matelli was on a mission.

A mission from God! she reiterated, thinking of the diner scene from the movie with the Blues Brothers. It was a favorite of hers, and she immediately began to picture it happening here, with herself as one of the characters. All the place needed was Righteous 'Retha singing "Think."

She already loved this place. *But it's not a part of my plan*, she warned herself, as Joni sat a plate of food down in front of her.

Maggie stared at the plate. Although she was not a connoisseur of morning meals, she immediately noticed that this was not the usual presentation for a breakfast "special." The food was neatly arranged on the oval platter, with the slices of rye toast neatly patterned, separating the eggs, fries and bacon.

Suddenly she looked around at all the other customers' plates to see if they were all that way, or if she had been given preferential treatment. She was amazed to see that every patron in the diner had been given the same preferential treatment.

Wow! she thought, looking again at the price listed on the marker board. *All this, and presentation, too, for that amount?* This was better than the prices in her college dives, *and certainly better looking,* she thought, recalling how dark they were, not allowing the customers, most of whom didn't care, to see how grungy the places really were.

There was nothing dark, *or grungy*, about this place, Maggie noted as she stared out the front, which was all one huge plate glass window, except for the door.

Her brain told her to wolf down the eggs, home fries and bacon, and ask for a to-go cup for her tea. But her body sat languidly as she watched the faces, and listened to the comments of the customers, most of whom walked right through the middle of the kitchen, engaging in immediate conversation, after coming in the back entrance.

A police officer came in and took a seat at a table with three other men.

"Morning, Ralph," one of the other patrons called to him.

"Morning," the officer called back.

"Here for your donuts?" another man joked.

"You know full well we don't serve donuts in here," Joni yelled out across the room, getting in the middle of the conversation. Her response caused a cackle amidst the crowd of customers, mostly men. "But the pies are fresh out of the oven and I've already sliced them."

The waitress walked past Maggie with the coffee pot in hand. "That's as close as we get to donuts in this place," she explained to the newcomer.

Maggie admiringly eyed the pies that were lined up on the racks behind the counter. There must have been at least a dozen varieties, freshly baked and demanding attention. It was all she could do to resist the meringue, piled so high that the baked concoctions barely fit in the glass display case.

Too bad I'm not going to be around at lunch. I'd treat myself to dessert. She looked again at the assortment of pies. *They probably don't have key lime, though. I'll get that soon enough when I get to Florida.* Her brain had kicked back into gear, reminding her of her "mission," and that she should ask for her check and leave.

A young couple walked in and found a table next to the front window, giving them as much seclusion as possible for a breakfast crowd in a small-town diner. Maggie caught the glimmer of love in their eyes as they took each other's hands instead of the menu.

The waitress greeted them from the back of the restaurant. "What are you doing in here this morning?"

"I took the day off to be with my husband," answered the woman.

"Well, you better take good care of her," Joni shouted to the husband.

So much for privacy and seclusion, observed Maggie.

That was what had unconsciously struck the visitor until that instant. Everyone who walked in this place knew each other . . . *and their business.* It seemed that they were all connected through some magical, mystical power that became a part of them from the instant they walked into the luncheonette.

"You going to the park to see the sculpture this week?" one of the Golden Girls asked the waitress.

"I thought I'd head out there tomorrow evening. There's supposed to be a cold front coming in, and I figured I could run some hot drinks out to the folks," came the reply.

The Golden Girl turned back to Maggie. "You ought to stay and see the sculpture at the park this week. There's a man here in town, Joshua Redford, that does a huge sculpture of Christ on the cross, and it's done entirely with sand."

"Yeah," the second of the Golden Girls chimed in, with her first words to the visitor. "It's just like a big sand castle, except it's Jesus. And this is the third year in a row he's done it."

Maggie sat there staring at the two women who were obviously entranced by this annual event that was about to happen. *Golden years, huh? I hope I don't get there for quite a while.*

She tuned in just in time to hear the first of the women explain, "Every year gets bigger and better."

"With both the sculpture and the crowd," Joni added as she put the plates of food in front of the two women.

"Uh, thanks," Maggie replied somberly, for a lack of anything to say. *At least I know where the sand trucks were headed*, she thought as she finished the last bites of her eggs and home fries.

Another man walked in and took a seat at a table by himself.

"Haven't seen you in a while," Joni said, putting a cup on the table and filling it with coffee.

"I've been in Florida for a couple of weeks."

He's talking my language! Maggie smiled as she glanced around at him.

"I'll have . . ." he began.

The waitress grabbed the fleshy part of his cheek between her right thumb and forefinger and squeezed it back and forth like an elderly lady grabbing a little tike with the words, "Oh, how cute!"

"I know what you want," Joni said with delight, screaming his order back to the kitchen like all the others she had taken that morning. Her tablet never left the pocket of her apron.

Maggie wondered why she bothered to have a pad and pen. It obviously wasn't a necessity.

Joni strolled from table to table with the coffee pot. Just

as she got to the table behind Maggie, the waitress grabbed her ear with her right hand while still holding the pot with her left. "I've lost my earring," she exclaimed, pouring coffee into the cup of the gentleman seated next to the wall.

"I heard something hit," he said.

Having been blessed with hawk eyes, Maggie looked around on the floor. "Any idea where it is?" she asked, trying to be of help.

"I think it fell in the coffee pot." Her words came out as gingerly as if she had announced, "We're serving burgers for lunch."

Maggie wanted to laugh aloud, for if the pronouncement by Joni were not hysterical enough, she continued to pour coffee for the gentleman. The look in his eyes as he lifted the cup was priceless.

Joni went behind the counter where she picked up a spoon and began to fish around in the coffee pot. Directly, she pulled out the earring and then fished some more for the back. When she had both pieces, she rinsed them off under the sink, put them back on her ear lobe, then continued to pour the coffee for waiting customers.

"Home town, here we are," Maggie chuckled to herself.

She turned slightly to watch the reaction of the gentleman behind her. He had put the cup back on the table without drinking any of the coffee, obviously waiting for a clean cup. When he didn't get one, he finally picked the cup up slowly, moving his arm up and down several times while trying to decide whether to drink it or not. Finally, either his need for caffeine or his thirst got the best of him, for he raised the cup to his lips.

What struck Maggie as most bizarre about this incident was that no one even seemed to notice anything out of the ordinary.

She looked closely as Joni again walked past her table,

and noticed that the earrings were small yellow Easter eggs, decorated with an orange zig-zag pattern. *They* are *rather cute. No wonder she didn't want to lose one.* Maggie still felt the urge for a belly laugh, but thought better than to make these people, who had thus far accepted her, think she was making light of their small-town customs.

The newcomer wished she had a video camera so she could enter the incident on America's Funniest Home Videos. *I could pay for my vacation* and *have enough for a sizable down payment on a new car.*

After the amusing entertainment of breakfast and the tasty meal, Maggie decided it was definitely time to go. She walked to the counter, where Joni punched a few numbers on the cash register and gave the customer her total. The visitor handed her a tip, and turned to exit.

That's the most memorable breakfast I've ever had, she smirked, walking toward the door. *I'll bet she wears bunny rabbit earrings tomorrow*, she said to herself, a huge smile spreading across her face.

"Don't forget to check out the sculptor at the park. It's quite an event around here," the waitress called behind her.

Maggie nodded and waved, having no intention of letting some small town artist get in the way of her carefully planned trip.

Not knowing what possessed her, she stopped on the sidewalk and looked inside the luncheonette at all the customers and the antique setting. It was like her mind wanted to make sure this magical place really existed, and that she hadn't been part of a dream.

Her eyes didn't deceive her, as she delightfully observed the interaction of the customers still dwindling in with the ones already inside eating and finding out the goings-on of their town from each other.

Probably sponsors ball teams for the neighborhood kids, she noted, thinking of her own childhood sports activities, and how proud she had been to wear uniforms that displayed names of businesses on the backs of her shirts. It was those businesses that also provided special snacks for the team members. *Perhaps I should make a stop at Dietsch Brothers*, she speculated, remembering that her shirt had borne the name of Bob's Scoops. *No wonder I love ice cream so much*, she smiled again as she pulled out of the parking space.

୦୫৪০

It appeared that the drive to the interstate was not going any faster than the trek to the diner had been. The road that passed through town taking her farther south to the interstate happened to pass by Riverside Park, the place where Joni had told her the action for the week was to be. Maggie noticed that the reporters and news van were still on the premises of the site for this small town's gala event.

Suddenly the driver in front of her slammed on his brakes, causing Maggie to have to do the same. Rubber-neckers had traffic at a dead stand still.

Great! If I had wanted to spend my vacation in the park, I'd have joined those students from the school that were going on Alternative Spring Break to do mission work. As I recall, one of those groups was planning to spend this entire week in a dilapidated park somewhere fixing it all up for the kids of a deprived neighborhood. But my mission is much more urgent than theirs. I'm sure I'll go back to U-M with a much greater reward than they got after sitting around in a park all week. Besides, I'm on a mission to find love. All they're going to do is give it away.

Tired of meandering thoughts and sitting still, she put down her window and leaned out to see how long the line of cars was. *Not too bad*, she thought, counting the vehicles in front of her.

Maggie, too, tried to get a glimpse of the activity in front of her that appeared to be such a showstopper. *After all, I did inherit my father's natural Italian love for sculpture. And music,* she added, as she turned on the radio and began to sing to pass the time.

When she got to the park's driveway, Maggie turned in behind the cars leading the way in front of her. *I'll watch for a second,* she reasoned, *more for the Golden Girls than for myself. A seventy-five ton sand sculpture* is *quite a feat. Besides, maybe I can pick up a pointer or two for my own sand castle for the beach.*

She had no idea why she was getting into this crowd rather than for the benefit of the women who made such a fuss over the whole deal. There was much more important business waiting for her on the sunny coast of Florida. As she turned down the small street that led to the parking lot, Maggie caught a glimpse of a small fire hydrant painted like a toy soldier.

Great! Here I am looking for the perfect man, and the first guy I find is some cute little dude hardly more than a foot tall. I can hardly wait to tell the girls about him.

The crowd continued to grow in anticipation of the giant project. Five huge sand trucks were lined up, stretching out the entire length of the road that led past the picnic shelters and to the volleyball court where the sculpture was to be done.

Donning her sunglasses and ball cap, in the glaring sunlight that was already hinting at above-average temperatures for this area, Maggie drifted among the people who were standing on the grounds to get a good view, but kept far enough back to stay out of the way of the convoy of trucks.

The oversized vehicles moved forward, then backed up to the volleyball court, one truck at a time, each dumping their contents into a large pile, until there were five gargantuan mounds of sand lined across the playing area.

The truckers had lined up their vehicles, now facing the mounds of sand, side to side in the parking lot like humongous monsters on display for all the children, and overgrown children called adults, to see.

Maggie grinned as she thought of the wheeled machines as real-life Transformers, complete with their drivers. Each man stood beside his truck, with his name written beside the driver's door. *I wonder if that's so they don't forget which truck is theirs*, she laughed, still making light of this happening that everyone around her saw as so spectacular.

I just don't get it, she shook her head. *Don't these people have anything more exciting to do?*

But then she looked at the number of boys and girls who had run up to the trucks, shaking hands with the drivers and snapping pictures of them, like they were some big celebrities.

In the background, she could see the houses that lined the side street facing the park. Every one of them looked "lived in." Most were white frame; their yards had stalks of green shooting out of the ground, ready to burst open at the first hint of spring that, from the looks of things, would be within the week.

Her mind returned to the truckers who stood beaming with pride, every tooth in their mouths showing, at their roles in this event that had brought out so many of the town's residents. She couldn't help but notice that these five men appeared to have not a care in the world, no lack of self-esteem, content to deliver mounds of dirt and gravel from one point to another, enabling various and sundry projects to be done all over northwestern Ohio.

Quite a responsibility, she mused, as she watched their

interaction with the children and adults who had moved forward to talk to them. *There's more to these guys than what you expect*, she realized, noting their jobs entailed more than dropping off huge loads of sand. They were delegates of peace. Maggie chuckled, for in her mind she heard the theme song of those vehicular robots, *"Tranformers – more than meets the eye!" They really* are *like Transformers!* she exclaimed to herself, now staring at the five men in amazement as they signed autographs for the small children.

It seemed strange that she had spent most of her life within three hours of this place, having grown up in Cleveland, then attending college in Ann Arbor, with Findlay nestled between those two cities, and she had not experienced this segment of life before.

If nothing else, this will be good information for my Public Policy skills, Maggie reasoned, as if there were some importance to her being here instead of driving south on I-75. *I can hopefully make use of what I discover about this activity as it pertains to society – the public.*

She forgot about her own mission for a few minutes and took a good look at the scene around her. The five truck drivers and the sculptor suddenly took on a new image in her mind as she thought of the saying, "Men never grow up, they just get bigger toys."

Maggie pictured them as six little boys in a large sand pile, five of them pushing around their large plastic dump trucks with big rubber wheels, while the other one made sand castles, using his mother's small gardening tools.

And here they were as men, in a park, standing next to the largest sand piles she had ever seen, surrounded by swing sets and see-saws. What more perfect setting could there be?

These men were a team, perfectly content, proud of their work, showing no signs of stress. They took their jobs seriously.

Seriously about having fun, that is. No wonder they didn't seem hassled by stress. *Six grown men standing in the middle of a huge playground!*

One of the truckers handed the man who appeared to be in charge of the operation an invoice. Maggie had correctly pegged him as the sculptor. She could hear their conversation as she strained her ears like all the others gathered around her.

"You know the first year you brought the sand? When you handed me a bill for eight hundred dollars, I nearly choked. But would you believe that before the week was over, I had recouped nearly every penny of that from people who came by to see my work? They'd come by and drop a dollar or two in a bucket that found its way beside the sand.

"It all started with a woman who made a daily walk through the park. She always carried a couple of dollars in her pocket in case of an emergency. One morning she passed by and saw the sculpture taking shape. She came back around the park and stopped to see what was going on. The sculpture of Christ impressed her so much that she wanted to feel she had a part in it being here, so she handed me the two dollars to contribute toward the sand."

The man gave a quizzical smile. "I wasn't quite sure what to do with it, so she found a bucket and set it beside the fence where I was working. Her two dollars grew as other people came by and saw the donation. By the time the week was over, that woman's two dollars had grown into nearly eight hundred dollars without anyone saying a word, or me asking for a cent."

His words took an assertive direction. "Even if there had been a doubt before, I knew for sure at that point that God was in my work and my endeavor. Now the woman comes each year on the day I start this project and hangs the bucket out, and somehow the sand for the sculpture miraculously gets paid for during the course of the week. And there are always some individuals who volunteer to haul the sand away and see that it gets to needy organizations after it finally becomes too weathered to resemble a sculpture."

After listening to the sculptor's story, the drivers all hopped into their trucks with great ceremony. The one closest to the street started the procession that looked like a small-town parade with dump trucks rather than fire trucks.

"See ya next year, Joshua," the last driver called out as he rounded the turn and headed up the street behind his comrades.

Joshua. Now that's a fitting name for some guy who's about to spend all week doing a sculpture of Christ on the cross. It has a very . . . Biblical *ring to it,* she discerned with a hint of sarcasm.

Then the five mounds of sand stirred something inside her. *Perhaps it's that natural Italian love of art making its presence known.*

She eyed the sand intensely, trying to imagine what must be inside the sculptor's mind, and how he was going to get the piles of dirt from where they were into the impressive sculpture that everyone was anticipating.

Memories of Maggie's first trip to Italy with her father took over her thoughts. She could still remember holding her father's hand, walking down the streets in Florence with a group, *not unlike the one gathered in this park,* and listening to a tour guide talk about Michelangelo.

"The people of his day thought it nothing unusual to see men carrying a huge slab of marble down the street," the guide had explained, "for they knew it was nothing more than Michelangelo beginning a new sculpture. What amazed them was that he never used models or had patterns, for he saw the finished piece in his head the whole time. The artist said all he did was let the figure out of the marble."

Maggie envisioned the streets of Italy filled with towns-people in the days of the great master. Then she looked at this artist, standing in the midst of a crowd, talking to the bystand-ers. He showed no concern or anxiousness about the giant task that lay before him.

He, like Michelangelo, must see the image inside the sand. All he has to do is let it out, release it from its bondage.

Having no clue as to what made her do it, Maggie walked back to her car and opened the trunk. The chair that had been intended for the sand on the beach got its initiation in the sand that had spilled out from the dump trucks as they were leaving. Maggie unfolded it and staked her place like the others around her who had come to watch seventy-five tons of dirt take shape.

She drew a scrutinizing evaluation of the man who had already taken on the role of a great and talented master in her mind. Joni had told her that he was a landscape artist. Dressed in khaki workpants, a colored, pocketed t-shirt and tan work boots, Joshua Redford looked the part.

Her attention was drawn not to the man, nor his physi-cal appearance, but the vigor with which he approached the job before him.

Joshua climbed atop the mound of sand in the middle of the piles. His hands quickly began to pull handfuls of the tiny particles away from the peaked top. Before long, the oval image of a face was visible.

Maggie watched closely as the man cupped his hands in a sloping motion and made a nose. Then he took the palms of his hands and pulled them away from each other to form the eyes. His fingers followed the same curvatures to make the brow – *that brow that was so much a part of the story of the thorny crown*, she vaguely remembered.

It seemed odd to watch someone mold a man from dirt - handfuls at a time. *But only God could breathe life into that man*, she heard from the depths of her subconscious, her mind turning to all the scientists who tried to play God through their cloning.

Memories of Maggie's childhood crept into the forefront of her thoughts. She could remember sitting in her little rocker, beside her grandmother in the matching big rocker, listening to Bible stories that the grandmother loved reading to her. The first story she recollected was about Adam and Eve, and how God took clay and made the man. Then He took one of Adam's ribs and made a woman to be his mate. God breathed life into those two persons. She could hear her grandmother's voice as she finished the story, "And God said, 'This is good.'"

Myths, Maggie reminded herself. It was simply a myth, like all the other creation stories from all over the world. She refused to let her educated mind become caught up in all that religious hogwash.

But then as the speculative observer kept watching the body that was taking shape before her, she also remembered her grandmother reading her another story – *the one of the brow with the thorny crown*, she said aloud.

The mind-wandering episode stopped as Maggie stood looking around at all the people who were gathering to watch this artist, a man not big in stature but obviously huge in heart, as he moved toward a small front-end loader over by the fence. There was no expression of fear, anticipation, or any other strained emotion on his face.

It is there. The image of this whole sculpture really is there inside his head.

She watched as he drove the piece of machinery toward the middle pile of sand, which was looking more like a body all the time. He carefully added to it from the mounds on either side of the large section on which he was working.

Maggie's eyes and mind analyzed how the metal scoop

on the front of the machine became his chisel and hammer, *technically speaking*. She couldn't help but think of Mozart and Beethoven with laptops. *We are in a technological age, so technically speaking is okay*, she tried to reason.

The look in the sculptor's eyes, as he skillfully lowered the scoop and manipulated the sand to precisely the right spot, was as intense as a surgeon working on a patient. So was the artist delicately, yet intricately, working on his creation.

His creation? How odd that His creation is his creation, thinking of her memory of the creation story from moments ago.

Joshua climbed back on top of the pile of dirt and began to scoop more sand with long, pulling strokes, a motion that resembled a swimmer with beautifully precision form. He shaped the sand from underneath Christ's body until, in just a matter of minutes, the image of a cross appeared, looking much the same as if the artist had whittled it from a large tree trunk. The entire sculpture was being formed exactly as his mind saw it.

Like everyone around her, she was so mesmerized by the artist's command of his talent that she didn't move for fear of missing something. Finally, Maggie went to the car and dug a bottled water out from under the ice in the cooler and grabbed a snack from the packed basket Ebony had provided. How convenient it was that she had something to stifle the mounting hunger pangs so she could sit and watch as fingers, ribs, and limbs emerged from the pile of dust.

As she again sat in the chair, a memory of climbing onto her grandfather's lap and listening to him read from that same Bible storybook flashed across her mind. For he, too, was fond of telling her the story of God creating Adam, then Eve. She could envision Him taking a handful of dirt, like this man, and forming something beyond belief. Then Maggie pictured the Creator breathing the breath of life into the man.

"The Master's Hands," her grandmother was so fond of

saying about God's creations.

Perhaps it wasn't a myth at all, Maggie inferred as she watched the man in front of her at work. But the theory she had heard in her head sounded more like her grandmother's voice than her own.

Maggie tried to dismiss the thoughts of her ancestor. Ever since she had begun to work at the club four years ago, she had lost all contact with her dad's mother. And after the grandmother's death two years ago, she refused to have any thoughts of the woman who had once been so close to her.

She knew it must have hurt her father terribly when she didn't show up for the memorial service, but she couldn't overcome the feeling of sin and shame that ate at her every time she thought of her grandmother. And she felt it would have been most disrespectful to attend a celebration of life for this person she had once loved so dearly, when she was afraid everyone would see through her fake mask of being the Miss Prim-and-Proper Maggie Matelli.

Working at Northern Exposure was not something she had wanted to do. It was not her life's dream, and she had no intention of staying there once she found another job. *A real job.* But this job had allowed her to pay the rent and have spending money while in school.

She had managed not to tell her parents for a long time where she was employed. But when they found out, she had pulled away from them, as well. They tried to stay in touch for a while, and Maggie knew it was her that caused the distance that had grown between them.

Her memories of her parents and grandparents, though pushed to the far depths of her mind, were still pleasant ones. It seemed almost therapeutic, in a sense, to be aware of those memories trying to surface now that she was away from Ann Arbor and nearby Northern Exposure.

Chapter 7
Afternoon, Holy Monday

The weather report had predicted there would be a high of 84 degrees in Findlay for the day. Maggie was shocked that the temperature here was as warm as what she was expecting in sunny Florida. Her sweatshirt and coat from last night had been traded for a long-sleeved denim shirt, with the sleeves rolled up, over a sleeveless top and capri pants.

Youngsters ventured outdoors to take advantage of the afternoon's warmth for all sorts of reasons, she observed as she saw a couple of adolescents walking across the other side of Riverside Park. One was carrying a fishing pole over his shoulder, and had on a big-rimmed straw hat that gave him the appearance of being a dead-ringer for Huck Finn. There was a girl with him who was toting the tackle box. *Huck's Becky, I suppose.*

Talk about taking a stroll back in time, she chuckled, feeling the need to shake her head to make sure she wasn't imagining things. *This is definitely a scene from Americana.*

Maggie watched to see the whereabouts of their destination. The couple walked across the street and went in the block that was caddie-cornered from where she sat.

She decided to walk in that direction to stretch her legs for a few minutes, wondering what could attract them to that particular spot. What she discovered was a circular walk lined with huge granite stones, each one giving a bit of history about a man named Tell Taylor, a long-ago Findlay resident, and some song that he had written. Behind the stones, Maggie noticed, flowed Blanchard River.

Waterfront and sand. Imagine that. And a bright, hot sun. She strolled along the water's shore, watching the number of teenagers, on spring break from the local high school, who had gathered to fish or feed the ducks, or simply congregate with their friends. *Nice, but it's not Florida!*

Maggie began to calculate how much longer it was going to take her to reach Florida's sunny coast and that "perfect man."

Walking back from the river, she saw that the song written by Taylor was *Down By the Old Mill Stream.* Her curiosity was piqued as she began to make the circular walk, stopping at each stone to read about his life and humming the tune as she went. Maggie knew that song. Her grandmother had sung it to her as a child.

"Your grandfather would sing it to me during our courtship. He was fond of singing it to me as we would take evening strolls or sit in the front porch swing," she could hear her grandmother saying with a slight blush.

She began to sing softly to herself, "Down by the old mill stream, where I first met you . . ."

The visitor read until she found that Mr. Taylor had penned the ballad while sitting on the banks of the Blanchard River in 1908, getting his inspiration from a gristmill seven miles upstream.

She read each stone with more enthusiasm, now that she knew the song. Maggie couldn't resist the urge to smirk as she came upon the next large chunk of granite in the circle. "Tell

Taylor's career was launched when Joe Howard, comedy star of that day, heard him sing in a restaurant in Buffalo in 1901 during the Pan American Exposition and offered him a singing role in his company."

Exposition, huh? I guess you could say my career was launched because of an exposition, too.

The smirk fell to a serious expression. Maggie had no desire to work at Northern Exposure – *then or now*. It happened, with the grueling schedule of graduate school and keeping her grades up, to be the easiest way to get the money she needed for tuition and books. Now she wondered why she had been so stubbornly adamant about being responsible and paying for her own education. Her parents had offered to help, but she had been determined to do it all on her on.

Well, I did it on my own, alright, her conscience scolded as she moved to the next stone.

There are worse things I could be doing, she tried to console herself.

Besides, my whole purpose in trying to find this "perfect man" is to be able to get out of the club sooner. I'm ready to settle down, have a family . . . all those things that normal people do.

She kept walking and reading about Tell Taylor. "He died in Chicago, November 23, 1937, en route to Hollywood, California, to film the story of this, his most popular song."

How sad that one is finally going to receive recognition for his work, and he doesn't even live to see himself on the big screen. What a bummer!

The other stones told what a significant life he had led, most of his years being spent in Findlay, and how much he had done for the school system, and the public music instruction in the county. He had even donated his farm's acreage for the city's first public golf course. Mr. Taylor also had a music publishing company in Chicago.

At least he didn't spend his entire *life in this small dive. He obviously got around.*

Maggie's sadness turned into a healthy respect for a man she didn't know, but could appreciate. She sang the words of the song all the way through, hearing her grandmother's, then her grandfather's, voice with each note.

"Down by the old mill stream where I first met you. With your eyes of blue, dressed in gingham, too. It was there I knew, that you loved me true, You were sixteen, my village queen, By the old mill stream."

⊂ℨ℺

She had barely gotten back to her beach chair when she noticed a teenage boy who appeared to be fifteen or so riding his bike on the river side of the park, then down the street toward the sculpture site. His long, lanky limbs, so customary of male adolescence, looked like they were going in all directions as he pedaled the bicycle. Short blond hair that stuck up on his head, obviously having missed its comb this morning, stated that this guy had no cares for the day and intended to enjoy every moment of spring break.

Maggie watched him as he peered through his thick glasses with a definite determination in his eyes. She began to wonder what he was up to, for in his right hand, he had a long branch from a forsythia bush, full of small, bright-yellow blooms.

It was obvious that the teen had broken the branch from one of the shrubs near the Tell Taylor Memorial, for she had appreciated an entire row of them when she was there earlier. She wasn't up on the rules of Findlay, but where she was from, picking the park's flowers was a big no-no.

Still peering through his glasses, he stood, holding his bike in place, and watched Joshua, who was hard at work on the image of Christ. At the precise moment that the sculptor moved to the back of the sand pile, the teenager shot across the street on his bike, darted through a small opening for pedestrians in the chain fence, and rode right up to the sculpture. He quickly laid the branch at the base of the cross, next to Jesus' feet, and rode off as hard and fast as he could before the artist had time to get back to the front of the sand pile.

The boy had taken off across the street and ducked into the parking lot for the river's reservoir so that he could make a faster get-away.

Maggie watched for the look of surprise on Joshua's face as he walked back around the sand.

"Where'd this come from?" he asked, seeing that at the present moment, he and Maggie were the only two people there.

She looked across the street to see the boy, now a good ways down the sidewalk and taking his time, peeking back over his shoulder to make sure the artist found the token he had left. "See the boy on the bike way down there?" Maggie asked.

Joshua started to wave, but Maggie's next comment stopped him.

"He didn't want you to see him. He obviously went to great efforts to leave an anonymous gift of appreciation," she continued.

Maggie recreated the teenager's antics for the sculptor, who was visibly touched by the boy's actions.

"At first, I was shocked that he 'd broken a branch from one of the park's shrubs, but after watching what he did with it, I don't think the rangers would have minded," she concluded.

"And just think of all the negative things that boy could have been doing," Joshua responded. "There really still are a lot of good people in this world," he finished, a look of gratification making its way across his face.

The artist went back to work, packing down the sand around the base of the cross with his steel-toed boots, and adding definition to the facial and bodily features with a small hand-held tool.

Maggie looked back in the direction of the teenager, who was nearly out of sight, as he mounted the top of the hill on Osborne Street then disappeared down the slope. She thought about his gift. It was not solely for the artist. In fact, she began to wonder if it was for the artist at all, for he had laid the branch at Jesus' feet. She suspected that his offering came as a tribute to both the master, *and* the Master – in the form of the Son.

That's the way all offerings and tributes are to be made.

Maggie, with her eyes on the unfolding cross, allowed her mind to consciously recall her namesake. *Giving.* The word that best described her grandmother. *But why did she do it?* she questioned. *My grandmother walked into the places where she worked, like the boy – quietly, with a smile on her face, giving of herself to others. And I know why. It was all because of her love for Christ and her appreciation of her fellow brothers and sisters.*

She thought of her grandmother's perfect man – *my grandfather. They didn't have material possessions. But,* Maggie realized as she now rationalized about that couple, *I never saw her without a smile on her face. Not one of those plastered-on smiles, or one that turns into laughter and is contagious to everyone around it, but one of those soft, gentle smiles that spreads through a crowd by the peace and contentment it makes them feel – like the feeling within the smile's owner.*

It suddenly occurred to Maggie how many gifts her grandparents had given to people. Not once did they expect something in return. They gave because they wanted to. *And they gave anonymously.*

She watched the hands and the eyes of the sculptor. Maggie saw that same look, that *possessed* look, on his face. This man, whom she had observed spending most of his time on his knees while doing his work in the sand, was giving - to a community, a town, the world – through himself and his talent. *Without speaking one word*. She looked directly into the intensity of his face as he labored over his project. *There he is, toiling with love, expecting nothing in return.*

The onlooker wondered what had caused her grandmother to spend her life in that giving manner. From a story she had heard her mother mention only once, Maggie's grandmother was planning to be married to her childhood sweetheart when she decided that there was something more for her in life. A short while later, she met Maggie's grandfather, a missionary, whom she married, sharing in his life's work. As she recalled, her grandmother could have lived quite comfortably, never having to work, had she married her first suitor, the son of a wealthy lawyer.

Her thought stopped with the realization that had things been different between her grandparents, she would not be sitting here. Not here in Findlay, nor in sunny Florida. Maggie Matelli would not be in search of her own perfect man.

"Part of the plan. At the Master's Hand," she heard her grandmother's voice, stating words that Maggie had grown up hearing from her elder.

Flashing back to the teenager, it dawned on Maggie that Joshua was right. That young guy could have been out doing any number of things at his age. *Things like all the creeps who visit Northern Exposure. Or lonely people that come, too*, she conceded. But he chose to sit back and watch, and when he did move, it was in silence.

"It's the silent ones, the ones in the background, that are the real *servants of God,"* her grandmother would say. *"They're the ones who are never recognized here on earth. But their re-*

ward comes in heaven."

Right after some proverbial statement like that, her grandmother would say, "*Let's pray.*" Then she'd take Maggie's hand and continue, "*Now, Maggie, when you pray, remember not to do it for show, or think about who sees you. It is between you and God.*"

"Yes, ma'am," Maggie would answer, and then bow her small head and clasp her tiny hands together.

Why all this sudden thought of a grandmother who died two years ago? Maggie dismissed her thoughts as being stirred up by the words of *Down By the Old Mill Stream.*

The slamming of a car door alerted Maggie that another person had come to observe the sculpture.

Maggie watched as a woman in jeans and a t-shirt hastily made her way across the grass toward the sand.

"Hi, JJ. I got here as soon as I could. I had an all-day meeting in Toledo today and have another one tomorrow."

"Chic, boy am I glad to see you. I'm just now ready for you to start the packing."

The woman, noticing the visitor, put out her hand. "Hi, I'm Chic. Are you here to help JJ, too?"

"Uh . . . no. I'm actually on my way to Florida. I just happened to stop when I got behind the sand trucks this morning. I had intended to pull off here only long enough to get gas and some breakfast, and," Maggie paused and looked down at her watch. "Oh, my gosh, I had no idea it was this late!"

"Why don't you help us?" Chic offered. "It's too late to take off for Florida now. You can leave in the morning."

"Well, actually, I am supposed to . . ."

Maggie stopped in mid-sentence. For she was already standing in a huge pile of sand, the sun was beating down making the temperature hotter than today's expected high on the Florida coast, and she was not about to explain her search for a man.

"I have two of the levels I use for packing. I'd love to have your help," Joshua urged.

She looked down at her watch again, then back at the two smiling faces that said, "Welcome."

"Sure. Why not? I guess you're right. I can get an early start tomorrow."

"And what's your name?" Chic asked.

"Oh, sorry, I'm Maggie Matelli. Just graduated from the University of Michigan." The visitor glared at the two who had just given her a job.

A job on my vacation! She wanted to laugh, but she decided against it. *Working in the sand in the park on my spring break! I could have been with those other students on* their *mission trip if I was going to spend the day doing this*, she felt like blurting aloud. But then, she didn't want the two who had made her feel so welcome to take her comment as disdain.

"So you're from Ann Arbor?" Chic asked, stepping out of her clogs and handing Maggie a long wooden tool.

"Just the last six years while I was in college. Originally I'm from Cleveland."

Joshua interrupted the women's conversation to show Chic and Maggie how he wanted them to pack the sand. He took one of the wooden masonry levels and pounded down on the sides of the cross and the sections underneath the cross that gave the sculpture its three-dimensional effect.

Chic immediately followed suit, taking the tool from the sculptor.

Maggie looked at the piece of wood in her hands and then at Chic, who made the task look as simple as a child playing in the sand with a brightly-colored toy bucket and shovel.

Seeing the overwhelmed stare in the newcomer's eyes, Chic offered an encouraging consolation. "It took me a while to get used to this, too. This is the third year I've done this with JJ. He and his wife, Lynn, are my best friends. That's why I can get away with calling him JJ. He hates for anyone else to call him that, but I get away with it." She flashed a huge grin at the sculptor. "Probably only because I come and do the grunt work for him here."

Maggie nodded, still trying to get the hang of the tool.

"Advertising, huh?" Joshua asked, beginning to work on the second pile of sand.

Who, me? rushed through Maggie's head as she wondered what she had done to give away her secret occupation.

"What?" Chic asked, wondering what brought on that question. "Oh, the shirt," she grinned, looking down at the bank logo splattered across her chest.

Maggie breathed a sigh of relief.

"I grabbed this on the way out of the meeting this afternoon. I didn't have my spring and summer clothes out of the attic yet. Who would have ever thought we'd have temps in the eighties in Findlay this week?"

"Yeah," Joshua replied. He looked at Maggie, "You'd think we were in Florida if you didn't know better."

Well, I wouldn't go that *far*, she wanted to say. Again she just nodded.

"Chic works for the bank. She's actually a manager of the downtown office."

Maggie eyed the woman beside her more closely. Here she was, with her blond hair hanging straight down around her face as she pounded in rhythmic motions in the sand. She was not in the least bothered by the dirt getting underneath her manicured nails. Her business image was completely lost as she stood there working; she could have easily been mistaken for one of the laborers who hold up construction signs along the highways. And her energetic stamina had caused Maggie to consider Chic not much older than herself.

Her words took flight before Maggie could stop them. "But you look so young."

"Thanks, dear," Chic laughed. "I have three grown children."

Maggie stopped her motion entirely. "You're kidding?"

Chic shook her head.

This time, Maggie turned to Josh. "She doesn't *really* have three grown children?" Her voice of shock expressed a question rather than a statement.

"Yep, she really does."

Maggie looked at Chic again, trying not to stare, but searching to find the slightest hint of crows' feet on the woman's face.

"What is it here?" she asked, thinking back to the Golden Girls and the waitress. "Nobody here looks their age. Is there something in the water?"

"Blanchard River? Are you kidding?" Chic laughed. "There's nothing in the water here but old yucky dirt." She stopped her pounding for an instant. "But thanks for the compliment. I'm sure you'll see my son and his girlfriend at some point during the evening."

With that, the banker looked at Joshua. "People will be getting off work soon. If they hear you're out here, this place will get swamped."

"The newspaper photographer didn't come out until this afternoon, so it will be a couple of days until the story runs. They may put the picture of the trucks in, though. Several photographers and journalists were here during the morning hours when the drivers unloaded the sand."

Yeah, if it hadn't been for them, I'd be halfway to the Florida line by now, Maggie wanted to say.

Chic's prediction was right. People driving down the street

saw the sand and turned into the park. Then they must have gone home and called their neighbors, for people continued to come in growing numbers.

"Aren't you hungry?" Chic asked Joshua. "I know you haven't eaten all day."

"I'm working against the clock. The rains are supposed to move in tomorrow afternoon and continue for the rest of the week."

A good reason for me to get out of here, Maggie told herself.

"The wind's been blowing so hard and fast today that I feel like I'm in Desert Storm," Joshua said.

"You've got to eat," Maggie offered, wondering why she had gotten into this conversation. "This is a huge job, and you have to keep up your strength. You've worked non-stop all day. I've watched you."

Joshua paused for a minute. "You know what I'd like to have? I'd love a big cheeseburger and some fries and a pop."

"Here. Let me go get it for you," Maggie said. "Can't I find a burger joint out on the main drag down there?" she asked, pointing toward Tiffin Avenue.

Chic laughed. "She's only been here a day, and she already knows her way around the town."

Oh, great! Maggie wanted to respond.

"There's money in my shirt over on the picnic table," Joshua offered.

"No, this one's on me. This is the cheapest entertainment I've had in months."

As she drove away, she thought of her remark, and how much "gentlemen" paid for the entertainment of watching her work. Suddenly, Maggie felt even more ashamed of her past. Tears welled up in her eyes as she thought of the image on that cross, his hands extended, the legs limply dangling.

What she was seeing at the park was not entertainment. What *she* offered was entertainment, *a quick fix*, something that did no one any good, and left everyone involved with nothing.

But the scene at the park, the image. . . Maggie realized that it left her with a longing. But it was a very different kind of longing. She felt so drawn to the man she saw portrayed in the sand, and he wasn't even a real man.

Her heart yearned. Her soul longed. Maggie suddenly wished that her grandmother were here. She would have the words of wisdom that her granddaughter needed to hear.

That thought caused Maggie's heart to ache even more, for she realized how detrimental it had been to herself to shut her grandmother out of her life. During her high school and college years, though, it came to seem that the elder was "too religious."

Maggie had not been one to be outwardly rebellious. In fact, she had been the quiet sort. So for her to go to work at Northern Exposure had not been the typical adolescent run-away, or the "in your face" attitude. It had merely been a "quick fix" for her, an easy way to earn money. And being the quiet sort, she didn't have to say much. She had been able to do her job without being recognized by college peers. For in the establishment where she worked, they appealed to a higher class of clientele, not people on a student's, or even a professor's, salary.

She stopped the car at the first fast food chain she saw. Although she had intended to enter the drive-thru, Maggie felt the need to be alone for a few minutes so she opted to go inside the eatery.

As she turned off the engine, she stared up at the sky and wondered if God were looking down at her. "Hey, God, it's me, Maggie Matelli. I haven't spoken to you in a long while, but you know my grandmother very well. In fact, if you *are* watching and listening to me, she's probably there right beside you.

"I know this distance between us, and between my grand-mother and me, was all my fault. I guess in the shame and dis-grace I've felt because of my job, I thought I could hide by not looking for you . . . or talking to you," she added slowly, letting her head lower in guilt.

Maggie felt a huge lump in her throat. She knew this was nothing like she had intended or expected from her vacation. Yes, she had fully intended to get away from everything and ev-erybody. *Like in those quiet places where Grandmother always said God talked back.*

She lifted her head again, feeling the need to continue. "Well, God, perhaps my grandmother is haunting me from the grave. If anyone could do it, she could." Maggie shook her head, fond memories replacing her feeling of unworthiness. "You know how much I really did love her. I just couldn't bear to face her after making the wrong turn that I did."

The tears that accompanied the lump in her throat turned into a smile. *A wrong turn. I'm beginning to think my exit into Findlay was a wrong turn.* The smile grew larger. *Or maybe, thanks to you, Grandmother, it was a right turn.* Maggie laughed.

"What's that Ohio motto, God? With you, all things are possible? Maybe two wrongs *do* make a right!" she blurted aloud as she got out of the car and slammed the door with confidence, not caring who heard her.

She went inside the restaurant and ordered a cheesebur-ger combo with ketchup, mustard and pickles - just like Joshua had requested - and smirked at the idea that she was at least taking food back to some man, that she was providing a man with something he really needed and wanted.

For the first time since she could remember, Maggie felt needed, a necessary part of society. And she liked it.

The quest for my man will begin tomorrow, she assured herself, walking back to the car, bag in hand.

Chapter 8
Evening, Holy Monday

Joshua had to be pried away from his work to eat.

Maggie had suspected that would be the case after having watched the diligence and discipline with which he had worked all day. She had seen enough students of the arts at U-M to know how they were when they got caught up in a project.

It was Chic who finally placed her hands on Joshua's back and pushed him to the picnic table, where he sat down beside Maggie's chair – the one meant to take its place beside her man.

The visitor had not bothered the artist during the day, but she took this opportunity to compliment Joshua on his work. "I'm really glad I got sidetracked here today. Your work is awesome. It's been an incredible experience for me to watch you."

"Thank you for your kinds words. And thank you for the burger. I didn't realize how hungry I was."

"You're welcome. Now you'll be set to work the rest of the night at the rate you're going."

"I may need to, with the weather the way it's supposed to

be."

"You remind me of the stories I used to hear in Italy about Michelangelo," Maggie went on.

"You flatter me too much," Joshua said humbly, wiping his mouth, but showing delight with her praise.

"No, really. A guide in Rome once told us how the artist never used models or patterns because he saw the images in the marble, and his job was to let them out. That was truly a gift from God. Watching you, it's obvious that you see the figures inside these piles. You just have to scoop away the excess sand."

The sculptor stopped eating and looked at his admirer. "I guess it is a gift from God. But all I want to do here is to give the people of Findlay a gift . . . something to offer them a way of relating to Christ."

"From the looks of the people I've seen and heard today, I'd say your wish is coming true." Maggie's sincere expression said that her words were genuine.

"I had no intention of spending the day, much less the evening, here. If truth be known, I was livid this morning when I got stuck behind the sand trucks. I wanted *nothing* in my way of getting to Florida. I'm looking forward to the sun and the sand, something I've never been exposed to in Cleveland or Ann Arbor, and it was my reward to myself for completing grad school." Maggie muffled an embarrassed chuckle. "My real goal, *or mission*, this week was to find myself a man . . . my perfect man."

Chic burst into laughter. "Honey, don't you know there's no such thing?"

Joshua smiled at Maggie. "She is right, you know."

"I guess," Maggie conceded rather sheepishly. "But you know what I mean. There's supposed to be someone out there for everyone, and I'm ready to find my mate, settle down, and have a family."

"That's an odd switch for a college student, especially of

grad school. Most kids are anxious to get out in the world and make their mark, thinking of nothing but bringing in the almighty dollar." Chic stopped pounding the sand. "But I guess it's a good thing people think that way or I wouldn't have a job."

Maggie thought of the people who visited Northern Exposure. *Too bad they don't think like all the others. Then I wouldn't be trapped at the club. I'd love not to have that job.*

"Your art really does touch people," Maggie finished, changing back to the original topic of discussion.

"It is a most rewarding undertaking. You wouldn't believe the people who come to see it." Joshua wolfed down another bite and washed it down with pop. "I love doing these things on the beach whenever we go to Florida to visit my relatives."

"You do these large figures of Christ in Florida?" Maggie asked, her voice full of bewilderment.

"Yes," Joshua answered. "There are people everywhere who worship Jesus and appreciate the sculptures."

"I know," Maggie tried to explain, "it's just . . . well . . . on the beach, I expected to see sand castles, or people covered in sand. You know, things like that. I figured people were trying to get away from home routines and religion."

It was clear to both Joshua and Chic, as they exchanged glances, that this young woman had a lot of maturing to do.

The artist had prayed that at least one person would find Christ through his sculpture. Perhaps this was his answer to prayer. He prayed silently to God as he continued to talk with Maggie that he would be given the right words that she needed to hear.

"I did one of these near West Palm Beach. It was way down behind a plastic fence, but I did it there so that it would be protected. One morning, as I was out working on it real early, a man ventured down to where I was.

"He walked slowly toward me, like he wasn't sure he was

supposed to be there, but when he got close enough to see what was pictured in the sand, he moved up closer to view the image. After a few minutes, he fell to his knees in prayer."

Joshua took another gulp of the pop. "I didn't want to disturb him, so I kept quietly working."

Maggie thought of her initial reaction to Joshua and the truckers, *Little boys who never grew up.* She realized how right she had been as she listened to his story. This man's work really was play to him.

"When the man stood, he moved closer to me. 'I'm a minister here in West Palm Beach,' he began. 'My father has been ill for months and I've been caring for him. I walk down the beach every morning to have a few minutes each day away from the situation and to try to clear my head if only for a short bit. His condition has really gotten to me lately, and I came out this morning praying, actually begging, for a sign from God of His strength to be used through me.'

"The man's face relaxed for the first time. 'I never walk this far. But this morning, I felt the urge to keep going. When I came to the fence, I knew I was supposed to turn back, but my feet and legs wouldn't let me. Something made me step over the green plastic and keep walking.

"'Now I know what it was. If I hadn't crossed that line, I would have never seen this, and I would not have received my sign from God.' The minister took another step toward me and extended his hand. 'God has used you as a messenger, my friend,' he said, encasing my hand with both of his and shaking it as hard as he could."

Joshua stared into Maggie's eyes. "I knew from that moment that nothing I did with these sculptures was ever done in vain."

Chic walked over and took a break, sitting down beside the artist as she reached for her water bottle. "Do you remember the woman in the wheelchair who came last year?" she asked him.

"You mean the one who was so large, and all the men went over and helped to carry her to the sculpture?" he asked back.

"Yes, that's the one." Chic turned toward Maggie and began to relate the story. "Last year, we were sitting here relaxing one afternoon after JJ had finished the sculpture. We saw a woman helping another woman out of a van. It had one of those lift-gates for getting out the wheelchair. The driver of the van removed the wheelchair and went to the passenger side and helped this woman into the chair.

"As they got to the grass," she continued, indicating the spot with her hand, "the woman pushing the wheelchair struggled terribly to get it to move."

Joshua picked up the story here. "There were a good number of people hanging around at that point. They saw me looking in that direction. When I started to move toward her, some of the other men offered to go get her. They went over and picked up the woman, chair and all, and carried her close enough that she could see the sculpture."

"'Thank you,' she said. 'Thank you so much. My sister is dying with cancer and I had to come here and see this sculpture that everyone was talking about. I knew it would make me feel better. And I had to come and pray for healing for my sister.' The woman looked down at her hands in the wheelchair. 'No matter what form that healing takes.'"

"She sat there like that for a few minutes," Chic finished, "with no one saying a word. Most people bowed their heads and prayed with her. She finally raised her head and asked who the sculptor was. JJ moved over to her and shook her hand. The woman pulled his head down and kissed his cheek. 'You are a blessing from God, my son.' Her words came out as a whisper to him, but there was such a silence here that everyone heard her. There was hardly a dry eye in the place."

At this point, Joshua looked directly at Maggie. "You see, it doesn't matter where people are – whether at home, at work, or on vacation – faith is a part of our lives. It doesn't take a coffee break or a vacation. We can leave God behind, but the fact is, God *never* leaves us behind. He is *always* with us . . . in *every* circumstance."

Chic took Maggie's hand. "If you stick around this week, you'll see all sorts of incidences like the ones we mentioned. It's really something how people come here and bring their burdens and lay them at the feet of this Christ figure. It's almost like a shrine for them in a way. The visual image somehow makes it easier for them to feel a personal relationship with their Lord."

"That's why I'm adding a sculpture of Christ praying beside the empty tomb this year," Joshua stated. "I hope the people who come to see will be able to think about Mary Magdalene, and Peter and John, and their reactions to the Risen Lord."

Maggie stared at the sculptor with a blank stare.

He feared he'd said something to offend her.

"Is anything wrong, Maggie?" Chic asked, noticing the change of mood in the young woman's face.

"No." She started to speak, but paused. Maggie looked at the pile of sand where Joshua had pointed when he mentioned the tomb. "No, it's nothing. You know how you sometimes get a tingle in your spine. I've heard some people call it a cat walking over your grave. Just one of those weird deja vu sensations."

Several people walked up, grabbing the attention of the three who sat talking.

"Chicadee, I'm here and reporting for duty," one of the young men called out.

"This is our work crew," Chic explained to Maggie. "Looks like we're in trouble, doesn't it?" she grinned at the five young adults, one of whom was her son, who had come to help with the packing.

Joshua and Chic got back to work, speaking to the helpers and giving them instructions, and leaving Maggie to contemplate the empty tomb.

Or more importantly, the visitors to the empty tomb, she said to herself, still viewing the sand waiting to be made into the third sculpture.

C3&O

Maggie glanced at her watch again, totally unaware of how late it had gotten to be. She watched the artist and his faithful crew work for a few more minutes, then packed up her chair and went to the car.

I'll find a place nearby to spend the night where I can get back on the road in the morning. If I leave right after breakfast, maybe I can beat the crowd who will be making their way here. That way I can get to the interstate with no delays.

She was a little disgusted with herself for allowing some trivial thing to get in the way of her vacation, not to mention her search for a mate, but Maggie knew better than to worry about the time she had lost.

I'll make up for it tomorrow, she vowed, planning to drive from sun-up to midnight the next day. *I have enough snacks so that I won't have to stop to eat. I can stay on the road for the long haul.*

The long haul, she mouthed. *The long haul to finding a real man.* Maggie gave a long, exasperated sigh. *Real men love Jesus . . .*

Chapter 9
Morning, Holy Tuesday

Maggie neglected to set the alarm on the clock, figuring she would wake at the morning's first light. Despite her intention to leave at sunrise, yesterday at the park, *and all that packing*, had taken more of a toll on her body than she had suspected. When she saw that it was nearly eight o'clock, she jumped in the shower, and then quickly got her things together. Before checking out of the motel, she made sure the cooler was full of ice and the snacks were easily accessible.

She was not in the mood for another cholesterol-packed breakfast, but Maggie figured it would be easier to find her way back to the interstate from the diner where she had eaten the day before. Besides, she knew where Miller's was and going there would save her from wasting any more time in search of another place.

Ah, a space with my name on it, she voiced, parallel parking in the only empty spot in front of the luncheonette.

"I see you're still here," Joni smiled, handing Maggie a

menu as she walked through the door.

"Yes, it *was* rather interesting watching the sculptor in action yesterday. But there's some sand in Florida calling my name, so I just came by to grab a bite of breakfast before getting back on the road."

"You know, a lot of people are going to be flocking in here over the next couple of weeks 'cause they say *this* sand is callin' their name."

"Hmmm," Maggie scowled, wondering how this sand could possibly hold that kind of attraction to anyone. "How so?" she asked.

"I'm not real sure. But I thought I'd walk down there after work tonight and check it out myself."

The breakfast seemed even better than it had the previous morning. In fact, Maggie found the French toast very tasty, similar to what her grandmother used to make for her when she was a child.

"Why don't you stick around?" the waitress asked as she poured more tea for Maggie. "Maybe this sand can call your name. It's a lot closer than driving to Florida."

"No, thanks. There's also a man waiting for me down there."

"Oh, really. What's his name?" Joni asked, thinking back to the customer's brief mention of this the previous morning.

"I don't know. I haven't met him yet. But I fully intend to before this week is over."

Maggie chuckled inside, for she could hear Ebony saying, "I heard that."

"Gotcha," Joni replied, shaking her head, letting her customer know that she understood. "But if you change your mind, we have several nice single men around here. And there'll be one more before the weekend."

"Huh?" Maggie asked, a confused expression on her face.

"Never mind," Joni answered, her eyes twinkling with that 'I know something you don't know' gaze. "I was simply thinking out loud."

Maggie looked around her at the people who had come in Miller's for breakfast this morning. It was a little later than yesterday, so she saw a different crowd. The patrons sitting around her now were by themselves, most of them seated on a bar stool at the counter. Each of them was reading a newspaper, and it struck her as odd that each publication was different.

What was more noteworthy to her was that the waitress and grill cook weren't yelling back and forth as loudly as they had yesterday, and the clatter of the dirty dishes being washed carried a softer drone so that it, too, did not disturb the air of quietness that had settled on the luncheonette.

There was only one table that had any conversation going on, and that was at the front corner table where the young couple had retreated for seclusion yesterday.

This must be the designated table for important issues, Maggie thought, glancing over her shoulder to get a peek at the two men who were discussing a land deal in Florida.

Florida? I'm supposed to be almost there by now.

She downed three more bites of the French toast, pulled some money for the tip out of her purse and went to the cash register to pay.

"See you this evening if you're still around. It's supposed to be getting much colder during the afternoon due to a northeasterly wind coming through. By tonight, the temperature is supposed to drop at least fifty degrees. I'll bring you some hot chocolate."

"Thanks," Maggie nodded. "I really appreciate your offer, but I'll be long gone by then. I have no intention of spending my week in the cold and the rain that's supposed to be coming."

"Very well, then. But come back and see us sometime."

"I may just do that." Maggie reached out her hand and shook that of the waitress. "It's been a pleasure."

"That's Findlay for you," Joni offered. "Folks leave sometimes when they get out of school, but they most always come back." She winked at Maggie, still looking as if she knew a secret and wasn't about to share it.

With that, Maggie walked out the door, got in her car, and headed toward the interstate. *Sun, sand, and my man, here I come.* She could almost taste the key lime pie as she drove from the ramp onto I-75 South.

☙❧

She had only gone seven miles when she saw both lanes of traffic stopped. *Not again,* she mumbled to herself. When she got a little closer to the next exit ramp, she could see an officer directing traffic up it, and another officer at the top of the ramp giving detour directions.

Maggie heard the officer tell the people in the car in front of her that the southbound lanes would be closed most of the morning due to a tractor-trailer truck accident that had fuel leakage. She decided rather than to wait in traffic, she'd go back to the park, sit in her beach chair, and begin the novel she'd brought. *Besides, a good juicy book will have me in a romantic mood when I get to the sunny coast. The temperature's not supposed to drop until mid-afternoon. I'll be long gone by then.*

People were already congregating at Riverside Park when she arrived. She grabbed the chair from the trunk, pulled her book out of her tote bag that had been carefully packed for the beach, and threw on her visor and sunglasses.

She looked at the sculpture that the artist had begun the day before. It was obvious that he had spent the entire evening working on it. Maggie noticed that the branch of yellow forsythia had been carefully placed so that it was standing right at the base of the cross in front of Jesus' feet.

"Rains are supposed to be coming in this afternoon. I'm working against the clock to finish as much as I can before they get here." The sculptor stopped long enough to stick his finger up in the air. "Winds are coming in from the northeast. We don't need that." Joshua was talking over his shoulder to some of the spectators as he continued adeptly moving his hands.

Maggie looked at the sky. *Not a cloud in it*, she observed.

"We'll pray that the weather doesn't destroy your work," one of the men in the crowd offered.

"Can you believe that every year I'm up against something, but it has yet to mess up my sculptures?" Joshua asked, not really surprised, but more in a tone of making conversation about the goodness of God.

"Look who you're talking about," replied the wife of the man who had begun to pray.

Maggie recalled the comment of another man who had placed his chair beside hers the evening before. A couple of women had mentioned that they hoped no one came and did harm to the sculpture. The man leaned over to Maggie and said, "You know, it's funny that people don't come in here and tear this up. But I've been coming out to watch Joshua every year. No one ever touches it. It's like the place becomes a sacred ground when he does these sculptures."

She had gathered that by the moods of everyone who had come to observe what was happening in the park. Even in the midst of people walking their dogs, or children on the playgrounds, or exercisers riding bikes, jogging, or walking, there was a presence in the air pervading all the activities that were a part of the environment around Joshua's mural.

His work goes beyond human expression, she reasoned.

It's that Master's Hand that's leading the master's hand.

The vacationer sat straight up. *There go those words again!* They were the words, the phrase, which her grandmother was fond of using when she saw God at work in someone's life, someone who was making a difference in the lives of others.

CBXO

There was a quiet lull just before lunch when no one was around besides Maggie and Joshua. She didn't dare talk to him, for she was as touched by his actions and his work as she was by the art being produced. Feeling he needed some private artistic space, she decided to go grab a bite of lunch.

She had also made another decision, one she had tried to escape all morning, but she was going to find a room for one more evening. At the rate Joshua was going, Maggie felt the sculpture would be done enough that she could see the full mural by tomorrow morning.

As she folded her beach chair, she saw a woman getting out of her car and hastily walking toward the volleyball pit. This was a woman who, too, was on a mission. She had been here before, Maggie was sure, from the determined look in her eye.

A fan, she smiled. The newcomer tried to make eye contact with the approaching woman to greet her, but the "fan" was so caught up in getting to catch the artist alone that she didn't even notice Maggie.

Before the woman had walked halfway across the park, she yelled ahead to Joshua. "I knew you'd be out here. I just *had* to come and see you."

It was then that Maggie noticed the camera in the woman's hand. By the time she had reached the sculpture, she was snapping pictures as fast as the film would advance to the next frame. Then she held the camera down by her side as she looked at the portrayal of Christ in the sand, tears forming in her eyes.

Joshua put down his trowel and walked over to the woman. Putting his arm around her shoulder, he said in a low voice, "Thank you for coming back to see my work this year."

She looked up at his eyes, not at all bothered by the sand on his arm getting on her shirt. "I had to come. Ever since that first sculpture, two years ago, I've made daily trips to see them until they were gone. I just live a couple of streets over, so this is on my way to everywhere." The woman wiped her eyes. "You don't know how much this means to me. It does this to me every year."

"What's your name?" Joshua asked.

"Jewel," she replied.

The woman didn't give her last name, and it wasn't important. But Maggie knew that the woman truly was a jewel, and wondered if God had specially named her.

Names can say a lot, Maggie thought as she got in her car, trying to decide on something besides a burger for lunch. *I wonder if I'll ever be able to use my* real *given name out in the world of Public Policy.*

Heading down Tiffin Avenue, or "Restaurant Alley" as she had heard the locals refer to it, she noticed a sign up in front of Cheddar's that read, "Key Lime Pie is back."

Key Lime Pie! Did I make it to Florida and someone forgot to tell me? Maggie stared at the sign. *And it says, "is back." It must have a reputation for being good or they wouldn't be advertising its return.*

Maggie whipped into the parking lot of the restaurant. *There'll be no burgers today.*

Lunch consisted of a huge slice of pie, topped with homemade raspberry sauce, then a bowl of soup for dessert. The key lime dessert was excellent, as scrumptious as her anticipation of a slice from the Florida coast.

I'll have another piece on the coast later this week, she promised herself, still tasting the sweet tartness from the slice she had just devoured. *And another piece this afternoon*, she grinned as she ordered a slice to go. *After all, it is vacation*, Maggie smugly told herself, trying to excuse all the extra calories.

She used the payphone in the restaurant to call about a room reservation. Flipping to the yellow pages, she found a Victorian bed-and-breakfast that sounded "homey" to her, so she dialed the number to see if there was an available room.

"There is one room open currently," a male voice told her.

Not even bothering to ask the price, she replied, "I'd like to reserve it, please. My name is Maggie Matelli, and if you'll give me directions, I'll be there shortly."

Chapter 10
Early afternoon, Holy Tuesday

About two steps from the door, she heard its knob turn and saw it open.

"Welcome to Rose Gate Cottage," spoke the man holding onto the knob. His natural, congenial smile offered an even warmer welcome than his words. It was heightened by the exuberant twinkle that danced in the eyes of the woman who stood behind him.

"I'm Charlie Brentwood and this is my wife, June. Please make our home your home while you are here."

Maggie's eyes were already scurrying around her surroundings, taking in the many sights that were visible from the spot where she stood just inside the front door.

"And if you happen to play the piano, please feel free to use the one in the parlor," he added, noticing her stare in that direction.

Her searching eyes caught sight of the original sheet music to *Down By the Old Mill Stream* that stood on the music rack of the piano. Beside it was the music to *Bring Back My Baby Bumble-Bee*, another song that her grandmother had sung to her as a child.

Maggie knew that she was in the right place, and for the first time since her arrival in Findlay, she was cognizant that her being here was not merely by coincidence. *It really* was *a right turn, Grandmother! Something I should have recognized sooner,* she mused, thinking not only of all the little instances that had hinted toward this realization, but also the fact that she had a newly acquired Master's degree – a fact that should have made her somewhat intelligent about the things going on around her.

A white Maltese came flying through the door, barking and wagging her tail as she jumped up in Charlie's arms and held her nose out toward Maggie. "And this is Emmy," introduced the host.

"Hi, Emmy. You remind me of the dog I had as a child. Her name was Lucy." Maggie reached out and petted the white neatly-groomed body of the cottage's pet and guard dog.

"Let me show you to your room," Charlie offered, putting Emmy back on the floor and taking Maggie's bag. "You'll be staying in the Garden Villa."

Garden Villa? That's sure a far stretch from the ocean-front room I was planning on. Oh, well, at least it has a nice ring to it.

As they wound their way up the flight of stairs, which made a turn halfway up, Maggie noticed a lovely, most pristine bronze bust of a woman sitting atop the post.

June, seeing their guest's interest said, "That's our guardian of the stairs."

"Really?" Maggie asked, her interest mounting. "Is there a story behind this statuette?"

"No," answered June. "And actually, that's the first time

I've ever called her that. But for some reason, that title hit me all of a sudden."

"Hmmm," mused the guest. "Perhaps it's my presence. This whole town seems to me like one big guardian angel."

"It is a wonderful place to be," Charlie noted. "We've been here for thirty years, and we wouldn't think of going elsewhere."

"That's a nice recommendation. But I'm only here for the evening. I'm actually on my way to Florida. I have big plans to spend my week in the sun and sand, and find my perfect man."

Charlie winked at June. "Here's your room," he said to the guest, placing her single suitcase on the luggage rack in an obscure corner.

Maggie looked around in amazement. What she saw before her was a vision like something from one of the travel magazines she loved to leaf through. She imagined herself, and her "perfect man," touring the world and staying in places like this, rather than the "same old, same old" rooms of the motel chains.

"It's lovely," the guest said, whirling around to see everything in the room. "It's so elegant, yet so cozy," Maggie added as she walked toward the gas fireplace that gave the room a visual aura of warmth.

"We'll leave you to relax and enjoy. Again, please make yourself at home in our home while you're here, and help yourself to the selection of teas and coffees on the sideboard in the hallway outside your room," Charlie finished.

The guest took a peek in the hallway, trying to catch everything she had missed on her way to the room. There was a small wooden bench beside the sideboard that had antique stuffed animals on it. One in particular caught her attention.

"This looks just like the velveteen rabbit in the storybook," she said with a childlike excitement. "I love that story."

"Me, too," June replied. "This was actually my father's stuffed animal," she added, picking it up and handing it to their guest. "We found it in his attic, after he died, when we were go-ing through and cleaning out things."

"Wow," Maggie commented. "How great to have some-thing of your family's heritage like this. Especially something that he treasured as a child."

"June makes stuffed animals," Charlie explained. "She crafts them to look like the antique bears and rabbits."

"I used to. I don't do it so much anymore, but it gave children a bit of happiness to feel they had something similar to what their grandparents had played with and loved as children," June added.

It was not surprising to find that this woman, who still possessed her childlike spirit, had designed and created stuffed bears and rabbits to be held and cuddled by adults and children alike. She looked at the couple's faces, both of which were cov-ered with smiles that said, "I'm glad you're here. Sit down and rest a while." There was quite a difference from the fake, though suggesting, smiles that welcomed the paying guests to her club.

"I'm so impressed. And I'm so glad I found this place," Maggie ended.

"We'll be around should you need something. All you have to do is let us know. We want this to be a memorable stay for you," Charlie said, already heading down the stairs.

"I'm sure it will," the guest ventured, not knowing what made her say those words, or why she had that feeling. For she knew that statement was more than simply a polite act.

As soon as her host and hostess were down the stairs, Maggie plopped backwards on the four-poster bed, with her arms outstretched, and lay staring up at the full canopy above her. The room was filled with antique pieces, each one possessing a distinct personality. Already she loved the ornate lamps in the room - especially the pink one, shaped like an Easter egg, that set in front of the window.

She looked around a bit longer before walking the few steps into the bathroom. It was incredibly spacious, and the fully-mirrored wall around the huge tub made it seem even larger. Maggie loved the pale aqua color that melted into the cream accents, and the columns that stood at the corners of the tub. The shell-shaped lavatory helped to create a mood of romance and femininity.

Maggie thought how wonderful it would be to share this space with someone special, someone who loved her and only her. She grabbed the bottom of one of the plush white robes that hung beside the bathroom door and held it up to her face, basking in its rich softness that made her feel pampered just by touching it.

And how wonderful it is going to be to wrap up in this tonight and lounge in the high-back chair with my romance novel beside the fireplace. Sometimes being alone isn't such a bad thing.

The temperature outside was dropping noticeably and dampness was overtaking the air. Together, those elements of nature made for a frigid chill, so Maggie decided to get back to the park while she could still enjoy the artist's labor of love. She thought about making a cup of hot tea for the road, but decided that would be better with the book later.

Chapter 11
Mid-afternoon, Holy Tuesday

On her way back to the park, she passed a brick building with a green awning. "Dietsch Brothers," Maggie said aloud, reading the white letters on the awning. "That's the ice cream place that one of the Golden Girls told me about," she added, still talking aloud.

Forgetting the chill in the air, she turned around and went back to the establishment that had become a landmark in Findlay. The building was so clean that it looked brand new, not like it had been here since the thirties, serving lots of customers and bringing them pleasure with its frozen dairy concoctions.

This place has probably cured more ills than the pharmacy down the street, she smiled as she opened the door and caught a whiff of all the chocolates that lined the aisles directly in front of her.

From the moment Maggie entered the door, and the carefully arranged tiles on the floor proudly pronounced in the same green-and-white letters as the awning, "Dietsch Brothers, Fine

Chocolates, Ice Cream," she knew she was in love. It wasn't the same as finding the man she had set out in search of, but from the looks of all the flavors in the cooler, it was a close second.

Next to key lime pie, Maggie's favorite dessert had always been ice cream. But she didn't think of it as dessert. It was one of the simple pleasures of life, to be consumed and enjoyed at any hour of the day.

And from the looks of this place, I'm not the only one who feels that way.

She remembered the suggestion about the banana split, but for now, the pink of the peppermint ice cream seemed to be what beckoned her palette. The visitor decided to check out the framed newspaper articles on the back wall. *This place, too, must hold a prominent place in the town's history.*

Maggie discovered that the family business had been taken over by the sons, and that their father, in his eighties, still came in most days. She wondered how many rewards had been granted at this place for good grades, birthdays or anniversaries. The chocolates, with messages molded into each bar, lined the walls indicating that these candies were indeed used for a variety of occasions.

"May I help you?" a man asked as she walked back toward the counter.

"Yes, I'll have a scoop of the peppermint in a cup." Maggie watched him, recognizing him as one of the owners from the newspaper's picture. "Great place you have here," she said, as he handed her the cup. "Do you still make everything in house?"

"Right back there," he pointed.

The place was immaculate. Maggie couldn't believe the family pride that must have accompanied this place. But then she remembered the year her parents had taken her grandparents and her to see the Passion Play for Easter in the village of Oberammergau, Germany.

The farmhouses had been so clean that they could have eaten off the floor, a fact that had struck Maggie as she listened to her mother and grandmother comment on the way the townspeople took such care and pride in their belongings.

That same pride must have passed down through this family, for with a name like Dietsch, they've got to be German, too.

As she spooned a bite of the ice cream into her mouth, Maggie remembered that particular Easter, and all the other Easters she had spent with her family. There were many years that she wasn't able to see her grandparents, due to their work, but there was never a time that spring wasn't heralded in by a basket of treats, an egg hunt and a delectable noontime meal on Easter Sunday.

Her parents made sure that Holy Week received the spiritual significance it deserved, and Maggie grew up learning and memorizing the events of that week. But over the past few years, that part of her childhood had taken a back seat, along with many of the other memories of her family.

It seemed almost amazing that here it was Holy Week, and she had planned such an eventful happening for so many months. But for some unknown reason, her plans were not getting off the ground.

Hey, who can complain? Maggie grinned. *I've got a tasty ice cream, a great room, and I'm having a blast.*

She let her thoughts drift away as she continued her drive back to the park, still thinking of a way to encounter a man, her "perfect man" before she got home. Maybe Joni's tip about the eligible bachelors of Findlay would come in handy before the week was over.

CR&O

Maggie hauled her beach chair out of the car and found a spot that provided a great vantage point for the section of mural that Joshua was currently sculpting. The portrayal of Christ on the cross was pretty much done, minus some of the minute details, and the image of Christ carrying the cross uphill was now visible as the artist continued to mold and shape the pile of sand.

Three boys came riding their bikes toward her. They stopped when they saw Joshua at work.

"Hey, look," exclaimed one of the boys. "It's the sand-man."

All the bikes came to a sudden halt as the boys stopped to observe the artist and his worthy endeavor.

"I've never seen him before. I've only seen the sculpture after it's finished and he's already gone," added the boy who had called their attention to the 'sandman.'"

"Me, too," replied another of the boys.

The third boy was dismounting his bike and laying it on the ground so that he could get a closer look. Both of the other boys followed suit, not to be outdone.

"Hey, mister, you did an awesome job on that," called the first boy, apparently the spokesman for the group.

"Thanks," Joshua responded.

Maggie watched as the boys sat down outside the circle of sand and began to let their own hands make small shapes in the dirt.

The sculptor mounted his tractor and began to move more of the huge pile of sand into a workable area. He suggested to the boys that they move to a safer distance.

Being careful not to block Maggie's view, they backed toward her chair, but one of the boys was still in the way of the tractor.

As Joshua moved closer to them, the talkative boy cried out, "Don't run over my friend. He's the only friend I've got."

Maggie chuckled to herself. "Surely you have at least one other friend," she said aloud, pointing to the third boy.

"He's not my friend, he's my brother," was the reply she got.

She wanted to laugh. *Typical siblings.*

With that, the third boy - the brother - spoke up. "You do have Jesus for a friend."

Maggie was touched by the serious insight of the boy's statement. *He must be the brains of the group.*

The boys sat on the seat of the picnic bench beside Maggie's chair, intrigued by every movement of the artist.

"I sure wish I could do that," spoke up the first boy again.

"Why don't you guys go around to the back of the sculpture and work on your own creations?" she suggested.

The talkative one looked at her for a moment. Noticing her empty container from the pie with the fork on top, he asked, "Hey, lady, are you going to use that?"

"No." Maggie handed the plastic fork to him. She opened the Styrofoam box and took out a knife and spoon. "And here's something for your two friends." She chuckled aloud. "Excuse me, your friend and your brother."

A huge grin spread over the boy's face. He knew he had made a new friend, now giving him two.

"Here, guys, let's go," he said, handing each of the other boys a plastic utensil.

They trotted to the back side of the sculpture.

Maggie loved the way these young guys were using their imaginations to do something creative and stay out of trouble instead of wasting the afternoon away seated in front of a television set, or glued to a video game or computer. *Too bad more kids aren't like them.*

But then, in the short span of time she had been in Findlay, she recounted the number of children who had passed through the park and begged their parents to let them stay longer to watch "the sandman." She thought of all the hype of modern society and "dysfunctional families." It seemed that epidemic had not made its way into the confines of this town. This was definitely the kind of place you wanted to raise your kids.

The longer she was here, the more Maggie was dazzled by the "good-old-American-apple-pie" feeling she got. Watching the people who wandered through Riverside Park reminded her of the books she had read in grade school.

Watching the three boys left her speechless. Here she was with a graduate degree yet there was no way she could explain this man's talent, or more astounding, his absolute love given so unselfishly to all those around him, many of whom he didn't know. And, on top of that, his ability to inspire the three boys to mold their own creations, with an artistic subject that offered meaning to their futures.

"Let's go tell my grandparents we saw the sculpture dude." There was a bolt of excitement in the first boy's voice as they walked away, pushing their bikes instead of riding them. His eyes were lit up like he'd just seen his favorite sports hero.

Maggie smiled. *Those guys will never forget this moment. And it will certainly have more of an impact than any two points scored on a basketball court!*

As they walked away, Maggie's smile grew larger. *Chalk up one more for the sculptor.* She could imagine the cheers of the crowds who came here to watch the volleyball games. An odd analogy occurred to her. *Sculptor – 2; Satan – 0.* Maggie's smile resembled that of her grandmother.

Two women walked over to the green stand that was erected beside the volleyball court and placed a couple of sandwiches, some chips and a drink on it. They exited without saying a word as they left their gift of appreciation for Joshua. Maggie noticed that this stand, which was probably for the scorekeeper of the spring and summer games, was the place where onlookers left their peace offerings for the man who left a piece of himself here each year for the town of Findlay.

A father and his young son who had come to see the sculpture stopped beside her, not wanting to distract the artist. The youngster hopped up on the picnic table and sat with his legs dangling over the bench.

"Who is that man?" the child asked, pointing to the image in the sand.

"Jesus," answered the father.

"Why?" shot the boy, his eyes glued to the work of art.

"Because it's Easter," the father offered.

"Why?"

Maggie turned to look at the child full of questions. She knew enough about children to realize this poor father was in for a hundred "whys?" during the next few minutes. As much as she wanted to feel pity for the father, her classes had taught her that an inquisitive child was a learner.

The father's face showed that he was trying to find the right words. "You know in your Sunday School class how you've learned about Jesus?"

Oh boy, now you're in for it! Maggie thought.

But she watched as the child simply replied, "Yeah." He appeared to be satisfied with that "you've learned about Jesus" comment.

The string of expected "Whys?" came to an end. His need for information was fulfilled with two words, "about Jesus."

Obviously, the boy had learned quite a lot about Jesus in that Sunday School class. *At least enough to tell him everything he needs to know about this image for the moment*, she surmised, watching the child who was still staring at the sculpture.

Suddenly, Maggie wondered how it was that all the children who had come through the park understood about Jesus and accepted him without question. Yet how many adults did she know, or had observed come by to see the image in the sand, who were unable to do the same.

Somewhere she had heard the words, "Through the eyes of a child," or something like, "you must become as a child." She found herself wishing she could remember the exact words that were depicted by the scene with this boy.

Another man approached the sculpture. He was leading a huge Bassett hound by a leash, and carrying his infant son in a carrier on his back, holding the baby comfortably in place.

"How old is your child?" she asked, noticing the child's eyes drawn to all the motion going on in the sand.

"Eleven months," answered the father, proud of the attention his son was receiving by this onlooker.

What the man didn't realize was that the fascination came more from him, already instilling a respect for Christ in his son by taking the time to expose him to this sight, even at such an early age. She was sure the man would return with his son year after year, each time building a relationship between the young boy and Jesus.

Maggie found it most interesting that Watson, the man's dog, also stopped dead in his tracks and stared at the image in the sand. She loved the fact that even the dog's eyes were taking in every inch of the sculpture, although she knew his thoughts were quite different from those of his master. But still, the fact that this monumental task caught his attention as well as that of the humans spoke to her of the relativity of all God's creation.

Her vision turned back to the child as she recollected a favorite picture in the Bible storybook from which her grandmother read. The caption said, "Let the little children come to me." She could see the picture vividly, with some children seated on Jesus' lap and others seated on the ground around him. Maggie was amazed that she could even remember the color of the hair and the clothing of each child in that picture.

The memory allowed her to envision this eleven-month-old infant as one of the children in that picture. Although this child was too young to have any idea of what was going on around him, Maggie was sure that in coming years, he, too, would understand "about Jesus."

Her thought caused a touching sentiment to surface, brought about by the number of fathers who had taken their role as "head of the household" seriously enough to instill that basic spiritual knowledge within their offspring by bringing them to this symbolic event.

That's the type of man my man will be. He, too, will bring his beloved children to see Christ, to know him. Maggie sat rigid in her chair, chills running up her spine. *That's odd. That was most certainly not one of the necessary qualifications on my list for the "perfect man."* She looked at Joshua, the sand, the father, the child and Watson. *Although it's not a bad quality to possess.*

Her mind thought of the bumper sticker from Sunday night when she had left the club. "Real men love Jesus." *Too bad I didn't get a good look at the man in that truck. I'd like to see the kind of men who love Jesus.*

"C'mon, Watson, let's go," the man called to the dog.

"Elementary, my dear Watson," Maggie heard in the back of her mind. Those words would have been a perfect explanation to the dog for what was going on. Through his master's voice, he would have learned that another master was being led by the Master.

Chapter 12
Late afternoon, Holy Tuesday

At precisely four in the afternoon, the temperature took a straight nose dive and within seconds it had become a good twenty degrees cooler. There was only a gentle breeze, more like a sea's breeze blowing lightly off the ocean waves, but it was definitely present.

Maggie was aware of it, for she had gone to get Joshua a bottled water from her car. Just as she opened the door of the Honda, it felt like someone turned an outdoor air conditioner on full blast. She assumed it was a passing wind, and that the air would resume its warmth from the sun in a few seconds.

As she returned to her beach chair, the chill bumps running down her arm and the back of her neck didn't go away.

Too bad this steamy romance novel can't warm me up, she thought. Maggie had already placed the book on the ground. It had somehow seemed inappropriate to sit and read the pages she had intended for the beach, *on my quest for a man,* when here she sat, in front of Jesus. *Sand or no sand.*

She suddenly got another chill, this time down her spine as she heard her grandmother's voice. *"My dear Maggie, don't you know that Jesus doesn't have to be there in front of you to know what you're doing, saying . . . even thinking?"*

Maggie's contorted mouth showed she did know that. She had allowed her occupation to disavow many of the lessons she had learned about anything of a religious nature - whether they were from her grandmother, parochial school, or anybody. It seemed if she didn't think of those things, she didn't feel the reprehensible shame.

Until I think of my grandmother, she recognized, the despair of wretchedness consuming her.

Thankfully, two women approached who caused Maggie's thoughts to switch gears. Although they were entering their "golden" years, it was unmistakable that they were identical twins. And it was obvious from watching them, as they talked and looked at each other while making their way across the grassy patch to the sculpture, that the bond formed by twin-ship was very much at work in their lives and relationship.

Maggie couldn't help but think of two girls, a set of twins, who had been in her class in parochial school. They looked so much alike that the nuns who were teachers couldn't tell them apart. A logical solution to the problem, it seemed to the nuns, was to assign the girls each a ribbon – one a pink ribbon and the other a blue one. Each morning, when the girls arrived at school, they were to pin their assigned ribbons on their navy jumpers.

The girls, whose names Maggie couldn't remember, couldn't have cared less about what the nuns called them, so without fail, they lollygagged into class and picked up a ribbon and went on about their business of daily school life. No one ever told the nuns, the nuns never knew the difference, and the twins lived a full and happy life.

Maggie returned to her thought from only seconds ago.

But Jesus knew them each by name.

The chill in the air had set in and made it explicitly clear that it had no intention of leaving anytime soon. After an hour of fidgeting in her chair, and trying to stay warm by walking in the sunlight, Maggie went to the car to find the blanket the girls had given her. She laughed at the fact that she was indeed using it to wrap up beside a man. *Not exactly what my friends had in mind!* She wondered if she would confide the irony of the use of her gift when she returned to Northern Exposure.

By dusk, a dampness accompanied the cool air, and it was evident that rain was on its way. Even under the blanket, Maggie felt shivers running rampantly up and down her spine.

Joshua went to his truck and found coveralls and a coat to shield his body from the cold.

He noticed Maggie shaking when he returned. "I have another pair of coveralls if you need them," he offered.

"No, thank you," she replied appreciatively.

Wouldn't that have been a sight for the girls? Me, sitting out in the sand beside some figure of a man, all wrapped up in Carhartt coveralls and a fleece blanket. The image brought a huge smile to Maggie's face.

A group of ladies came by from work to see the progress of the artist. One of them, whom Maggie recognized from the day before, must have told her co-workers about the sculpture. They hurriedly walked toward the pile of sand, holding their arms tight across their chests, trying not to let the cold air inside their sweaters.

"At least it's not snowing this year," one of them commented.

"Yes, do you remember last year when we came? There was snow all over the ground," another recalled.

"I have pictures of that," a third woman remarked. "I thought it was especially touching to see snowflakes on the crown of thorns on Jesus' head."

Maggie listened to their conversation as they quickly took note of the sculpture and rushed back to the parking lot.

Thank God there's no snow on the ground now. How would I ever explain those pictures to the girls? She laughed aloud. *I can see it now. Here I sit, all bundled up in coveralls and a fleece blanket, in my beach chair with its umbrella, and snow all over the ground.* The visual image of Ebony's reaction almost made it worth wishing that actually were the scenario.

The cold did not stop the master at work. His bare hands continued to move over the sand - scooping, molding - each stroke with perfection, to recreate the model that existed only in his head.

Maggie saw Joni getting out of a car. Noticing that she was reaching in the backseat for something, the visitor went over to help.

"I'm fine," called the waitress when she caught a glimpse of the approaching visitor. "I thought maybe Joshua might need some hot coffee or cider to keep him warm. I knew he'd be out here working, no matter what. There's also some hot chocolate here, if you'd like some."

"I'd love a cup," Maggie replied, taking one of the tall Styrofoam containers from the tray. "Don't you ever quit playing the part of a waitress?" she joked.

"That's my lot in life," Joni answered, lightly, but with serious eyes. "That's my way of serving others . . . not to use a pun."

"Hi, Joshua," she called over to the artist. "I knew you'd be needing this about now."

"Ah, Joni. A woman after my own heart," he said exuberantly as he walked toward the woman who had come bearing the tray. "If I weren't already happily married, I'd be calling on you."

The waitress laughed, touched by the sentiment of appreciation. "Yeah, I'd be way down the line after all those other ladies who are such big fans of yours."

He paused briefly to enjoy a cup of hot coffee and some light-hearted conversation with the woman who had taken time to make sure he stayed warm, on the inside at least.

Chapter 13
Evening, Holy Tuesday

The evening dragged on slowly. Rain had begun to creep in with the wind, and by nightfall, it felt more like winter on the Great Lakes than a spring evening. Only a few stragglers ventured out into the penetrating dampness to view the sculpture.

Chic, who had come again after work, looked quite different in her navy pea coat, with her pants legs rolled down, and heavy leather shoes.

"At least it's great weather for packing the sand," she commented, trying to find something pleasant about standing outdoors in these uncomfortable conditions.

Maggie felt the warmth of the gas logs in her Victorian room at Rose Gate Cottage calling her instead of the sand, but she somehow felt that her steadfast presence gave the artist moral support, if nothing else.

Besides, it was *my mission to spend my evenings beside a man. Now I've got not one, but* two, *right by my side. I may not be in sunny Florida, but at least a part of my prediction is correct.*

Lynn showed up, but instead of bringing the packed dinner that was expected, she informed Joshua and Chic that they were getting out of the cold. "You're not going to do the town of Findlay any good if you're not here to do this again next year," she said with a loving smile, her voice full of truth.

Chic looked over at Maggie, who was gathering her belongings. "Maggie, have you met Lynn?"

Joshua made the introduction as his wife moved toward the stranger. "Lynn, this is Maggie Matelli. She just graduated from the University of Michigan and was on her way to Florida when she stopped down at Miller's and got waylaid here at the park. She's the one I told you about who brought me the burger yesterday afternoon." He put his arm around his mate and kissed her, letting his actions show his deep affection for her. "And this is my wife, Lynn. She's the one who takes care of business and the house so that I can do these frivolous projects."

"Why don't you come with us, Maggie?" Lynn invited.

The tone in her voice proved that Joshua was not exaggerating when he said this was the woman who took care of him. Being of Italian descent, Maggie knew the artistic temperament, and she knew how fortunate this man was to have this woman. What really touched the young woman was the fact that this sculptor knew his blessing and was grateful for it. *That's the kind of man I want,* she thought to herself, *someone who knows me and loves me.* She looked back at the trio.

"I hate to impose," she answered politely.

"It's no imposition," Lynn acknowledged. "We'll show you the hang-outs. Findlay's not West Palm Beach, but it is a pretty nice place."

"Yeah, then you'll really know your way around the town," Chic laughed.

Maggie found she couldn't refuse their welcome invitations. Company did seem like a fun way to spend the evening. "Only if you let me pay for dinner," she acquiesced.

"Absolutely not," Joshua blasted. "What kind of a reception is that to our fair city?" He jerked off the coveralls. "Besides, I never paid you back for the burger yesterday."

"My small contribution to the on-going work of the sculpture. Remember? We have to keep the artist alive," she smiled.

"I'm glad to see that somebody else sees it my way," nodded Lynn, knowing she already liked this woman.

CRURED

When the foursome returned to the park after dinner, they decided that their time would be better spent sleeping for one night. They could pray that the next day would bring a break in the weather.

Before he would agree to leave though, Joshua had to check his work and pack up all his tools. His demeanor showed his reluctance in leaving his artistic baby, but he had finally agreed that it was not a good idea to stay out in the night air. He had too much work still ahead of him.

The rain had beaten down on the sand just enough to give it a sense of tension and intensity in the features that the artist could not accomplish by his own abilities.

"Hey, Chic, come over here." Joshua called. "I want you to look at how Jesus is."

"Jesus is frozen. Let's go!" Lynn ordered.

Ah, the power behind every good artist - his woman, Maggie laughed, while at the same time, seeing what she already suspected was the truth.

Joshua, Chic and Maggie laughed at Lynn's abruptness,

but none of them could argue with her reasoning. They all ran for their vehicles, waving their good-byes and promising to see each other tomorrow.

Chapter 14
Morning, Holy Wednesday

The bed proved to be as comfortable as it was gorgeous. Maggie awoke, feeling like a new person, when she saw sunlight dancing through the lace curtains. *Ah, a perfect day for travel!*

There was a part of her that hated to leave this room for one on the beach. As she pulled the plush robe around her, feeling the same luxurious warmth that she had after last night's bath, she sat in the chair that looked out the window.

There was a small garden right underneath her window with a bench, perfect for sitting and reading beneath a towering pink-saucer magnolia – Maggie's favorite tree. She thought what a shame it was to have to leave this perfect setting and drive for so many hours.

But my man is calling, she reminded herself.

Maggie got dressed and went downstairs to the dining room with its carved wooden furniture. All of the linens and accessories were exquisite and matched the furnishings and house so well that they appeared to have been designed by the same person.

She loved the pampered feeling she got as Charlie came out of the kitchen carrying a tray with juice and a freshly-made apple puff pancake baked in a ramikin, the cottage's signature dish. When she had come in the previous evening, he met her at the door asking her pleasure for breakfast and what time she would like to be served.

Now, the exceptional food and service were making it doubly hard to leave these surroundings.

Maggie breathed in the luscious aroma of fruit and spices with each bite. She thought of the woman in the kitchen with her multiple talents. And she thought of the man who had done so much of the repair and maintenance on Rose Gate Cottage. This couple perfectly complimented each other, just as did Joshua and Lynn.

And here I sit, savoring every bite of this delectable meal when I am supposed to be in search of my own partner, my own mate for life.

Now she felt guilty for not moving ahead with her mission, yet her conscience was trying to offer hundreds of reasons why it would be more beneficial for her to stay right here in Findlay, at the Rose Gate Cottage, and Miller's, and Dietsch Brothers – *and the park.*

Maggie finished the pancake and extended her compliments to Charlie and June on the fabulous breakfast. As she rounded the post with the "guardian of the stairs," the host asked, "Would you like to leave your things and pick them up later? One of us will be around and they won't be in the way at all."

"That would be terrific. I want to run by the park for just a few minutes before I leave, and I could stop back by here and grab my bag on the way to the interstate."

"Fine. I'll be watching for you," June said.

The houseguest wondered whether this couple had any children of their own. They appeared to Maggie to be the epitome of loving parents.

CRISC

As she neared the park, she could see the addition of a tent beside the sculpture. One of the local funeral parlors had brought it to shelter visitors from the impending wind and give Joshua a place to rest. The picnic table had been moved underneath it and pictures of the artist's past work had been hung with large S-hooks on the walls of the tent.

With each stroke the sculptor made, Maggie had the strangest sensations. Sensations that seemed to affect every part of her – physically, mentally and emotionally. And what seemed odd about it was that the sensations seemed to be stemming from a part of her that had been lacking for several years – her spiritual being. It was as if, with each scoop of sand that was scraped away, she felt the sin and shame of her own life being scraped away, also.

The few minutes at the park turned into three hours. Spectators now came and stayed longer. This was becoming more than a sight. People began to see it as a Mecca, a place to make their own personal pilgrimages. They, too, found it hard to leave.

Maggie took a break and went to Miller's for lunch. She wasn't hungry, but she knew that Joni could supply her with needed directions.

CRISC

"Do you have a good bookstore in town?" she asked, while reaching for the menu.

"Why, yes. It's less than a mile away. You come close to it on the way to the park," came the answer.

"Good. I knew if anybody would know, you would. Can you give me directions?"

"Sure." Joni took her pen, pulled a napkin out of the container on the table, and drew a map on it.

"Thanks," Maggie smiled, noting that this was the first time she had actually seen the waitress use a writing utensil. She jumped up and headed toward the door.

"Don't you want anything to eat?" Joni called.

"Oh, yeah, I almost forgot. Fix me an egg salad sandwich and a small cola to go. I'll be back in a few minutes to pick them up."

Joni shook her head wondering what was going on with their strangest visitor of the week. Even with her odd actions, you couldn't help but like her.

"Order to go," she yelled back to the short-order cook while putting the pen back in her pocket.

CR&O

June greeted her at the door when she reached the Rose Gate Cottage. Before the hostess had a chance to say anything, Maggie threw a question at her.

"Is the Garden Villa still available?"

"Why yes, it is."

Those were the words Maggie had been praying to hear ever since she left the park. "I'd like to stay through Saturday night if that's a possibility."

"You're not going to believe this, but there was a couple who had reserved it several months ago. Something has come up and they're not going to be able to get here. They had to go to

Florida to be with the woman's father during surgery."

A strange look of understanding came over Maggie's face. "Yes, I would believe it," she said, the words trailing off through the air more than being directed at June.

The hostess stared at the guest, and wondered what was going on inside her mind, for the expression of peace on Maggie's face was nearly breathtaking. Whatever it was, June was sure it was a good thing. The young woman possessed an energy – a placid energy – that had appeared since her arrival yesterday. And as much as the owner of the bed-and-breakfast would have liked to credit the young woman's change to their establishment, she knew there was another reason for it.

"Shall I tell Charlie to move your bag back to the room for you? He had placed it down here for your convenience."

"Yes, please. And June, I'm not sure what time I want breakfast. I have a feeling that I'll be at Riverside Park fairly late this evening, and I'll want to be back there early tomorrow. It will be Holy Thursday."

"Perhaps Charlie and I will see you there. We hear the sculpture is most fascinating."

"It's much more than fascinating. I'm not sure exactly how to describe it, but it has given me a feeling like I've never had before."

"I see," June replied gingerly. For indeed she did see. She saw a change in the young woman that could have only come from one source. *Ah, love, the sweet mystery of life*, she mused as she sang the old Victor Herbert song of the same name in her mind.

She was sure that she and Charlie would have to make a trip down to Riverside Park that evening and see the man that had put this look on Maggie's face. *Springtime definitely has a way of opening one's heart to hear the message of love*, she smiled.

Chapter 15
Afternoon, Holy Wednesday

As she pulled out of the diner's parking lot with her bagged lunch and cola, Maggie began searching for the street to which Joni had directed her.

When she reached it, she saw the sign that she had noticed the past two days but had given little attention. "Maranatha Bookstore," she read aloud. She made a quick dart into the parking lot.

Somehow the juicy romance novel that she brought along for beach reading had lost its appeal, so she had decided during this morning's hours at the park to choose a title that might fit her present mood a little better.

Maggie walked into the front door and glanced around at the aisles. The posters in stands throughout the store did not look like those of the typical bookstores back home. After looking around for a few minutes, Maggie realized she was in a Christian bookstore.

A lady, who was stocking the shelves, noticed the lost

look on Maggie's face. "Good morning. Are you looking for anything in particular?"

"Not really." After another couple of turns of her head, the prospective customer turned back to the salesclerk. "Perhaps you *could* suggest something. I'm here for the week and thought it might be nice to have something to read. I think I'd like something that would offer some inward peace, maybe help me to reflect and think, but I don't want anything that's too deep."

"I guess you already have a Bible," the lady offered, fully suspecting that the young woman in front of her didn't from the questioning eyes that were roaming the aisles.

"No, actually I don't. Well, I did, but . . ." Maggie saw no easy explanation for her predicament, so she launched forward with as little detail as possible. "I'm sorry to admit that during the past few years, I've tried to steer pretty clear of anything that dealt with religion. Besides, I never could get into all that jargon. It was too hard to read and understand."

She thought back to all the legal trivia and jargon she had been exposed to during the past six years at U-M and realized what a lame excuse that really was. *Perhaps the reason you couldn't understand it is that you didn't care to, Miss Maggie Mae.* The customer immediately turned off her subconscious that had taken on Ebony's voice. She could even hear her co-worker's "I heard that" response to the statement in her head. Maggie directed all her attention to the saleswoman in front of her.

Leading the young woman to the middle of the store, the clerk took advantage of the opportunity. "There's several new translations of the Bible that are easy to read and understand. They're written in modern-day language. There are even translations specifically written with helpful tips for women."

"You're kidding. I guess I've only seen my grandmother's old Bible. And the one in motel rooms. You know the one, supposedly translated for some king, and my grandmother used to laugh at the number of people who actually thought this king translated it."

"King James," the helpful employee interjected.

"Yeah, that's it. I remember that now as you mention it."

The clerk picked up three translations and handed them to the woman whose attention was now obviously piqued by all the books lining the shelves on either side of the aisle on which they stood. "These two have study tips, answers to lots of common questions, and even offer suggestions for passages to deal with particular problems in the reader's life. But this one is written almost in story form, more like a novel. It is available both as the entire Bible or the New Testament."

Maggie took the books and carefully leafed through the pages of each one.

"Perhaps it would be easier if we looked at the same passage of scripture in each book and let you see which you like best. If you're looking for something both peaceful, yet reflective, this might be a good place to start." The clerk politely took the Bible on top and turned to the fifth chapter of Matthew. "These are the words of the familiar Sermon on the Mount. I think they're the most beautiful in the entire Bible."

While the helpful woman stood finding the same passage in both the other translations, Maggie began to read. After looking at each of the books, Maggie quickly selected the third choice she had been given. She loved the words that read like her usual books. "Thanks. I think this one is perfect for what I'm looking for," she smiled, visibly appreciative of the assistance.

"Great," said the clerk, while putting away the other two Bibles. "Would you like the entire Bible version, or just the New Testament?"

"I think I'd like the one with the entire Bible," answered Maggie. "There are some stories from the Old Testament that I've been remembering this week. Stories that my grandmother used to tell me. Maybe this will spark my memories of them."

The clerk handed her the book she requested. "Let me know if I can be of further assistance." She started to walk away, gratified that at least this customer knew the difference between the Old and New Testaments.

"Thanks, I will. I think I'd like to browse around a little more while I'm here."

"Help yourself. There's plenty to see." The sales assistant started to turn away. "By the way, are you in town on business?"

"Not exactly," Maggie chuckled. "You'll never believe this, but I was on my way to Florida to spend the week in the sun and the sand. I got a little sidetracked watching Mr. Redford doing the sculpture down the road at Riverside Park, and this is as far as I got."

"That's quite an awesome project, isn't it? People have always come from miles around to admire his snow sculptures, but this is a way to truly speak to people, to minister to them. We're expecting record numbers of people to visit the park to see his work. It's like watching a master at work, for you know that God is using that man's talents. I think this should become an annual tradition."

"I don't know what it's like usually," Maggie offered, "but there has been a constant stream of visitors at the park observing his work. They seem to come from all walks of life and lots of different places. But what has drawn me to the site is that the people who are coming to view the sculpture have a purpose in mind. Like they're paying homage to the sculpture rather than just coming to see it. It's the strangest thing. I've never seen anything like it. This is most definitely the best place to go people-watching that I've ever found."

Maggie took a tour of the store, slowly walking up and down every aisle. She was mesmerized by the books, apparel, cards, posters - anything a person could want - all displaying pictures of Christ or religious symbols. She had no clue that there was such a market for this type of store.

As she stood looking at a row of posters bearing profound statements with pictures of Christ, her subconscious called her attention to the music playing in the background. She listened for a moment to the words that were floating through the air. "There's room at the cross for you, there's room at the cross for you. Though millions have come, there's still room for one. Yes, there's room at the cross for you."

Her eyes focused on the poster in front of her. There beside Christ on the cross were two other men, also hanging on crosses, one on each side of Christ. Maggie imagined herself on one of the crosses as she listened more intently to the words. As soon as that song finished, she heard a male voice singing, "Kneel at the cross. Christ will meet you there, come while he waits for you."

The words and the melody were noticeably several decades old, probably from about the same time period that her grandmother would have been the same age as she was now. But the rhythm, combined with the instrumentation and the smoothness of the voice had a bidding effect. A bidding effect that made the words of the next stanza speak to her in the same way as the previous song. "Kneel at the cross, there is room for all."

This time Maggie was consciously praying. "Lord, you obviously are speaking to me. Whether it's through my grandmother, or it's you, I feel the call of the words, 'Come, there is room.' I'm not much on spiritual issues, but I do have enough sense to know when this strong of a presence is surrounding me. I feel cradled. I feel loved. And most of all, I feel forgiveness – from You, from my parents . . ." She felt the drip of a tear fall across her cheek. "And most of all, from my beloved grandmother."

Maggie wiped her cheek with the back of her hand. "I

know you're taking good care of her, God, because she's there with you. I can feel her presence here, too."

Before letting the tears and her emotions get out of control, she made her way to the aisle marked "Music" hoping to find the CD that was playing. The aisle was packed with row after row of discs by various artists. Maggie was amazed that the people on the covers so closely resembled most of the singers that she listened to on a daily basis on her radio stations. They weren't at all like her idea of "Christians." Her eyes caught the small sign that read, "Now playing," and she went in search of that particular recording. She found it with no trouble, grabbed a copy and headed toward the counter, not wanting to miss any more of the action at the sculpture site.

"Here," the clerk said, handing Maggie a bookmark as she rang up the purchase. "This is on me. It's easy to lose your place without one of these." She reached into a clear cylindrical plastic container on the counter and took out a highlighter pen. "Take this, too. It might come in handy to mark verses that you really like."

The customer's brows raised in astonishment. "You mean it isn't sacrilegious to write in this book?"

"Absolutely not! The Bible is meant for people to apply to their own daily lives. It isn't some sacred tabernacle. Think of it as a tool or a roadmap."

"Kind of like a textbook?"

"Precisely like a textbook. The greatest textbook ever written, in fact. And all those things you were asking about at first – peace, reflection – you'll find that and a whole lot more inside those pages." She couldn't help but notice the pleased expression on the customer's face that prompted her to make one last comment. "Not only that, but God can give you a peace that surpasses everything you'll find in that book. It's a peace that surpasses all understanding."

"Thank you," Maggie said, simply. Her expression showed that she was trying to grasp a lot of ideas that were foreign to her past way of thinking, and that she was anxious to go in search of peace via her new roadmap, her Bible.

The clerk watched the woman walk out the door and get into her car. There was something about that face that demanded attention. *Was it the hair, the mysterious blue eyes that looked so out of place for the rest of her coloring? What exactly?* It looked like a face the lady had seen before, but she couldn't quite place it.

As she turned to go back to stocking the shelves, she stopped cold in her tracks. For there, hanging on the wall behind the counter, was a painting that had been placed in that spot of prominence specifically for the Easter season. It was a portrayal of Jesus standing beside the tomb, resurrected, with Mary Magdalene bowed at his feet.

The woman looked back toward the door to see her customer backing out. *That's it!* The face was so strikingly similar, except for the blue eyes, that the young woman she had just helped could have posed as the artist's model for the painting.

"Are you okay?" the store manager asked, noticing the faraway gaze in his employee's eyes. "You look as if you've just seen a ghost."

"No, not seen, but felt," replied the shocked employee. "You know how you get those miraculous feelings of having been touched by the Holy Spirit? I just had one of those experiences, except instead of being touched, I was zapped!"

"Yes, I've had those experiences. It's like when they happen, you're not sure what's going on, or that you like it, but when it's all over and you look back at what just occurred, you're glad you had it."

"And you're grateful that God thought enough of you to allow you to be the recipient."

"Exactly," nodded the manager.

"Did you happen to get a glimpse of that young lady I was helping, the one who just left the store?"

"No, I didn't. I was working on a voided ticket so I wasn't paying any attention to the people at the counter."

"I have an idea she'll be back during the week," exclaimed the clerk with an assurance that the manager would have found most peculiar had they not spoken about the Holy Spirit's presence only moments earlier. "If she does come in, I want you to see her. I want to show you something."

"Okay," agreed the manager, knowing that the customer who left minutes ago and the conversation all had something in common.

CB&O

By the middle of the afternoon, Maggie had read the story of the Crucifixion and the Resurrection. The lady in the bookstore had been right. This was much easier for her to understand than the King James' translation - the one she had tried to read last night before going to sleep - that was in her Garden Villa Suite on the table beside the bed.

She had gathered several points through her reading, but the one that struck her most was that she wasn't going to get to the sunny, sandy coast of Florida.

Findlay . . . Florida, what the heck? They both begin with F. And who needs the ocean? I've got the waterfront of Blanchard River right across the street. And I'm certainly seeing my share of sun and sand. She chuckled. *Even the key lime pie is good here. All that's missing is my perfect man, and who knows, maybe I'll even find him before the week is over.*

Maggie looked at the second sculpture, with its finished

touches, of Christ carrying the cross. Her eyes wavered beside it to the portrayal of Jesus hanging on the cross. She had no clue as to what it was about that oversized pile of sand, but something regarding it had erased her longing to find another being - a man - to be her mate, to give her purpose. She was beginning to feel the rich heritage of her own purpose. A purpose that had been partially uncovered by her grandmother, but one she had allowed to become covered in dust and cobwebs over the past few years.

Maybe that's *what that strange sensation was this morning. Maybe as Joshua scraped away the sand to uncover Christ, he also uncovered the dust that hid me – the real me.*

Chapter 16
Evening, Holy Wednesday

W ord of the sculpture must have been spreading, for people were beginning to come by the park after they got off work. The crowds were picking up considerably, and by six-thirty, there was a steady stream of spectators. Traffic moved slowly up and down Osborne Street as onlookers came to a crawl to get a glimpse of the sculptured outdoor mural.

Suddenly Maggie heard a male's voice yell out from the passenger window of a passing car, "What the *hell* is that?"

She felt horrible embarrassment and humiliation for the parents who had brought their children, not to mention tremendous sorrow for Joshua. But she was actually surprised that there had not been more reactions of that nature. Had this taken place in Ann Arbor, she was sure there would have been more derogatory statements from the various cultural groups. And had it been in Florida on the beach . . . *I won't even bother to speculate about that.*

Her thoughts were interrupted by the comments of three

elderly ladies standing slightly behind her.

"What a shame," mouthed one of the women quietly, obviously sharing the same thoughts as Maggie.

"Can you believe some people? What were they thinking?" asked the second woman.

The third woman's response was directed to both the other women. "Why does that surprise you? Jesus was rejected in his own day, so why would you expect him to be accepted in today's society?"

"Your words do carry merit. I've heard it said that if Jesus Christ were in our pulpits today, there would be Christians that would complain about him," noted the second woman.

"Point made," agreed the first.

The women ended their conversation and continued to watch the artist at work for a few more minutes before writing their comments in the guest book that had been added to the burgeoning list of items that were accumulating on the picnic table inside the tent.

But their words had made a notable impact on the college graduate who overheard them. Suddenly, her embarrassment and humiliation caused by the curt apathy of the man in the vehicle turned to pathos for Joshua that he had to endure such rejection because of his art. She realized that the women were right and that the words had been directed toward Christ and not the artist. Not until that moment did Maggie realize the extent of perseverance and fortitude shown by this man of small stature.

Her entire perception of artists changed drastically because of that one incident. No longer did she see them as masters of their talents, but heroes who stood firmly in the face of adversity, for their faith and their beliefs.

Maggie wondered what it would have been like to walk the streets of Florence, Italy, in Michelangelo's day. There were surely those who ridiculed him, too.

Those thoughts stirred up visions of her grandparents, especially her grandmother, again. They, too, had stood in the face of adversity because of their love for Christ. It was a love they had tried to pass on to her, but a love that she had rejected. She began to feel that she was no better than the car's passenger who made the raucous comment. Only now, she didn't feel the weight of sin and shame that she'd felt for the past few years. *That I felt up until today.*

The graduate's mind had been so wrapped up in thinking of the heroes in her life, in both her ethnic and her spiritual backgrounds, she had forgotten all about eating dinner.

Thank goodness I brought my drinks and snacks back with my chair. She turned her head toward the street as she reached into her cooler to grab a pop. As she did, Maggie saw an old car, one from the era of her birth, which reminded her of an old battleship. Not only was it incredibly long, it was steel gray, adding to its military resemblance.

The driver of the car had his head shaved and wore no shirt. Even from where she was seated, Maggie could see the numerous tattoos that were on his upper body. At the exact moment he became parallel with the center of the mural, she saw he had an object in his hand, which was pointed toward the sculpture.

Admirers had been taking pictures since Monday, so she didn't think too much about it until she saw a small barrel rather than a 35mm lens. She turned her head back toward Joshua and saw that a woman, who was in the path between the artist and the passing car, literally jumped out of the way after having seen the car and its driver.

Oh, my gosh! A drive-by shooting! Maggie was terrified. She quickly looked back toward the car and saw that the driver held the barreled object up to his eye. Now she felt horrified rather than terrified. She had allowed herself to make a rash judgment based on the man's appearance.

It wasn't actually his appearance, she tried to convince herself. *It was that barrel shape rather than a lens. And when I first saw it, he wasn't holding it up to his eye. It looked more like he was taking aim.*

Maggie tried to allow her body to feel relief instead of scolding herself. *After all, it really* was *a drive-by shooting . . . of sorts. And he* was *taking aim . . . of sorts.*

She wondered who she was talking to. Even though the thoughts were directed at herself, it seemed she was trying to convince some other person, *or Being*, that she was not wrong in her misconception about the driver.

Was I talking to God? Again? She honestly didn't know whether she was or not. Consciously, her words had not been intended for Him, but her subconscious told her that she had been attempting to ask for forgiveness for stereotyping the man in the car.

After a few minutes, the gray car came back by from the opposite direction. Maggie watched as the driver took more pictures, this time completely stopping traffic. She laughed that none of the drivers of cars behind him were blowing their horns in impatience.

He's got two things going for him, she snickered. *No one's about to run into that battleship, and with his intimidating appearance, they're not about to make him mad. Not such a bad combination after all.*

This time she felt a ripple of relief, for she knew that he, like the other passersby, was merely admiring the work of art. To see someone of this man's description have such an appreciation to make *two* passes by the sculpture made up for the guy who had gone by earlier, putting a damper on her feelings about humanity.

As she sat watching the spectators come and go, she caught a peep of the man from the vehicle out of the corner of her eye. He had parked his car and was headed toward the volleyball pit.

Dressed in black leather pants, black leather motorcycle boots, and no shirt, he looked like he belonged at a bike rally rather than at a family park viewing a religious symbol. His scraggly beard hung halfway down his chest, but didn't bother to hide the continual mass of tattoos or piercings that covered his back and neck, as well as his chest.

It doesn't matter, she reminded herself, thinking of the teenager who had brought the forsythia branch earlier. *What matters is that he's here instead of somewhere else.*

With that, she thought of how much he looked like the typical guys who frequented the strip joint she had seen on the outskirts of the neighboring town. *Not like the "clientele" of my fine establishment*, she thought cynically. *At least not on the outside*, Maggie noted, thinking of the guys all dressed up in their business suits who paid big bucks to get into Northern Exposure. She looked at the man again as he passed her. *On the inside, they're all the same - at least with their needs.*

The man moved to the middle of the mural and stood in awe just like everyone else.

Why should I expect him to react any differently? Maggie rebuked herself, feeling increasingly ashamed of her reaction to the man. *I am no better than him.*

She looked around to see if anyone else thought it odd that this character had actually taken the time and effort to come and see the sculpture of Christ. It was obvious from their expressions that everyone had noted his appearance. Some she could even see silently counting the number of piercings that were visible from his chest up. Maggie had already lost count by the time she persuaded herself that it was not of importance.

After standing frozen for a few minutes, gazing at the huge work of art like the other spectators, the man made his way through the crowd. He stood behind the fence, having gotten close enough to be within earshot of the sculptor.

"Thanks, man. This is awesome," he spoke up.

Joshua turned around, while continuing to mold the sand with his hands. "Thank you for coming out."

"I had to stop. Driving by don't do it justice."

The man continued to look for a few more minutes, still snapping pictures with the camera that had been misconstrued as a weapon, before quietly retreating to his car, nodding humbly to those around him as he left.

No one said a word about the man, or his appearance, but the stares he got made up for any dialogue. The expressions on peoples' faces indicated that their stereotypical molds had also been broken. Yet, his sincere appreciation of both the artist and his subject made up for the earlier disrespect shown by the other young man.

As he cranked the battleship-replica-of-a-car, Maggie noted how this man had no thought or need for things of material value. He was what he was, take-him-or-leave-him, and there was no pretentiousness about him. And he humbly bowed to all those who had at first snubbed him, much like a servant would have done.

As she watched him drive away, the young woman who had become lost in the crowd knew that her heart was again talking to God, although she had no idea of the words that it spoke.

Chapter 17
Morning, Holy Thursday

For the first time since her arrival in Findlay, Maggie awoke thinking about the club. Not actually about the club, but the girls with whom she worked that had become her family over the course of the last four years. Several young women had come and gone; some had disappeared briefly and then come back intermittently. And then there was Valerie, who had hung around like her sole purpose in life was to be the "den mother" of Northern Exposure.

She thought of that first evening she had shown up for work there. It was a most awkward situation for her, having grown up in a household of believers, and modest ones at that. Her lot seemed to have gotten thrown into a hopper and badly entangled with someone else's as she listened to the women talk about the customers, about the problems of their own backgrounds, and mostly, how they couldn't wait for the day when they could escape that wretched place.

It was Valerie who stepped over to her and quietly gave

her the words that allowed her to cope with the job and the situation that would have otherwise been unbearable. Maggie could still feel the tenderness of a mother's hand as the woman of seniority touched her shoulder and whispered, "Honey, while you're here, forget it. Think about anything else, everything else, but this place. Don't think about being here. Don't think about the customers. And most importantly, don't think about having to come back and face it all again tomorrow. Just plant a big smile on your face and no matter what happens, keep smiling."

The woman tried to flash a gingerly smile of her own at the new kid on the block, but the pain for her, another victim of needing money so badly that she'd go to any extreme to keep from depending on her family, was evident in Valerie's glare. She finished her words of encouragement with the warning, "And just remember one thing. They can look, but they can't touch. And if they do, you tell me. The owner will have them permanently kicked out of here. These guys get a reputation for stuff like that and pretty soon, they can't pay their way into any strip joint, no matter how sleazy it is. To them, this is just another drug, so they're not about to lose that privilege."

At that point, the halfway smile turned into a consorted effort. "We may get the upper echelon of society in here, but it's all the same, no matter where you go. These guys simply appear cleaner on the outside. On the inside, it's the same old dirt."

Ebony, who had been like a sister from the beginning, etched her place in Maggie's heart with the three words she could be counted on for any conversation, "I heard that!" She slapped Maggie on the back and said, "When I was a little girl, my grandmother told me, 'Sin is sin is sin.' Well, girl, it don't matter whether it's in Northern Exposure or the el cheapo strip joint down a couple of blocks, 'Dirt is dirt is dirt.' Whether it's those white-collar dudes that come in here all spiffed up in their suits and ties, or the tattooed jeans-and-t-shirt guys from down the road, it's the same old dirt. Don't you ever forget that, girl, and you'll be alright."

Maggie never did forget that. In fact, she repeated those words to herself every time she walked into Northern Exposure after that. But she never did tell any of the girls what her grandmother had said to her as a child, all the stories of truth and love. This morning, she felt like the time for that had come.

Yes, she nodded, *the time has come for me to share those words of wisdom as soon as I get back to the club.* It occurred to Maggie exactly what it was that she wanted to take each of the girls as a souvenir from her trip. *I'll take care of that little chore on the way out of Findlay.*

Satisfied with her decision, she began to sing. *"Down by the old millstream, where I first met you . . ."*

Chapter 18
Early afternoon, Holy Thursday

Maggie found it increasingly amazing at the number of fathers who walked the park with their children. She could have understood it better had they come during the late afternoon and evening hours, giving their wives a break after a long day of work or while cooking dinner. It struck her odd that most of them came during the mid-day or early afternoon hours.

Maybe the parents work different shifts so as to provide home daycare for their children. As she watched the children at play and coming to see the sculpture, Maggie pondered on the difference of the day's society from when she was a girl.

She loved the confidence she saw in the eyes of the children. *That's one thing that hasn't changed.* It reminded her of the walks in the park that she had taken with her own father. She could remember the cozy feeling of security as she held his hand and tried to take big, long steps to keep up with his. In fact, they had made a game out of stepping together.

A little girl walked up with what appeared to be her

mother and grandmother. Her thick blonde curls and bright blue eyes gave her a look of perfect innocence, but the vibrancy on her face told another story.

As Maggie looked at the young child, she noticed the strong resemblance to a picture, of a little girl with her tea set, hanging in the hallway outside her room at the Rose Gate Cottage. All that was missing was the pink dress of the Victorian era with the full bow hanging down the back.

"Look, Granny, it's Jesus," the child pronounced.

"Yes, it is, Clara."

The child's mother looked at the grandmother. "They learned all about the Easter story yesterday in chapel at the daycare."

Maggie, who was touched by the child's recognition of the figure on the cross asked, "How old is Clara?"

"I'm three!" the child spoke for herself, not giving either of the women who accompanied her a chance to open their mouths. She was all smiles as she made her announcement.

And not a shy bone in your body, thought Maggie.

The two women smiled at each other and then at Maggie, as if they could read her thoughts.

"Clara, can you tell me about Jesus?" the grandmother asked.

The request caused the young girl to beam. She looked like not only could she tell the grandmother, but she was bursting at the seams to share the story.

Too bad everyone can't have Clara's attitude and exuberance about sharing the Gospel.

"They put him up on the cross." There was the tiniest lisp to the child's voice that gave her storytelling even more character than her eyes that danced with every word.

"Who did?" came the next question from the grandmother, as the elder bent down so that she was on Clara's level.

"The soldiers. And they nailed his hands and feet and put somethin' on his head and the blood came out."

Then the child leaned way in toward her grandmother as a huge smile burst across her face and her eyes began to sparkle like fireworks. "But he's comin' back!" Clara said loudly enough for everyone in the park to hear, with words that were boldly enunciated on every syllable.

Maggie wanted to laugh aloud. She had never heard the Easter story told with quite that much energy. The only element the child lacked was a closing statement, like an ad for a sequel to a movie that said, "And he'll be bigger, and badder, and better than ever!"

The grandmother reached out and hugged the child, then the mother took Clara's hand and led her to the other two scenes of the sand sculpture.

How touching that three generations can come and share this experience. What a rich heritage of faith they're planting in this child. Then she recalled her own rich heritage she had shared with three generations . . . *and how I strayed from it.* With all her being, Maggie prayed that this young girl, so innocent even in her vitality, could continue to walk the path of the straight and narrow that was being embedded in her.

As the three females walked away, Maggie silently asked, *And who says they're the Terrible Three's? Clara is most certainly a* terrific *three.* She chuckled. *And nobody will surely ever get in her way!*

Another threesome was walking toward the sand. Maggie saw that one man was leading a younger man who had a tall, hand-carved walking stick. A woman was walking closely behind them at a very slow pace.

Yet another person who has come to this site for healing, to feel Jesus, Maggie thought, bowing her head. Without realizing it, she had begun to pray for individuals that made their way to the sculpture.

"Would it be alright to touch the sand?" the older man asked, approaching Joshua.

The sculptor looked up slightly, while continuing to work. You could catch the regret in his voice as he answered slowly, "Well . . . not really." He paused for a second before giving an explanation. "I'm sorry, but it could cause a part of the sculpture to disintegrate. "

"I understand," said the younger man. His comment was directed at the man with him rather than at the sculptor.

"Do you have any tools?" the older man asked. "Anything that you might use in the process of making the sculpture?"

"Well . . . yes, actually I do," replied Joshua, again a slight hesitation in his voice.

He moved to the white plastic bucket that held his hand tools and removed one of the trowels he had used to define the features of Christ. He handed it to the older man, who then handed it to the younger man.

At that point, the woman reached out and took the cane as the young man held the trowel in his hands, running his fingers around the edge of the dull blade's surface. Then he held the wooden handle in his hand and stood there, facing the sculpture.

After a couple of minutes, he held out the trowel in the direction from which it had been handed to him. "Here, you can have it back now."

The trio started to move away.

Joshua, watching them, walked alongside the fence and asked the older man, "Do you mind if I ask why you did that?"

"Not at all. My son is blind and feeling is his way of seeing."

The sculptor wished that he had granted the father's first wish, but the younger man didn't seem to mind. In spite of his blindness, he had been able to feel the touch of the Master's Hand through the trowel, the same trowel with which he also felt the touch of the master's hand.

Feeling deeply humbled by the young man who had just left, Joshua turned toward the few people who had come to sit, visit and meditate for a while. "I do this sculpture as my gift to the town and the people of Findlay." You could hear a slight crackle in his voice as he continued, "But I'm the one who always goes home with the gift."

He watched the two men and the woman get in their car and drive away, and imagined what it must have felt like for Jesus to have someone touch the hem of his garment.

Joshua was so totally engrossed in the people who had just left the site of the sculpture that he didn't notice the tall man who had stepped up directly behind him.

"This truly *is* quite a gift that you give to the town of Findlay, Redford."

The artist turned. "Hello, Mayor," he said excitedly, brushing the sand from his hand onto his trousers before extending it.

"It's an honor for me to see the lives of people who are touched by your artwork here. You should be very proud of yourself."

"Thank you, Mayor, I appreciate that. But what I do here is not *for* myself, and not *of* myself." Joshua looked back toward the sand. "I'm just glad that it serves a need for people."

"Well, that's an understatement," the Mayor said, slapping the sculptor on the back.

Maggie sized up the man around whom people had begun to flock. He was a man of maturity, full of the graceful strength and style that was absent of younger men. His nylon Notre Dame jacket and monogrammed cabby hat denoted his Catholic background, and his sweater indicated that he was a fan, and judging from his tall, athletic build, probably a player of golf. Mayor Lawrence Anderson didn't look anything like what she would have expected from a public official.

But then, this town is not like any place you've ever been before.

The man who was solely responsible, *with a little help from above,* for getting permission for Joshua to display his artwork in the city's largest park was not only reachable, but he reminded Maggie of a grandfather with whom any child would love to climb up in his lap with a good book.

She listened to the humorous anecdotes and funny stories he shared with the citizens of the town. His quick wit stood out as she observed his mannerisms and his way with people. Maggie fell immediately in love with him, for she realized in watching the man that he was exactly like her grandfather. He gave her a feeling of comfort on the inside and he made her feel at home on the outside.

The listener observed the way he spoke to everyone around him, leaving out no one, not even the children. *A perfect politician*, she grinned, wondering how many babies he had kissed in his lifetime.

During the past few days, Maggie had heard this man's name mentioned on more than one occasion. And what amazed her was that all the comments were good. Politicians were supposed to be crooked, they were supposed to be "above" the law and others, they were . . .

Wait a minute, Maggie. Who ruled that?

Here stood a man who, from all she had seen and heard, was completely fair. His kind face spoke of honest and genuine care and concern for the townspeople of Findlay, and Maggie was sure that any babies he had kissed had been because he truly wanted to show his love for them.

After all, she'd heard that he had been a high school coach

and principal for years, and that, in itself, said eons of his character and nature as far as she was concerned.

Mayor Anderson and Joshua exchanged a few more words before the artist went back to work and the official took a seat at the picnic table beside her chair.

"I don't believe I know you. Are you visiting Findlay?" the mayor asked her, a congenial welcome in his voice.

Maggie was shocked. Shocked that this man obviously knew his subjects. And shocked that here was a man of importance, "real" importance, not like the men who visited the place she worked, noticing her and introducing himself. She felt humbled and honored at the same time.

Immediately, her mind began to wonder what would have happened had a man like this been in office at the time of Jesus' crucifixion.

I know what would have happened, she stated confidently, based on the words she had read - *from reputable sources, I might add* - over the last couple of days. *Barabbas would have been crucified and the sins of the world would not have been taken away,*

Maggie looked at Mayor Anderson, sizing him up even more closely.

And God's plan would not have been carried out as prophesied in the Old Testament scriptures.

This man - this mayor, a man of the public's eye, a man of importance - this man had been a messenger sent from God to Maggie. She had been wrestling with the fact that her arrival and her stay in Findlay were not of her own choosing. They were a part of God's plan. This man had just revealed that truth to her.

Suddenly, she felt the need to get out of her chair and bow at his feet. But she knew that was not what God wished, and she was sure it would embarrass this man, whom she could see, was loved by his community. Maggie was sure Mayor Anderson had no idea that through his choice to acknowledge her, he had made one of the most diplomatic rulings of his entire career.

Realizing that he was staring at her, waiting for a verbal response, she dropped her analogies. "Yes." Maggie looked into his eyes that exuberated a dominance, but, at the same time, a gentleness of deepest concern for his citizens. "Yes, I am."

"Come to Findlay to see the sculpture?"

"Uh . . ." She paused for a second, not wanting to admit that she actually had no idea of stopping, in what these people considered their fair city, for fear of insulting the kind man who was bidding her welcome. "No, not exactly. I was on my way to Florida for a spring break, but I kind of got detained here after seeing Mr. Redford at work on the sculpture."

"Yes, I can see why. He's an incredibly talented artist, and his work goes beyond human description." The mayor took a second look at the visitor. "Spring break, huh? Are you a student?"

"I was. I graduated from the University of Michigan this past January. This vacation was my reward to myself for my hard work and sacrifices." She gave a small, light-hearted chuckle. "At least, the trip to *Florida* was my reward. Guess I didn't get too far, huh?"

"I'd say you hit the jackpot. Findlay is a fine place to live. We have a few eligible bachelors here. Maybe you'll get a chance to meet some of them before you go back to Michigan."

Maggie didn't want to offend such a gentleman by telling him she had no intention of meeting someone in Findlay, Ohio. That was definitely *not* her idea of the place to find the perfect man.

Mayor Anderson didn't give Maggie much of an opportunity to respond. "I'm a graduate of the University of Michigan, too." His Notre Dame jacket gave no hint toward that tidbit of knowledge.

"That's where I got my undergraduate degree." He leaned in just a little and said in a more hushed tone, "And my wife."

"Really?" asked Maggie, now intrigued by their common ground.

"Yes," he said, again louder and sitting back in an upright position. "Proposed to her right there in the sparking room of the Martha Cook dormitory."

"What?" Maggie asked, full of astonishment. "You mean people actually used that place?"

"You've heard of it?"

"I sure have. I've spent six years of my life in that dorm. We've all heard the story of the sparking room, but we didn't think much about it."

"Oh, that was the place to be in my day there. I was a law student and the Law Quad was across the street. Mr. Cook, who donated the money for the Law Quad, had the dorm built and named after his mother. His intention was that the young women who stayed there could look out across the grounds and find suitable husbands." Once again he leaned in toward Maggie. "That dorm was *the* place for women to live on campus back then."

"It still is," she confessed. "It's the only female dorm that isn't co-ed after all these years. And they still have the finest food with the best chef on campus." Maggie's pride in U-M and Martha Cook Dormitory showed in her speech.

"Is it as formal as it used to be?" Mayor Anderson asked, noticeably enjoying this conversation as much as the female.

"We had a couple of nights each week when we dressed a little more formally and were actually served our dinner. The rest of the time it was more like a college cafeteria except for the fact that the food and the atmosphere were much better. And we had to take all our meals there together. If we had a conflict on any given evening, a roommate or a friend would take a plate to our room for us so that we didn't have to miss a meal." Maggie thought back to how many evenings she had eaten and then disappeared, or had a plate saved for her, her colleagues assuming she was hiding away in a secluded corner of the library, which was across the street from the dorm, studying until the wee hours of the morning. She had been fortunate enough to escape to her job without being noticed during the past four years. That was one convenience that being a student on such a large campus had afforded her.

But then, it also meant there were a large number of staff and administration for her to have to dodge. She had found it most strange that one of the professors on campus, who looked the most distinguished and seemed to own the world, was the one who sought refuge in the club. It had become increasingly difficult over the course of her last two years to disguise her identity between the building that housed the Rockham School of Graduate Studies and Northern Exposure.

Mayor Anderson noticed that the young woman was lost in thought. He mistook her far-away look as a longing for a beau, or a time of her life that she missed.

Maggie realized there was a lull in the conversation from the fact that she had gotten lost in her thoughts. "They still serve tea at four every Friday afternoon," she continued, a hint of glee in her voice. "I don't know what it is about tea time that I love, but I looked forward to that each week. In fact, I was hoping to go to the Swan House Tea Room tomorrow, but I found out they had no openings."

"Why don't you come as a guest of my wife and me?" the mayor invited. "We have reservations for tomorrow and we'd love to have you join us. That is a habit my wife still loves from her college days, too. I'm sure she'd love comparing notes with you and seeing how things have changed, or stayed the same," he chuckled, "after all these years."

"Are you sure I could get in?"

"I don't think there would be a problem, but I'll call to make sure."

Maggie watched as the mayor took out his cell phone and called the Swan House without looking up the number. *Wow!* she thought, most impressed that he had this establishment etched in his memory bank of important phone numbers. It must be quite a place. *Or a wonderful spot of habit for this married couple.*

She was so engrossed in her thoughts of how romantic it was that this couple still attended tea each Friday afternoon that she missed the entire phone conversation until he turned to her and asked, "Can you be there at eleven tomorrow morning?"

Maggie gave an affirmative nod.

"We'll see you then," he said to the person on the other end of the phone. "That will make four of us at our table." As he hung up the phone, he explained, "They're only having one seating tomorrow due to Good Friday. We usually go at one, but we have a Tenebrae service to attend."

The visitor wasn't sure if the fact that her head was spinning was the result of this man's memory, his love for a tradition with his wife, his clout, his devotion to his faith, or his kind spirit. But for whatever reason, this man had made his mark on her. *No wonder the people of this town love him.*

She watched the attentiveness he gave to the citizens who had come up and were shaking his hand and sharing stories with him. Maggie again reflected on the position of Christ and the politicians of his day. It was hard to believe that there were people out there who would not be drawn to this man's fine and upstanding qualities, but like Christ and other political figures, she was sure there were enemies lurking about for Mayor Anderson, too.

When he turned back to her, she shook his hand, hoping

her expression told him how appreciative she was of his generous offer and kind gesture. "Thank you. I don't know what to say."

"I think you'll love our little tea room. It happens to be listed in the great Tea Rooms of America. Our table is directly across the street from a lovely Victorian home whose stained-glass window sits in clear view for us. It's a wonderfully quiet way to end the hectic weeks, which usually find me trying to tie up lots of loose ends before the weekend so that I can begin a new agenda every Monday."

One of the other female visitors who had overheard the conversation turned toward Maggie. "And you'll love the shoppe. Be sure you get there early enough to look around at everything. I could spend hours in there."

"Sounds like my kind of place," Maggie smiled. "Thanks for the information."

"I'll see you tomorrow then. Do you need a ride or can you find the Swan House?"

"I'm staying at the Rose Gate Cottage, so I'm just around the corner. I think I'll walk."

"Fine. See you there."

Maggie lounged back in her beach chair. *All is not wasted. I have a date with a wonderful man in a lovely romantic setting. I'll bet even my Florida treasure would not have treated me to such a memorable date.* She grinned. *No matter that he's married and his wife will be part of the date. What a lovely experience.*

He stopped long enough to speak to one last couple that was making their way across the grass from the parking lot.

I'll bet he still calls his wife his cookie, she smiled, thinking of the name dubbed on all the females who had stayed under the roof of the Martha Cook Dormitory.

Mayor Anderson walked back to the sculpture and

stretched his long arm over the green plastic makeshift fence and patted the artist on the back. "Great job, Joshua. You and your work are an asset to Findlay. I need to run now and get back to work, but I had to come and say hello and check on things."

"Good-bye, Mayor. Thanks for stopping by."

The sculptor acknowledged everyone with that same phrase, but it was never said in a monotonous tone. Each time the words came from his mouth, there was feeling in them, delivered specially to the individuals who received them at each usage.

"I couldn't let the week go by without checking this out for myself. You know this *is* the talk of the town this week. People all over Findlay are commenting on how special it is to have you here and how this makes them feel a pride in the community."

"They are most kind," Joshua responded. "I feel like the one who is fortunate to be able to share my faith through my talent in this public place. You do know, Mayor, that without your support, this would not be possible."

"Redford, you give me too much credit. The authority for this artful project came from a Power greater than mine."

Maggie squinted her eyes, trying to sum up the two men in front of her. Joshua had become predictable after spending so much time around him during the past few days. His emotions and words were sincere, and she had become familiar with his pattern of actions. But here stood another man, obviously much in control of the situation, who was giving credit to a Higher Power. Not like some of the professors she knew from her college classes in similar positions of status. *And especially not like those 'self-proclaimed' higher powers who come into the club!*

Joshua stepped outside the fence, in respect of the man speaking to him, and once more brushed his hand on his trousers as he reached out to shake with the city's leading official.

"Thanks, again, Mayor."

"My pleasure."

Mayor Anderson glanced at his newest admirer and smiled. "I hope you enjoy your stay in Findlay. Please come back anytime."

"I will," she replied, wondering why she had said those words. She had no intention of spending much time in such a quiet place.

The mayor started to walk away, but turned back to Maggie as if he had forgotten something. "Why don't you go to the Holy Thursday service this evening at St. Michael's?" he invited. "We've just built a new sanctuary and we've got a brand new pipe organ and piano. The musicians are wonderful and it will be a lovely communion service. I won't be able to attend, but I think you'll love all the sculptures that have been specially commissioned for each of the stations."

"Thank you. I might just do that."

Maggie sat spellbound. She certainly had no intention of attending a Holy Thursday service when she left Ann Arbor. And had she planned on going to church, communion was probably the last thing she would have considered. She remembered communion and Holy Thursday from going to church with her grandmother, and she found both of those quite depressing. But she was sitting here now, because of an invitation of a kind gentleman, a sculptor who had given up a week to touch the lives of others, and a depiction of a man – *a perfect man* – with the inclination of going to a worship service. *Not exactly what I had in mind for a rollicking night out on the beach!*

She thought back about the three men she had just blamed for her change of plans. *A father, a son, and the Holy Ghost.* Maggie looked up at the sky that was showing signs of an afternoon storm. *I'm sure you're up there, Grandmother. And I'm sure there's probably a big smile on your face right now.* As she folded her chair, she glanced back up at the increasing somberness of the gray clouding over the blue. *I love you, Grandmother. Thank you.*

Maggie walked to her car, still thinking of Mayor Anderson, a man so gentle, yet with the power of a giant. She knew she would think of this man, his character and his humor many times in the days to come. His simple recognition of her presence made her feel like a real person again. A person who could hold her head up and walk with pride and dignity. And it also said to her that her past didn't show and that it didn't matter.

Thank you, Grandfather, she wanted to say, knowing he must be smiling right alongside of her grandmother.

Chapter 19
Late afternoon, Holy Thursday

The crowd became so thick that it was difficult to move in and out of the opening in front of the sculpture. People began to congregate for longer periods of time rather than walking by and leaving after a short look at the sand art.

Emotions were more expressive than they had been earlier in the week. *Probably because of the events of Holy Week and the symbolism that's visible here.*

Maggie saw a woman stoically walking toward the crowd. There was a look of purpose in her eyes, which appeared red around the edges, indicating that she had been crying. In her arms, she carried an array of flowers. They were not ones that had been picked from a flower garden, but were obviously cut stems from a floral arrangement.

As she came closer, a man, who had been a step behind her, moved up so that he was beside her and took her arm, which he held firmly. His action resembled a mark of comfort more than one of physical need.

The fact that people moved aside to let the woman pass through showed that they, too, saw her need to make an offering to Christ.

With everyone watching her movements closely, the woman laid the flowers at the foot of the cross where the image of Jesus was nailed. You could see tears forming in her eyes. "Thank you, Jesus," she said. "Thank you for taking my baby home."

The woman fell to her knees, not bothered by the fact that she was in dress clothes, and bowed her head. She prayed silently, the tears running down her cheek. When she raised her head, the man beside her took her arm and helped her back to her feet.

When he was sure he would not interrupt her, Joshua moved over to the woman. "Thank you for coming," he said softly, placing a hand on her shoulder.

"I had to come for my daughter. We buried her today, and these flowers are from her grave. She's suffered so long, and I had to come and pay tribute to God for allowing His Son to come and take her home."

Joshua was totally speechless. He wanted to cry himself, but dared not. All he knew to do was put his arm around the woman and hug her.

"May you feel God's peace in the days to come," he offered, as he backed away from her.

She nodded simply as she regained the stoic posture with which she had come to the cross, while the man with her led her back to the car.

All of the spectators were spellbound by the effect of the sand on this woman. No one said a word during the next few minutes.

Maggie noticed several nearby heads bow. She wondered whether they were praying for the hurting woman, or for their own grievances.

I wonder if Joshua has any idea of the number of people whose lives have truly been touched by this work of art.

She remembered her last trip to Italy. It had been during her high school years. Even though she had been an adolescent, her maturity level allowed her to appreciate the craftsmanship of Michelangelo, but more deeply, the spiritual effect that his sculptures had on her.

The sinewy muscles sculpted by the Italian master, like the ones on the Christ nailed to the cross in front of her, touched her soul to the very core. Although the famous artist had been dead for hundreds of years, he was still able to reach into peoples' hearts and their spirits through his work. You couldn't help but notice the influence of the Master, the Spirit, in his art.

Even though Maggie had felt a similarity in the two artists – Michelangelo and Joshua - on her first day here, she was now more convinced that the inspiration for their work came from the same Source. She thought of Rodin, another master who had been greatly influenced by Michelangelo. His work was to be on exhibit at the university's Museum of Art in a couple of weeks after her return to Ann Arbor. She made a note to take a day and let those sculptures inspire her and allow her to become reacquainted with the work of both of those masters.

Chapter 20
Evening, Holy Thursday

"Going out somewhere special?" June asked as Maggie bounded down the steps.

"I guess you could say that. I'm going to the Holy Thursday service at St. Michael's."

"Really?" Charlie had come around the corner just in time to hear the guest's answer. "That's where we're going."

"You could sit with us, but we're helping with the serving of communion," June apologized. "I'm sure we can find someone for you to sit with."

"Oh, don't worry about that," Maggie replied. "I haven't been to church in a while, and I think maybe I'd like to be alone to think through some things."

"Would you like to ride with us? The church is not exactly in the back door anymore. We usually attend the mass at the old building right behind us, but both parishes are meeting together in the new sanctuary during Holy Week."

"I appreciate the offer, but I'm not sure where I'll go when it's over."

"I can understand that," June commented. "One of those things where it's how the mood strikes you."

"Yeah," agreed Maggie. *Or how the* Spirit *strikes you!*

CЗEО

"Hi," Maggie heard as she got out of the Honda. "We're glad you could make it."

She turned to see who was calling to her and saw the woman who had told her about the gift shoppe at the tea room. *Talk about small towns!*

"Are you sitting with anyone?" Before Maggie could make her excuse and explanation, the woman had hooked an arm through hers. "Why don't you join us?" she asked.

The woman's husband nodded in agreement.

Just then, another couple joined them as they made the walk toward the sanctuary. "This young lady is visiting Findlay this week. We met her out at the park today where Joshua Redford's doing the sculpture. Have you been out there yet?"

The foursome was busy catching up on the business of the community, and the woman still had Maggie's arm locked in hers, so she was dragged into the building with them.

She watched as they each reached into the baptismal font and took water, giving the sign of the cross, thereby blessing themselves and recalling their baptismal dignity. The woman who had escorted her into the building explained that the awe-inspiring font had been designed in the shape of a huge cross especially for St. Michael's.

"How's this?" the woman asked as she walked into the sanctuary and pointed to a pew. She didn't wait for an answer, but proceeded to sit, taking Maggie down with her.

The guest breathed a sigh of relief as the woman and her husband knelt to pray, giving her a chance to sit quietly and take in the lofty, yet simply reverent, majesty of the building. She could only imagine how glorious the service would be on Easter Sunday, but for this evening, the somberness and austerity of Holy Thursday had set in the beige stucco walls, creating a mood that permeated into her very soul.

She felt her own spirit soar as she observed the hand-carved wooden stations and crucifix, commissioned especially for this sanctuary, and the gorgeous windows that had been given by the nuns. Even though the architecture relayed the message of a twenty-first century cathedral, the symbols and the cross on the ceiling spoke to her in a way that brought back very real memories of her childhood and the pleasant times of going to church with her parents and grandparents.

Maggie looked at the couple with whom she was seated. *They're about the same age as my grandparents would have been then.* She gave a silent laugh. *And this woman has as much spunk as my grandmother.*

The woman found someone to talk to in another row, giving Maggie a chance for more time of reflection. Just getting to a comfortable state in this surrounding took a few minutes, allowing the butterflies, not only in her stomach but her entire body, to stop their flitting.

She noticed the newly-installed pipes of the organ, which Mayor Anderson told her earlier had been built in Italy. That fact alone allowed the precarious visitor a feeling of belonging, of oneness, in her heritage.

The congregation began to sing as the priests and altar boys processed down the aisles. Maggie listened to the breadth of the music. She had been taught that there was something indeed spectacular about the singing of Mid-Westerners. Hearing the combined voices within the sanctuary assured her that was a trait that had gone unchanged during the years.

It amazed her that an electric guitar joined in an ensemble with a violin, a flute and the pipe organ on one of the selections. She had never seen an electric guitar used in the high church services in Cleveland. There was something about the informal instrumentation blended with the formal that appealed to her, that called her by name.

The music, an art that had been such a part of her life, caused a burning inside her soul like an inextinguishable fire, an unquenchable thirst, a desire like none other she had ever known.

She had worn red, the only dress she had brought that was remotely suitable for the service. *But then, how suitable is red for a Lenten service?* Maggie's thoughts again chided her conscience, reminding her that the color spoke of her profession. However, her worry of wearing a bright color to the service quickly passed as she saw that others were dressed in fairly casual clothes, also with red.

Maggie sat stunned as she watched twelve people make their way to the altar for a foot-washing service. The priest became the servant, *the lowly servant*, in the same manner as Christ on the evening that he had washed the feet of his disciples. She was reminded of the people who had become servants in so many various ways during the week.

As the priest moved from one person to another, both men and women, all of different ages, she finally understood the significance of this act, *this lowly act*, that showed how deeply Jesus had loved his brothers of the Spirit.

He came to one girl, a female soon to be a woman. As the water poured over her feet, tears poured down Maggie's face. The girl looked to be about the same age as she had been when she went to work at Northern Exposure. Consumed by the power of the moment, Maggie begged God not to let this young lady slip and fall onto a path of sin and shame.

Not wanting to miss any of the service, she forced the tears to stop. She rubbed her eyes so that she could again clearly see the expressions of each face as the priest washed and dried their feet.

She had opted to cover her chest with her crossed arms, indicating that she was not able to partake of the elements of communion, but after watching the service of foot-washing, Maggie felt compelled to join in the observance of the sacrament.

As the rows of worshippers were ushered to the altar, Maggie tried to look down at the stately marble floor while praying that her secret would not show in her expression. But as she made her way down the aisle, it struck her that not one person noticed her sin and shame.

When the father presented her with the elements and gave her his blessing, Maggie was sure that he saw into the depths of her soul as his eyes caught hers. Yet he offered her the same words as the other parishioners. She was forgiven, she was loved, she was one with all those around her.

Maggie went back to her seat and pulled down the kneeler. She bowed her head and offered her petitions to God, a practice in which she had not participated over the past few years. Yet the words flowed freely from her lips as she whispered them softly in the same manner as the other worshippers.

Everyone here is a sinner, she recognized. *Everyone here has been offered the same gift of forgiveness. Everyone here has experienced the redemptive love of God through His Son, Jesus Christ.*

She couldn't help but stare at the eyes of the priest as he administered the rites of the sacred elements to each person. Not once did his pleasant expression change as he offered the sacred feast. It was not his lot to cast judgment; it was his lot to let others see Jesus' love in his face.

Maggie's sense of belonging was intensified as she turned,

with the rest of the parishioners, toward a small chapel at the back of the sanctuary. Her eyes followed the steps of the fathers' procession as they carried the blessed sacraments and placed them on the Altar of Repose. She watched the parishioners who began to pray over the bread and wine, beginning the all-night vigil.

The couple she had met offered to take her out for dessert, but Maggie had another end to the evening in mind. She rushed back to the Rose Gate Cottage and ran up the stairs to her room. When she found what she was looking for, she headed back toward Riverside Park and the sculpture.

There were very few visitors at the park when she arrived. Most of them had been shooed away by the early evening rain. There was a slight mist in the air, perfect for the aura of the evening.

Maggie reached inside her purse and pulled out the bottle of perfume she had gone after in her room. While the stragglers walked toward their cars or were lost in conversation, she tiptoed inside the green plastic fence and laid the perfume, the most expensive bottle she had, at the base of the cross in exactly the same spot as the teenager had left the yellow forsythia.

Chapter 21
Morning, Holy Friday

"We thought you might like to see this," Charlie said, beaming as he placed the morning's *Courier* on the table beside the apple puff pancake.

On the front page, in a full-color shot, was a picture of Joshua standing atop one of the huge piles of sand, molding the shape of Christ praying beside the empty tomb. It had taken the place of endless days of photos of soldiers, and scenes from a raging war. And now, instead of bombs and terror, there was an image of peace glaring up from the headlines of the newspaper.

Maggie stared at the picture for a bit before reading the caption underneath it. Then she turned to the next page where the full story of the sculpture was in print.

"Can you believe this?" she asked the couple who stood looking at her, waiting for her reaction. "This is wonderful." Eating the pancake, she read the story again. "Not only is it a tribute to a great artist, but the reporter did a terrific job, and there are no mistakes. That's an accomplishment of its own in a town this size." Maggie noted the name of the reporter. *Beth Hendricks.* She would definitely send a note to the woman for the superb job she had done. "I do hope *The Courier* realizes the talent of this lady."

"She's very good," June agreed. "I always enjoy reading her articles."

"And look at this," Maggie shot. "It says here that some author is writing a book based on this sculpture. Can you believe that? And can you imagine the size of the crowd all this publicity will bring in next year?"

Charlie and June could already see the wheels turning in their new friend's mind as she mentally made plans to return for the event the next Holy Week.

"Shall we reserve your room for next year?" Charlie asked with a smirk.

"Absolutely! But you'd better save all of the rooms for me because I intend to bring some friends along the next time."

She gazed at the couple, beaming, yet with a faraway look in her eyes. *Isn't this a switch? And just yesterday afternoon, I was sure I'd never spend any time in this town!*

The guest finished her breakfast while chatting with her host and hostess. "Why don't you come down to the park today?" Maggie suggested.

"We plan to," Charlie answered. "There's been so much going on here this week with the renovation of the carriage house that we haven't had a chance to get away. But the workers aren't coming today, so we're hoping to get there in the afternoon sometime."

"Good, I'll look for you."

"Maybe we could grab a bite of lunch together," June suggested.

Maggie looked appreciatively at the couple, fully aware that it was not a custom to socialize with their guests outside the home. But this had come to be more than a business relationship. She had grown to love Charlie and June from the moment she first set foot inside the Rose Gate Cottage. It seemed they recognized her need for open arms from the moment of her arrival, and they had offered her just that – *no questions asked.*

They are just like . . . She stopped, searching for just the right word to describe what they meant to her. *Parents*, she realized, thinking back to her earlier assessment of them, as she nodded her head in acceptance of the invitation.

Maggie wondered what they would have said had she told them about her place of employment. But that didn't matter to them. What *did* matter was that she was a part of God's creation, and they accepted her as she was. She had feared what people would think once they found out about her past. But it dawned on her that not one person had asked about her line of work. When she told them she had recently finished graduate school, that was all that was said – besides asking her major.

Now she felt she could enter the world a new person, not only on the inside, but also on the outside. *That's odd*, she reasoned. *For most of the people who visited the site of the sculpture this week were looking for a change on the inside, not on the outside.*

She sat there, mentally patting herself on the back at the discovery she had just made.

Wait a minute, Maggie Matelli! How do you know that? Those people could be just like you. They could be strippers, or druggies, or alcoholics, or be carrying around any number of afflictions and pains – mentally, physically, and emotionally. Perhaps they, like you, have a past for which they are ashamed. And perhaps they have felt a sense of forgiveness by coming to the cross this week, also.

All this week, Maggie had assumed that the other people who came to the cross were there to observe, to see the work of art, to appreciate the artist. *Well, maybe I realized that a few came for healing – like the blind man.* But for the most part, she had seen this as a pleasurable event for the majority of onlookers that came.

It struck her that she knew nothing about the people whom she had seen and met this week. Perhaps they were like the people in the Bible who were hungry, thirsty, naked . . . *and would I have offered them food, drink, or clothing?*

She thought back, trying to visualize the faces of all she had encountered during the week. *Maybe I was sitting right beside that author and didn't even know it. Maybe I was standing next to a serial killer or rapist.* The young woman folded her napkin and placed it on the table. *Or maybe I was standing beside hundreds who simply needed a spiritual reassurance instead of an awakening.*

Maggie knew that she would not look at the sculpture, *or the visitors,* in the same way. In her mind, she began to see the people who had been to the park during the week. She wondered which of them could have been Jesus, or angels, in human form.

Deciding to let the subject rest for the moment, Maggie knew that her mind would resume these thoughts once she was back at the sculpture with the other people who were drawn to it.

What better place for Jesus to be than there, where all sorts of people, of all ages, come? she concluded as she took the last bite of her apple puff pancake.

Chapter 22
Mid-morning, Holy Friday

Mayor Anderson and his wife were already milling around in the shoppe of the Swan House Tea Room when Maggie arrived. He stepped over to her, extending the same graciousness with which he had greeted everyone the afternoon before at the park.

"Ah, here's our guest. Maggie, I'd like for you to meet a couple of people." He took his wife's elbow and pulled her closer to him. "This is my wife, Dora, the best thing I got at U-M."

The two women nodded simply and made their hellos as another woman stepped up behind them.

"And this is Beth Hendricks, a reporter at *The Courier*. She's doing an article on one of the city's upcoming projects, so I asked her to meet me a few minutes early to take care of the business then join us for lunch. Her office is only three blocks away."

"Aren't you the reporter who wrote the article about Joshua Redford in this morning's newspaper?" Maggie asked, feeling like she already knew the woman through her writing.

"Yes, as a matter of fact."

Beth looked pleased that she had not only been read, but recognized, by a visitor of Findlay. Also sensing a connection, she directed the young guest's attention to some of the more interesting items of the shoppe.

The hostess, one of the tea room's owners, stepped into the room and informed everyone that it was time to be seated. Maggie followed the mayor and the rest of his party to their table. *He was right. The view of that home and the stained-glass window across the street are gorgeous.* The window was so magnificent it looked as if it could have been designed by Tiffany, himself.

Maggie loved the selection of teas on the menu. After the group at her table selected a common variety to begin, they each made their own choice for later in the brunch.

She watched as the hostess brought out their three-tiered tray of individual-sized goodies. The puff pastry, made into the shape of a swan (their logo and feature item), immediately caught her attention from the bottom tier. But she selected the fruit and the finger sandwiches for starters, saving the baked item for the finale.

The women each commented on how they loved teas. For the first time, Maggie saw this experience as being akin to what she had observed between Joshua and the truckers on the first day at the park. *The female version of never growing up.* She eyed Beth and Dora and realized that they were enjoying this outing as much as she was.

Their conversation centered around everything that had happened, or was going to happen, in Findlay as the three locals tried to give Maggie a full knowledge of their small town. She wasn't sure which she liked best, the food or the fellowship.

Dora's next statement reiterated her earlier assessment

of girls' play.

"I must admit that I look forward to the Spring Tea at the Martha Cook Dormitory each year. I haven't missed one yet."

"Perhaps the two of you can sit together next year when they have that annual fundraiser and invite all the past cookies," Mayor Anderson suggested.

Maggie previously had no intention of being a part of that social group, not because she didn't want to, but because she was ashamed of the sinful choice she had made during her college career. She had been afraid her mistake was irrefutable, that the others would find out and scourge her. "You know, I think I'd really like that," she answered with a confidence that she knew would have been absent the week before.

"Can you believe he still calls me his cookie after all these years?" Mrs. Anderson asked, a girlish, blushful pride showing in her face as her husband placed his hand over hers in her lap.

I knew I was right! the young guest beamed.

The more Maggie learned of this man, the more she liked him. His devotion to his wife was evident both in and out of his spouse's presence as it manifested itself with the same vitality that it must have in their days in the sparking room. And Maggie increasingly adored his wit and humor, as well as his ability to make all those around him feel comfortable. Her love for him grew by the minute as he brought back many fond memories of her grandfather.

"You are a most remarkable man, Mayor Anderson, and I truly love your disposition." She felt comfortable enough with both he and his wife to add the next statement, knowing they would take her words in the vein of respect with which she meant them. "I wish I could take you home with me."

Mayor Anderson laughed and shook his head. "So do some of the residents of Findlay."

"I seriously doubt that," she bolted with laughter, while

enjoying the prevalence of his quick wit. But then Maggie remembered her thought from yesterday. That same thought raced through her mind now as she suspected Jesus would not have been crucified on Good Friday had there not been those who were against him.

She refused to let depressing thoughts cloud her mind and remove her from the frivolity and fun of the tea. This was the quaintest lunch she had shared in quite a while, and she intended to enjoy it to the fullest.

The mayor and his wife had to rush to get to the Tenebrae service, leaving Beth and Maggie to chat. "Take your time," he offered. "I'll take care of the check." He shook hands with the visitor. "Will you still be here on Sunday?"

"No, I'm afraid not," Maggie apologized.

"Too bad. We'd love to have you as our guest at church and then the Japanese restaurant for lunch. We go there every Sunday."

"Perhaps next time," extended Mrs. Anderson, offering her hand to Maggie.

As they exited the room, Maggie stared behind them in disbelief.

"They're quite a couple, aren't they?" Beth asked, reading the mind of the young woman left with her at the table.

"Yes, they are. They remind me a lot of my grandparents," Maggie said, with a melancholic tone.

"Lucky you."

"Yeah," Maggie said, still staring behind them. "I don't think I've realized how lucky until the past couple of days."

"Sadly, that is more often the case than not. We don't appreciate the people who are closest to us until it's too late."

The visitor wanted to comment further, but the lump in her throat made that impossible for the moment. Rather, she took one of the bite-size poppy seed loaves and nibbled on it.

Beth could see the look of dismay on the young woman who was seated beside her. "Have you ever tried the chai here?"

"No," Maggie was able to respond, swallowing hard.

"It's the best thing on the menu, but they don't offer it unless you ask specifically for it. Would you like to share a pot?"

"I'd love to."

The reporter called the hostess to the table and made her request.

Maggie saw a look of delight come across the owner's face as she exited to the kitchen. It wasn't long before she returned with another teapot. The hostess poured a cup for each of the women adding with a smile, "Enjoy!"

"Thanks. I'm sure we will," replied Beth.

"Ah," expressed Maggie, savoring the combination of the aroma and the flavors as she picked up on the taste of chocolate and honey in the tea.

"It's even better than I remember."

The women made small talk, Beth answering questions about the town for the visitor. They agreed that they could have each devoured the entire pot of chai by themselves.

It wasn't long before the hostess returned with a black bag that bore the name of the Swan House Tea Room in gold metallic letters. "Mayor Anderson asked me to give this to you before you leave," she stated, handing the package to Maggie.

Stunned, the young woman opened the bag to see an autographed copy of the book, *The Great Tea Houses of America,* that featured the Swan House. Maggie was ecstatic. "Can you believe he did that?" she asked the reporter.

"Yes, I can," Beth answered, sipping the Chai. "That's just the kind of person he is. Did you know he served in the Senate, and was named to the Senate Hall of Fame, before returning to Findlay to run the town?"

Again, Maggie's thoughts turned to the similarity of this

man to her grandfather. "No, I didn't," she answered, remembering how, as a child, she thought they should have a Hall of Fame for Grandfathers, and that hers deserved the tribute of being the first one inducted into it.

Not wanting to return to her melancholic state from moments earlier, she turned the subject to the morning's newspaper article. "I was most impressed with the story you ran this morning on the sculpture. It was a good feeling to see something besides bad news as the headline, especially for this season."

"Thank you. I was glad to see it on the front page and then a continuation of the story on another page with more photos. Did you know it hit the Associated Press?"

"No, that's great."

"Joshua deserved that. He does a lot for this community through his talents, not just at Easter, but also throughout the year. Anytime the park does some special event for the kids, he's always making a sculpture for them. One year he even made a dinosaur and a Volkswagen Beetle out of sand. The kids loved it . . . and so did the adults," she recalled, with a chuckle.

"This has been quite a week. I never intended to spend a day here, much less a week. And do you know this has been the greatest vacation I've ever had? I can't wait to go back to the . . . to school and tell all my friends about this." Of course, Maggie knew her friends would never understand. *Perhaps it's time I make some new friends . . . like the students who spent this week doing mission work for Alternative Spring Break. I bet they'd understand the magnetism of this place.*

"It's quite an event. Why don't you stay until Easter Sunday to see the crowd that hits the park? There's something even more spectacular about the sculpture on that day, like God adds His own special touch. I've heard people make that comment every year, but I've never gotten there on a Sunday. This year, I plan to see for myself."

"I don't know. I kind of need to be heading back."

"Think about it. If you stay, I'd love to have you visit my church. I play the organ there."

"You're kidding! What a multi-talent you are. I play the piano myself. Not in church, though." *Huh, not even in the club!*

Beth wrote her home phone number on the back of a business card. "Here. Call me if you change your mind. Besides, maybe you can still get in touch with the mayor and have lunch."

"No. If I do stay, it will be to hear you play and then see the sculpture one last time. Then it will be on the road for me."

The reporter had done enough interrogations to know that her lone captive audience would be sitting in her congregation come Sunday morning.

"I've got to get back to work. Another story is calling my name, but take your time in the shoppe. There's lots of interesting things. And they do have Chai mix that you can purchase."

"That got my interest. I think I will."

"Hope to see you Sunday," Beth urged, shaking the hand of her young admirer.

Maggie found that neither the woman from yesterday nor the reporter had exaggerated in their description of the gift shoppe. The walls were covered with gorgeous tea pots and magnificent tea sets that would claim the heart of any collector. And although she was not a collector, she had made up her mind to have one for herself as a souvenir of Findlay, Mayor and Mrs. Anderson, Beth, and the Swan House.

If I can't go home with a man, I'll at least go back with the next best thing, she laughed. *Besides, this is a lot less trouble.*

"*I heard that,*" she could hear Ebony's response.

Before leaving, she had selected a tea set that was white with mint-green trim and hand-painted pictures of dogwoods decorating it. There were miniature silver knives, spoons and forks held in their own elastic bands in the top of the white wicker picnic basket in which the fragile pieces were arranged and cushioned in a padded blanket of green-and-white gingham. Maggie, suddenly feeling a longing to see her parents, also selected a piece of antique Fenton glass for her mother and a hearty tea blend for her father.

As she exited the Swan House, shopping bags in each hand, she realized that a healing was taking place within her. A healing between her parents and herself, but also a healing for a barrier that had been self-inflicted. Neither her mother nor father had abandoned her when they found out about her job. It was her own guilt that had placed the, what had seemed, insurmountable space between them. Now, it seemed they were only a phone call away.

Maggie also sensed a longing for her grandmother, wishing to say she was sorry. Sorry for not being there in the last years. Sorry for not attending the memorial service. Sorry for abandoning her spiritual background. Sorry for many things. *Sorry for things for which Grandmother had already forgiven me*, she realized.

She wanted to go back to the sculpture, feeling the need to be there for Good Friday. But first, she had to take care of one of the two errands on her to-do list while still in Findlay.

Chapter 23
Early afternoon, Holy Friday

Maggie made a swift turn into the building with the familiar green-and-white awning she had spotted earlier in the week.

"Welcome back. What'll you have today?"

Maggie scanned the cooler, trying to hurriedly decide what her pleasure was. Dietsch Brothers was booming with customers, all scurrying to pick up last minute treats for Easter baskets and desserts for Sunday's lunch.

"Take your time," the man behind the counter offered.

"There's so much to choose from, but I think I'll have a German chocolate shake."

"One German chocolate shake coming up."

When he handed her the large cup overflowing with chocolate and pecans and coconut, Maggie asked, "How did you recognize me after all the customers you've obviously had this week?"

"We make it our business to know," he replied with a

smile. "And you had a peppermint scoop in a cup. The fact that you're not from around here also helped to point you out."

"But how did you know I'm not from here?"

"We've been in Findlay for a long time. Knowing our customers and what they want is what keeps us here. Nearly every family in town has been here at one time or another."

She gazed at the man, looking farther than his face and the apron that held a story all its own with traces of the various flavors wiped on it. Maggie imagined the man's father standing in that very spot, looking exactly the same, except with a few less flavors streaked across his apron, handing cones of ice cream across the counter to boys and girls who had ridden bikes or walked there for an after-school treat.

How many birthdays have been celebrated at these tables? she wondered.

Her eyes met the ones of the man facing her. "You're right. Knowing everyone who walks through that door *is* what has kept you here. You are *all* family."

For the first time, Maggie fully understood what it was about the town of Findlay that appealed to her so much. She had seen reruns of *The Andy Griffith Show* as a child, and Findlay was still the epitome of Mayberry, USA.

"Anything else for you today?" he asked.

"Yes, as a matter of fact, there is. I'll be right back."

She walked around the cooler to the shelves of handmade chocolates and grabbed two handfuls of the small bars that had sayings molded into them. They had caught her eye on her first visit to the store, and during the course of the week, Maggie had decided they would be perfect thank-you notes and souvenirs. After choosing the appropriate delectable sayings, she went back to the counter to make her purchase.

It amazed her that the owner remembered everyone's orders, not bothering to jot them down, and kept all the purchases and numbers in his mind. But he had grown up in this business. It literally *was* second nature to him. And the smile on his face clearly stated that this was more than a way of paying the bills. Even his manner of taking care of the customers gave Maggie a warm, cozy welcome feeling that brewed an emotion inside her that had been absent during her college years.

A feeling of . . .

She couldn't describe it, but she knew that somewhere in her past, she had felt it before. And she knew that before the approaching weekend was over, she would feel it again . . . *and recognize it.*

Chapter 24
Mid-afternoon, Holy Friday

Maggie found a strategic place to position her chair for the duration of the day where she wouldn't miss any of the action at Riverside Park. She expected this to be a most eventful evening in the Holy Week of Findlay, just as this day was in religious history.

Good Friday. She struggled to find the words that her grandfather had used to describe that day to her many years ago. *"The day of reconciliation between God and His children,"* the words finally formed in her mind.

As she gazed on the middle sculpture, the one of Christ on the cross with his arms outstretched and the one to the right, with him carrying the cross, the vertical timber of sand staring back at her seemed to pierce her heart.

Pierce. The vision of the man with all the piercings came rushing through her head. She remembered hearing her grandfather, as he read her the story about feeding, clothing, and offering drink to others, tell how Jesus appeared in all kinds of characters. That man suddenly took on the form of Jesus to her.

Maggie eyed the park ranger, nicknamed Yogi, who was talking to Joshua. He was a city employee, hired to keep a watchful eye over all the persons and happenings of the parks of Hancock County. And he stood there, his gun and uniform demanding authority, creating the portrait of the centurion in her mind. A man who was a hired official, yet recognized that "truly this man was the Son of God."

She thought back to one of Joshua's friends, a man nicknamed Buckeye, who had come riding up on his motorcycle the afternoon before. A man who, at the time, had seemed like a disciple to her in his renegade appearance, yet his humble and gentle spirit.

Maggie closed her eyes and pictured the entire story in her mind, recreating the events using the characters who had appeared to her during the week in her own personal message from God.

છાજી

Lynn Redford came running across the park. She whispered something to Joshua whose expression showed that his wife had just given him some exciting news. As the couple hugged, his cell phone began to ring.

"Hello?" He paused looking at Lynn, who was staring at him in anticipation. "Yes, this is Joshua Redford." A nod of his head told her what she wanted to know as she clasped his hand in support of whatever was going on between him and the person on the other end of the line.

Everyone seated near the sculpture could hear Joshua giving the details of how he came to do the sculpture and some of the stories of its effect on the people of Findlay and the town's visitors. They, suspecting the call was from someone important, sat eavesdropping on his every word, not wanting to miss any detail of what was happening.

Joshua said his good-bye and closed the phone's case as he and Lynn again hugged. "Can you believe that?" he asked, to the crowd as much as to his wife. "That was Marya Morgan, of K-LOVE FM radio. They're a nationally-syndicated Christian radio station based in Sacramento, California. Someone passing through Findlay saw the newspaper article, came by the park, then called the station to tell them about it, saying they thought others would like to know what's happening here in Findlay. She just interviewed me, and the picture that was in the newspapers around the country is going on their Web Site with her story."

"What's the address?" yelled one of the onlookers, already heading toward his car so he could go home and check out the site. Pencils and pens were flying as spectators, including Maggie, grabbed anything they could find to write on as Joshua called out, "www.klove.com."

Several people left to go and check out their town's prized artist on the Internet. Others commented on the fact that they regularly listened to that station and had heard Marya. Maggie made a note to check out K-LOVE FM on her radio when she got back in the car.

Chapter 25
Evening, Holy Friday

She wasn't sure whether it was the impact of last night's foot-washing or communion, or the significance of this being the day Christ was crucified, but there was an aura that blanketed the weekend – the air, the conversation, the feelings. Something had definitely moved into Findlay, Ohio, and staked its claim on the town's residents and visitors alike.

Maggie knew what the "something" was, but she was at a loss to describe it. And what's more, she didn't try to describe it. But she sensed that she, too, was caught up in the same trance as all the other people who were at the park. It was a feeling akin to being in the play *Our Town*, where you could move around and actually observe yourself – walking, talking, being – thereby creating an odd sort of eeriness. Not odd in the sense of being evil or frightening, but of being surrounded by a presence that had taken over complete control of every part of your existence.

And there was strength in knowing that "something", "someone" was out there - caring for you, holding you, keeping you from harm. Maggie's urge to stay the evening grew. She knew there was no way she was going to leave this scene before day was done.

With that thought, she left her chair in its spot and rushed to the drive-thru of the first fast food restaurant she came to, asking for the largest salad she could get. "And give me two large teas with no ice." She'd take her meal to the park and . . . "No, wait! Can you cancel that order?"

She heard a male's voice come through the crackly speaker. "Yes," he said simply.

"I'm sorry. I just remembered that someone made other plans for me for dinner."

Maggie pulled back onto the street, making her way to Riverside Park as swiftly as she could get there. She knew who that "someone" was. Her Father had requested her presence for dinner and she was going to be there.

Dinner was going to be communion. Not communion like she had partaken of the evening before, but a communion in Christ through the sharing of food and drink at the park with all the other spectators who were coming to join with their brothers and sisters.

Maggie stopped the car and got out. She looked up at the still sky with its few scattered clouds and yelled, "I belong. Thank you, God, for showing me that I belong. I am somebody. I am worthy. I am your child."

She hopped back in her silver coach, singing the words to "Tonight," her favorite song from *West Side Story*, knowing that something spectacular was indeed going to happen this night.

കൃ

The sun and mildly brisk wind had finally cleared all the dampness from the air so that it was a perfect evening for a picnic in the park. Others must have shared that idea with Maggie for families flocked to the grounds, most with baskets of food, some with balls and gloves, some with Frisbees, some with dogs.

But *all* of them with the idea that Riverside Park was the place to be on Good Friday evening.

As the crowd began to dwindle in, Maggie noticed that the group was different from any that had been at the park all week. She attributed it to the fact that people were off work for the weekend, their stress levels were down, they could sit back and relax, or that they felt the need to come and mourn, to come and pay tribute, or just to come.

The visitor had been right about the dinner plans. Families came with each member loaded down with something – a blanket, a chair, a cooler, a picnic basket, a grocery bag. And they came with the intention of sharing. Not with their own little family, but their extended family.

Maggie watched as the small groups huddled together, some under the park's shelters, some under large beach umbrellas, but most either on the ground, or on blankets. Men carried picnic tables from the nearby shelters to the sculpture site and people laid out offerings of food reminiscent of what you would see at a family reunion. *Which is exactly what this is*, Maggie surmised.

A young child, whom Maggie took to be about six or seven, walked over to her. "Would you like something to eat?"

She looked into his winsome eyes, full of expression yet no particular expression, and said, very plainly, "Yes." Maggie wanted to blurt out, "Yes, I've been expecting you. Father told me you would call me for dinner." But she knew that no one, especially this young child, would understand at all what she was talking about. So she simply stood, followed the child to the long lengths of tables and fixed herself a plate of food that far surpassed the salad and two teas of the fast food chain.

The atmosphere was of the most relaxed nature that she had ever known. People appeared to be eating and moving in slow motion. Conversations, although some were lively, seemed quiet and reflective. Even the children and pets, who had been bounding over the park during the course of the week, were in a calmer mode.

Maggie loved the spirit, *the Spirit*, she felt in the air. It was better than what she had imagined feeling in a warm and comfortable home scenario with her perfect man. *Funny,* she thought, *I'm not at home, but I* am *at home. I'm a stranger – all alone, but I have* hundreds *of friends by my side. I have no man, but I'm sitting right beside* the *perfect man.*

As darkness set in, people began to light candles, or turn on battery-operated lanterns, causing the ground to look like it was covered with stars, matching those in the sky. Everywhere she looked, there were small traces of illumination, all casting shadows around them.

There was an aura in the air that had intensified as the week and the trio of sculptures had progressed. Crowds had grown each day and evening, and now, it seemed that all of Findlay had turned out to take ownership and experience the "wondrous beauty" of this "wondrous attraction."

Maggie closed her eyes and imagined a hillside. She could barely catch a glimpse of it in her mind for it seemed so far away. But it was visible, like in a dream, and on it stood three crosses. Instead of the two thieves who were crucified with Christ, she saw her grandmother and herself.

Emotions that were beyond explanation welled up inside of Maggie until she felt her entire rib cage were about to burst. She was tempted to open her eyes, but she was afraid she would lose the daydream that had become a real part of her. Just then, she knew what this feeling was. It was the spirit, *the Spirit*, that Jesus had told his disciples he would leave with them. The Spirit that only he could give them. The Spirit that she felt in the air only moments earlier had penetrated her body, her soul, and had become a real part of her.

She began to wonder if she actually was in a dream world, or a dream where she would wake up and be back at the club with all those men she had been trying so desperately to escape, or if she had totally lost her mind. The answers to all her questions came back negative with the sound that began to waft through the evening air.

For at that moment, from a good distance behind her, Maggie heard a woman's voice from a far back corner as it began to sing. The words were so soft that they were barely audible, but as she listened, they became louder as the night air carried them, and the musical notes on which they floated, throughout the crowd.

She opened her eyes, as if that would help her to hear better. "On a hill far away stood an old rugged cross, the emblem of suffering and shame." Maggie had not heard that song in years, since her grandmother sang it to her while telling her about George Bennard, the author of the words who had lived in Ohio and Michigan. She couldn't remember the words, but they came back to her slowly as the woman continued to sing, "and I love that old cross where the dearest and best, for a world of lost sinners was slain."

The dearest and best. My man. My Christ. My perfect *man.*

"In the old rugged cross, stained with blood so divine, a wondrous beauty I see, for 'twas on that old cross Jesus suffered and died, to pardon and sanctify me." *He suffered and died . . . to pardon . . . and sanctify . . .* me *. . . Me . . . Me!*

Jesus loves me. I do belong. I really do belong. To Him,

to this family of friends . . . to my own *family.*

By the third refrain, Maggie joined all the people around her, most of whom were now standing, and began to sing. When she came to the final phrase, "I will cling to the old rugged cross, and exchange it some day for a crown," she closed her eyes, hoping to again see her daydream.

There was her image of the three crosses, with Christ on a center cross, and her on one of the other crosses. But her grandmother was standing beside her, dressed in a white linen robe, removing a jeweled crown from her head and holding it out to Maggie.

It hurt her terribly to think that it was her all along that had placed a barrier between them. That she had thrown aside a wonderful and loving relationship with her grandmother because of the guilt of her own misgivings and shortcomings.

Her ears tuned in on the final stanza of words as the woman sang. "To the old rugged cross I will ever be true, its shame and reproach gladly bear; then he'll call me some day to my home far away, where his glory forever I'll share." *Share . . . my grandmother . . . in her home far away . . . where that glory forever she'll share . . . right along beside her man, my grandfather.*

"So I'll cherish the old rugged cross, till my trophies at last I lay down; I will cling to the old rugged cross, and exchange it some day for a crown." Suddenly a rush of tears swept their way down Maggie's checks as she received the answers to all the questions that had been left unanswered this week as she realized that the "Something" that had staked its claim on Riverside Park this week was the same "Someone" that had staked its claim on her at this very moment.

Maggie had never cried tears like this before, and she didn't even know what kind of emotion caused them. But she did know that her mission, her purpose of setting out this week to spend it in the sun and the sand, and find the perfect man, had all been accomplished. Never had she sensed that it would feel so wonderful. Never had she known this feeling that she would take back with her to Ann Arbor.

Voices from all around her began to join in a final round of the chorus as she listened. "So I'll cherish the old rugged cross, till my trophies at last I lay down; I will cling to the old rugged cross, and exchange it some day for a crown."

As the last notes of the song filtered through the air, Maggie turned and looked at the woman who was singing. It was obvious that the woman did not have a trained voice like the ones with which she had grown accustomed in her days of listening to all the Italian opera singers with her father, or the many music majors she had encountered at the university. But the emotion evoked by the woman's simplicity and her love for Jesus, that soared through the air in the strains of words as she sang *The Old Rugged Cross,* literally ran through every vein in Maggie's body.

She looked around to see the effect this woman had on the entire crowd. People were swaying, they were crying, they were smiling. Whatever their reactions, it was clear that this woman's voice was touching everyone in the park in some way or another.

Maggie realized the beauty of the woman's song came from the fact that she knew these words. Not only in her mind as she sang them from memory, but in her heart and her soul. This woman, who was disabled in some areas of her life, knew Jesus in a way that many of the persons around her did not. And her voice was like that of an angel, sent down to offer everyone at Riverside Park the blessing of being able to share in that glory of the cross – *the old rugged cross.*

It wasn't long before every voice in the crowd had joined the woman and the entire park was united in song, the tones hovering in the air over the sculpture like musical angels. People who had flashlights turned them on, giving the effect of candles lighting up the park.

A spirit filled the crowd, making a mark on every person who had ventured out to experience this wondrous sight. Maggie was touched by the presence that overtook all visual and aural sensations. An invisible presence that scarred each person there as real as if they, too, had felt the nails being driven through their own hands.

She glanced across the street where she caught a glimpse of a stage, with a huge shell built around it, that was used for spring and summer concerts. Maggie wagered that never had any more inspiring or heartfelt music come from these grounds than the rendition of the hymn sung by this woman.

This woman who knew the love of God that was shed through the blood on that old rugged cross.

CS80

As the crowd sat back down and began to sing other songs that fit the mood created by the significance of Good Friday and the surroundings, Maggie clung to the image in her head of the three crosses. She had lost all feelings of unworthiness, and she felt the love that her grandmother had always extended to her.

Joni made a second visit to the park, again bearing trays of cups filled with hot chocolate, cider and tea. She asked Maggie to help her carry her offering to the picnic tables where people could take a cup of warmth at their own leisure.

Returning to her chair, it struck the visitor that each person here had a gift or a talent to share. Not to share, but to serve. They were all servants in their own capacity.

Maggie closed her eyes and listened to the hymn she still imagined drifting through the air and continued to envision the three crosses. *No longer will I serve those men at Northern Exposure.* Tears began to gently stream down her cheeks as Joni wrapped her arm around the visitor she had come to love. *From now on, I will serve this man,* my perfect man.

⊰⊱

By the time it approached midnight, Joni, like all the other spectators, said good-bye, promising to return before the weekend was over. Maggie couldn't drag herself away. She knew there was a warm, cozy bed and gas logs calling her name back at the Garden Villa, but the call she heard from these granules of sand was even stronger.

When members of the local chapter of Civitans had discussed who would be spending the evening with Joshua at the sculpture sight, Maggie readily volunteered. "Don't you want someone to be here with you?" one of the men asked, worried about her being there alone.

"Isn't the purpose of being here to greet visitors who might come? Visitors that, if they show up in the quiet hours of the night, probably have a need that may require an ear or a kind word?" She smiled politely, not with that painted-on flash that had become a part of her mask at the club, and answered her own question. "I believe I have those qualifications. I'll be fine."

"I'll tell you what," compromised the man. "I'll go home and sleep for three or four hours, then I'll come back and relieve you."

"That's a fair deal," Maggie agreed, pulling her hand out from under the blanket to shake, but not getting up from under the warmth it had created.

The still night air and the bright stars gave Maggie a security that she loved. Even though the great outdoors had not been her forte in the past, there was an undisputable calm about being here that made it seem familiar. Before she knew it, she had dozed off, sitting in her blue beach chair and wrapped in her blue blanket with the maize trim.

CZ&Q

She awoke with a start when she heard a beat-up old truck pull into the park and up on the grass, very close to the sculpture, before it came to a stop. It had no muffler, and it vibrated as it drove past her.

A tall, extremely stocky man opened the loud, squeaky door and got out, moving to where she could see him in the truck's headlights. His build and the scraggly beard on his weather-beaten face made him the epitome of a lumberjack. Maggie had never seen a bigger man. Even from where she sat, the liquor was so strong on his breath that he smelled like a brewery.

The quiet observer wondered if she should inch her way back to her car and get her cell phone in case a call to the police department was necessary. She knew the park rangers had made this a frequent stop on their rounds during the week, so she began to pray for one of them to make an appearance.

As Joshua turned around, Maggie could tell he, too, felt the uneasiness that came with the latest visitor to the park.

The huge specimen of a man stood looking at the sculpture.

Maggie found herself hoping that he wasn't going to do something destructive to the art she had watched in progress for the past five days. More than that, she hoped he wouldn't mug Joshua. She decided to watch his actions briefly before making any sudden moves since, tucked away in a corner of the tent, she had gone unnoticed thus far.

After a couple of minutes of staring at the form in the sand, the man walked over to Joshua, wrapped both arms around the artist, and lifted him straight into the air as if he were a tree trunk that the lumberjack was pulling out of the ground.

Maggie feared what was about to happen. She threw the blanket to the ground and stood up to go after the phone. But the sound of the stocky man's voice stopped her dead in her tracks.

She turned quietly around and looked at him, holding Joshua so that they were eye-to-eye, as he said in a husky, slurred, but still understandable voice, "Jesus loves me, too."

Huge tears that were proportionate to his stature reflected in his eyes and on his grimy face from the headlights still shining on the two men.

Joshua didn't make a sound, but nodded at the man.

Maggie wondered if this giant-of-a-person was in any condition to drive as he put the artist back on the ground, unharmed, only a little shaken. *But he was certainly alert enough to know that Jesus loves him, so surely he'll be okay.*

He got back in the truck, shifted it into reverse and backed up, then drove away, the motor rumbling loudly in the night air.

She watched motionlessly as Joshua looked down at the sculpture, lightly ran his fingers across the legs of the figure, and sat down, his face in his hands.

Chapter 26
Pre-dawn, Holy Saturday

She awoke in the morning darkness with words from the CD gently filtering through her head. Maggie slowly hummed along with the melody to "Alas and did my Savior bleed and did my Sovereign die?" The keeper of the vigil noticed that Joshua had gone home to get some rest so that he could be alert and cordial for all of Saturday's expected guests. No one, save the man who had come to sit with her, was at the park.

Wanting to have the sculpture all to herself in the pre-dawn moments, she quietly moved up to the green plastic fence, wondering how Mary Magdalene must have felt as she carried the pottery jars of anointing spices to the tomb, only to find it empty. And to be approached by an angel, and then to recognize the gardener as the Risen Lord.

As she looked down upon the sand, Maggie saw what appeared to be blood on the side of Jesus' ribcage, at the spot where the spear had been forced into his side, and on his forehead where the crown of thorns had been shoved into his forehead, and his hands where the nails had been driven.

The sight, which had become all too familiar to Maggie, caused her heart to bleed. Words from the hymns and scripture she had been reading, and the songs she had been listening to on the CDs, all ran together, creating visual and auditory images in her mind of both the past - from Jesus' time in history - and the present.

And the future, she thought, again silently reciting Luke 11:9 that had become her motto since opening her Bible to that passage when she got it to the park and began to read. *"And I say unto you, Ask, and it shall be given you; seek, and ye shall find; knock, and it shall be opened unto you."*

She had heard the words over and over again in the past three days. Her grandmother's influence told her there was a reason that those particular words were sticking with her. Yet Maggie had no clue as to what it was. All she knew was to recite them when they came to her, hoping their significance would make itself known at the appropriate time.

Maggie stood there in shock. She wanted to tell someone, but who would believe her? She wanted to know how this strange thing had happened, but whom could she ask? She wanted to reach out and touch the Savior, but she knew she was unworthy. She wanted to make the hurt and pain of Christ go away, but she knew she was incapable. She wanted to . . .

Suddenly, Maggie realized that all the feelings and emotions that must have been running rampant through Mary Magdalene's mind and body on that Easter morning, in the pre-dawn hours as she approached the tomb, were now running through her, causing the exact same reactions.

There was no doubt in her mind that she had truly been transformed during this week. And it was a transformation that had begun with the day of her baptism. *No,* Maggie told herself. *It began with the day I was named. The day that I was named after my grandmother. I was doomed,* no, chosen! *to follow in her footsteps. Footsteps that had been ordained long before even my grandmother was born.*

The man behind her slowly began to wake, stretching his arms and legs in the chaise he had brought.

"Would you care for some coffee?" he asked. "I'll run down the street to the convenience store and get some for us." He paused. "Or better yet, I'll call my wife and have her bring us some."

"No, thanks. Not just yet." She stood beside the fence, no longer able to keep away from the sand. Maggie ventured to step inside the green plastic and inch her way up until she stood beside the image of Christ on the cross. Every bone inside her body was screaming for her to reach down and touch the bloodied brow and side. But she remembered Joshua's words to the blind man about how it could cause the shape to disintegrate.

She moved to the sculpture of the empty tomb with the Christ figure outside it, kneeling in prayer. *If only I could touch the hem of his garment,* she thought, so loudly that she was afraid the man from the Civitans might have heard her. Maggie not only envisioned that act, but also felt the same as the countless persons who had encountered Jesus in the Bible, all wanting to experience his healing and forgiving powers.

And she knew why as words came to her. "All we like sheep have gone astray."

That time, the words actually formed on her lips, for the man asked, "Did you say something?"

"Oh, I was merely mumbling," she answered, walking back to her post inside the tent.

Her thoughts were captivated by the scriptural passage she had read during her evening's watch. Maggie reached into her tote bag beside the beach chair, pulled out her new Bible and hurriedly leafed through the pages, searching Isaiah to find the exact words. *Ah, verse 6*, she sighed, recognizing the words from Chapter 53. "All we like sheep have gone astray; we have turned every one to his own way; and the Lord hath laid on him the iniquity of us all."

We have all *turned to our own way.*

Maggie no longer felt imprisoned by Northern Exposure. She no longer felt like she was the lone unworthy person who had come to this park during the course of the week.

The Lord has laid on him the iniquity of us all.

Maggie sensed that every person who had visited the park during the week had a claim in that iniquity. *The iniquity that placed those thorns on his brow. The iniquity that caused his pain and suffering. The iniquity for which he gave his life.*

No longer did she feel the need to touch the hem of his garment, for she was free – free from Northern Exposure, free from the fear of being recognized, free from the guilt of disappointing her parents and grandparents - *free. Free!*

Maggie placed the Bible back in the tote bag and turned to the man who had been her company. "I think I'm ready for something to drink now, but could you make mine a hot chocolate?"

"You betcha," he answered, glad to be of service. "I'll zip down the block to the convenience store. That'll be quicker."

By the time Maggie had packed her belongings and placed them in the back of the Honda, the man had returned with the coffee and hot chocolate.

"Would you look at that?" he asked, glancing over at the sculpture. "He did it again."

"Who did what?"

"Joshua. He always slips back to the park during the Friday night of the sculpture and adds the red color to the sand to make it look like blood."

Maggie wondered how the artist had managed to come

without awakening either her or this gentleman, but she was not going to ask questions now. *Perhaps I can get a moment with Joshua when he's alone to ask him about it.*

"If I didn't know better, I'd think it was something like the Tooth Fairy who slips in and magically leaves that mark behind."

Tooth Fairy, huh? How about the Holy Spirit?

The bed at Rose Gate Cottage was calling her name, even if only for a couple of hours. Maggie thanked the man for the hot chocolate and bid him good-bye before making the drive to her warm gas logs and comfy covers.

She was already counting sheep by the time she got there.

Chapter 27
 Early morning, Holy Saturday

Maggie, although enraptured by the emotions and discoveries from the evening before and the early morning hours, felt wiped out and in terrible need of her Victorian bed. But knowing she was to leave later in the day for her return to Ann Arbor, something would not let her rest until she got her things together so that when she did awake, she could have an uninterrupted day at the park before her departure.

She thought about all she had planned to do this week and how long she had saved for this private present to herself. Funny, but she had saved a lot of time and money, in gas expense and driving alone, even with staying at the lovely bed-and-breakfast inn, by settling in Findlay for the week. *And I know just where that money will go*, she sighed, recalling her idea of what to take back to each of the girls. It will be much better spent than it would have had I made it to Florida.

As Maggie rearranged the garments in her suitcase, basically a matter of tidying up things since she had used so little, she dreaded the thought of leaving this little town even more than she had imagined she would the sunny coast of Florida.

Throwing in the last of the items, her hand brushed against a piece of paper in the bottom of the suitcase. It was barely sticking out from under the flap where the wheels were, having apparently gotten shoved away and hidden some time ago. She stretched her fingers to try to feel what it was. Buried under all the clothes was a small box that she could also feel. Maggie pulled the paper and box out to examine them.

The box was wrapped and the bow had gotten smashed under the weight of the objects in the suitcase. As she pulled off the bow, she slowly remembered her mother giving her this box a couple of years before. It had been something that her grandmother had left for her. Given Maggie's career at the time, she felt ashamed and unworthy to accept anything from her grandmother, "the missionary."

Maggie tore off the paper, still unsure of whether she felt comfortable with the contents. Yet, for the first time in years, she felt a strange connection with her grandmother. As the wrapping paper fell to the floor, a folded note came off the bottom of the box into her hand.

She unfolded the piece of lined tablet paper and began to read.

To dear Maggie, my namesake,

I want to leave this small token for you. It was the first thing my father, who was also a missionary, ever gave me. He bought it while on furlough once from the mission field. It has held a special place in my heart from the day he first gave it to me. Please understand that it is handmade in a unique hammered-metal style called damastine which is found in Toledo, Spain. I hope it will mean as much to you as it has to me all these years, and that it may remain in our family as a treasured heirloom.

From the day you were born, and named after me, I knew this would one day belong to you. I have prayed every day for you to grow up to be a fine, distinguished young lady who would also walk in the path of righteousness paved for you and shared by your ancestors.

Do you realize that I was given my name by my father, who had a great respect for its significance? Some people would see it as a curse, or blasphemous, but my father knew better. He looked deeper than the judgmental norm. I have carried the name with great pride and hope that someday, when you are old enough and mature enough to understand the responsibility that goes along with it, you will also proudly bear it and use it as your signature also.

And now about the keepsake in the box. I hope it is something you will always treasure. I will no longer need it, for in a few days, I will be exchanging it for a crown. Please know always that I loved you deeply even though I did not have the opportunity to spend much time with you, especially in the last few years.

Maggie ran her fingers across the box. The note she had just read made this seem like something very sanctimonious, and she wanted to give it the unveiling it deserved. She didn't know what possessed her to do it, but she closed her eyes and felt her heart take on a conversation all its own. Prayer had not been an active part of her life in a long time, but she remembered what it felt like, especially given the attempts of the past few days.

Suddenly, a phrase she had heard as a child shamed her, for she remembered hearing her grandmother tell her once that God knew everything in your heart and in your thoughts without you having to speak them. So many years of sin weighed down upon Maggie's soul that she couldn't bear to open her eyes, realizing that God was not only looking at her, but staring straight into her inner being. She imagined how Eve must have felt in the Garden of Eden in her nakedness in front of her Maker.

Tempted to place the box back into the suitcase unopened, she heard a small voice urging her to open it. Was it the voice of her grandmother? If it was, Maggie couldn't let her down by not even seeing what was in the box. She slowly lifted the lid to see a shiny object sparkling in the overhead light that was hitting against it.

There in the box, carefully wrapped around to fit in the small space, lay a necklace of beautifully-carved round, black onyx beads. In the center was a black cross with a gold design carved into the dark background, making it a gorgeous work of art. Maggie picked it up, moving very slowly to drag out the ceremony as long as possible, while feeling the load of guilt that ruled her present feelings.

She placed the beads around her neck and fastened the clasp, smoothing out the cross over her collar. As the golden object touched her skin, Maggie felt a strange transformation, much like the one she had felt as the artist sculpted the sand, except more intense. She looked in the mirror at the priceless heirloom, noticing the glow on her face that matched that of the piece of jewelry.

Placing the top back on the box, Maggie noticed another piece of paper. Seeing that the letters matched the handwriting of the first note, she pulled it out of the box.

> *Remember one last thing. It is not this sym-*
> *bol that's important, but the fact that it stands as*
> *the centrality of our religion, no matter what de-*
> *nomination we are. In dying on this cross, Jesus*
> *suffered our pains and sorrows so that all our sins*
> *are forgiven. Let this cross be a constant reminder*
> *that you are made whole by the blood of Christ.*
> *With love,*
> *Mary Magdalena Matelli*

Maggie sat numbed on the side of the bed. She couldn't believe that all this time, she had carried this heirloom in her suitcase. But even more shocking was the fact that had she opened it earlier, it would have held little or no meaning, and chances were that it would have been lost in the shuffle somewhere along the way.

She reached for the pen and tiny pad beside the phone and began to scribble in simple, childlike words of her own.

> *Dear Grandmother,*
>
> *I don't know much about God, and I don't*
> *know anything about angels, but if there's any way*
> *they can get this message to you, I hope they will.*
> *It's funny, I feel like you can see me right now. I*
> *hope you can. I want to make you proud, Grand-*
> *mother. And most especially, I want you to know*
> *that your prayers were not in vain.*
> *I love you,*
> *Mary Magdalena Matelli*

P.S. I guess I do know one thing about angels, for it must have been an angel that made sure I got your gift at this time in my life.

Maggie took the Bible from the bedside table and opened it to John 3:16 and laid the note on top of the page. She left it open on the table beside the window, then turned out the light and went to bed for what little time was left before daylight.

Chapter 28
Late morning, Holy Saturday

Maggie zipped into the parking lot of the Maranatha Bookstore on her way to Riverside Park. Her new mission, now that she had found her perfect man, was to find something to take back to each of the girls who worked with her at Northern Exposure as a going away present, and she knew exactly what she wanted. She hoped to find the woman who had been so helpful earlier in the week. In addition to making her purchase, she also wanted a chance to say both "Thank you" and "Good-bye."

Her eyes quickly spied the woman, deep in conversation with a man, down one of the aisles. Not wishing to be a bother, Maggie busied herself looking for the gifts.

The clerk happened to look up and catch sight of Maggie. She smiled and looked back at the store's manager, with whom she was talking about a new order. "Do you remember that young woman I asked you about a couple of days ago, when I mentioned feeling the Holy Spirit's presence?"

"Yes, why?"

"That's her," she answered, her eyes shifting in Maggie's direction. "Get a good look at her. I want to show you something after she leaves."

"You got it," he replied, walking toward where the customer stood.

"Good morning," he smiled at Maggie. "Hope you're off to the start of a great day."

"Absolutely," the young woman said, her face beaming.

Not a hard face to remember, the manager thought. *God has definitely blessed her with eyes that reach out to people.* He was anxious to see what it was that was so special about this woman. *Oh well, I'm sure I'll find out once she leaves the store.*

"How are you? It's nice to see you again," spoke the sales-clerk as she walked up the aisle toward Maggie.

"I'm fine, and I love my Bible. You made a perfect suggestion."

"Oh, I'm sure I had a little assistance with the helpful hint," the clerk said, pointing her index finger toward the sky. "We get a lot of that in here when our customers are looking for something in particular and we're unsure what to suggest."

"Hmm," nodded Maggie. "That's interesting." Her subconscious focused her attention to why she had made this stop. "Anyway, I had to come in today and thank you again for your help and to say good-bye. I'm leaving this evening to go back home. Plus, I wanted to pick up a few gifts for some friends that I used to work with."

"Do you need some help?" offered the lady, hoping to be as useful as she had been earlier in the week.

"No, thank you," Maggie answered, pointing skyward. "I got a little assistance on this one myself," proud that she was worthy of also receiving that gift.

"So I take it the Bible's not only providing some good reading, but it's working."

"I'll say. You know when I mentioned the stories my grandmother used to tell me from the Bible?" She paused long enough to see if the woman remembered the conversation. Seeing an affirmative nod of her listener's head, Maggie continued. "The strangest thing happened last night . . . *or this morning,*" she chuckled lightly, "before I went to bed. As I was packing to go home, I found a gift that my grandmother had given me a couple of years ago before she died. She had sent it to my mom, who on a holiday visit, gave it to me. There's a story behind why I didn't open it immediately, but I'll save you those details."

She knew she was simply saving herself embarrassment by leaving out the details, but she had gotten through the entire week without sharing them and she saw no point in starting now. "About the present, it had gotten tucked away in my suitcase and fallen behind the piece that covers the wheels from the inside. There was a note attached to it that my grandmother wrote to me right before she died. It's so odd that I found it in the wee hours of this morning . . . out of the clear blue." Her voice trailed off as if she was speaking to someone far away. "Like there was a reason for me just now finding it."

Maggie went on to tell her new friend about the cross and the beads, again focusing on the story rather than being lost in thought.

The clerk listened and stared in amazement. *Does the Holy Spirit continually follow this woman around?* she wondered, remembering how she had felt after their first encounter. The spine-tingling sensation running through her now was even more penetrating than the one she had then.

"I'd better get my items and go. I want to spend my last day at the sand sculpture reading my Bible, and I don't want to miss a minute," she finished with an enthusiasm that had been absent on her first visit.

Maggie turned to walk away, waited for a second, and

then went on to say, "You know, this started out to be the most spectacular vacation I could have ever imagined. The way it has gone was nothing like I planned or expected, but it has far surpassed even my wildest dreams."

"That's usually the way it is," explained the clerk. She pointed skyward again. "It's called divine intervention."

Maggie gave a smile and a soft sigh. "Somehow I think I'm going to get a lot of that from now on."

"I have a funny feeling that you are, too," nodded the clerk, as she returned Maggie's smile.

"By the way, do you have gift wrapping available?" the customer asked.

"We sure do, and on top of that, it's free," came the answer, with an even bigger smile.

"You can't beat that. It seems I've spent this entire week finding out that the best things in life are free," Maggie reflected, as she headed toward another aisle. "I hope you'll check me out again."

"I'll be glad to. Just let me know when you're ready."

"This won't take long. I know exactly what I want."

"Good! I'll head on to the counter. I need to catch the manager for a minute, but I'll be up there when you finish shopping, and I'll take care of wrapping the gifts for you, as well."

The clerk went to the manager's office. "I need you to come watch the front. I'm going to wrap some gifts for our young woman, plus I want you to get a really good look at her." She turned to go to the counter. "And while you're up there, take a look at that painting hanging behind the register, the one of Jesus standing outside the empty tomb."

"Okay," he replied, thinking it a strange request, but knowing better than to ask questions, as he went to assist another customer.

Maggie handed the clerk her items for purchase. "I'd like

to pay for these with my debit card, please."

"Not a problem. Let me get to the back to wrap all of these, then I'll come and ring them up for you."

As Maggie stood waiting at the counter, she noticed a most intriguing painting hanging behind the counter. She stared at it, feeling it speaking to her and wondering what caused its strange attraction. There was something about the piece of art that would not let her leave the store without it.

"Is that painting for sale?" she asked the manager, who was finishing up with his customer.

"Yes, it is," he answered, remembering that he was supposed to have taken a look at it.

The manager turned to look at the painting, wondering what it was he was supposed to see. His eyes stared into the eyes of the woman in the painting, then back to the woman in front of him. He hoped his face did not show the shock that he felt running through his veins.

"How much is it?"

"It's rather expensive. The artist is from Italy and is making quite a name for himself lately through his portrayals of the life of Christ. This one is signed and numbered. We were quite fortunate to be able to get this one for the store." He looked at the price hanging from the lower right corner of the painting.

Maggie did not even flinch when he told her the cost. "That's nothing compared to the price that Christ paid for me. I *must* have that painting." She looked at it intently as the manager watched her face. "Is there any way you could get another one? I'd love to give a copy to my parents."

"I'm sure we can, although it may take some time. I'll take the order and give you a call when it comes in."

"Could you possibly send it to me? I live in Michigan." Her eyes were still glued to the painting.

"We can do that. We can even have it shipped to your

parents if that would be more convenient."

"No, thanks," Maggie said, shaking her head. "I'd like to hand deliver it to them. I think that would be more meaningful." She looked directly into the eyes of the manager, the mystical quality of her own eyes quite evident. "This gift has been several years coming."

"I understand," he nodded, wondering if the young woman facing him had any idea that she was the spitting image of the female in the painting.

The clerk walked out with two shopping bags of wrapped gifts and began to ring them up at the register.

"Add this painting to the purchase," the manager instructed.

The blank stare from his employee told him that she was as shocked as he was.

"And we're going to order another one and have it shipped to her when it comes in." He looked back to Maggie. "We'll try to have it shipped directly to you from Italy if you'll leave your address."

"Gladly," offered Maggie.

The salesclerk ran the charge card through the machine and handed Maggie the copy for her signature.

As she signed the bottom of the receipt, the young woman added, "I was named for my grandmother. All these years I've been called Maggie. But last night, after finding her cross and the beads, I decided that I'm going to use my full name from now on. I think this is an ideal time to get started," she said, jotting out the lengthy signature with great pride.

The manager and clerk smiled at each other, both obviously thinking that there really was something special about this woman *and* this moment.

Maggie handed the top copy of the receipt back to the lady who had become a memorable friend and thanked both the people in front of her. She made her way out the door with the shopping bags in one hand and the painting securely tucked under her other arm.

The salesclerk relayed the story of Maggie's grandmother and the gift to the manager.

"So what's this name that we are using beginning today?" the manager asked, taking the merchant's copy of the receipt from the clerk.

They turned to each other in disbelief, both with dazed eyes and gaping mouths, as they read the signature on the piece of paper.

Chapter 29
Early afternoon, Holy Saturday

By the time Maggie arrived at the park, excited about spending the day there but grieved that she would soon have to leave this paradise, cars were lining the street. Dozens of children were running in all directions through the sheltered area of the park near the sculpture. She watched as they bent down, knelt or stooped, around every object, shrub and tree, looking for brightly colored eggs filled with candies, coins or coupons from their favorite stores and restaurants.

There was a huge, costumed-white bunny with a big, floppy-pink bow dangling around its neck, the satin of the bow shining in the sun. The character was walking through the playground, shaking hands with all the youngsters and stopping to pose for pictures with members of his energetic audience.

What shocked Maggie about the scene was not the oversized rabbit, or the number of tots at play, but the number of children who ran past the festivities of the Easter Egg Hunt and came flying on foot to the sculpture.

One little girl ran away from her mother, shouting as she ran, "Mommy, Mommy, I want to see Jesus!"

The mother caught up with the little girl, grabbing her hand, and said, "We'll come and see Jesus later. Let's go see the Easter Bunny now," she coaxed, waving her camera in the air.

"No, Mommy. I want to see Jesus first." The little girl wiggled from side to side trying to pull loose from the mother's grip.

When the mother saw the eyes of all the people who had already gathered to see the sculpture, or were walking through the park, she began to realize not only the scene she and her daughter were creating, but also the impact of the little one's words. It became obvious that everyone within earshot was staring at her, watching to see what her reaction would be.

Not wanting to give in to a child, the disciplinarian side of her felt a strong urge to yank the child from the scene, take her home and get away from the burning eyes she felt. But the motherly side won out as she said, "You're right, we *should* go and see Jesus first."

They made their way over to the sculpture, where Joshua came over and shook hands with the little girl.

"Do you like Jesus?" he asked.

"Yes, I do," she said emphatically, her eyes twinkling so vividly that they could have easily rivaled the brightness of the eggs hidden throughout the park. "Did you make him?"

"I only made a picture of him in the sand," Joshua smiled, a twinkle in his own eye. "Would you like to go inside the fence and see him?" the sculptor asked as he reached down and scooped up the little girl in his arms.

He carried the young child into the fenced area filled with sand.

Everyone, who had minutes earlier been all eyes, was now all ears as they listened to the artist tell the little girl about Jesus, the Easter story, and about how he created the sand sculpture. They were extremely touched when he explained that God, the same Father who *really* made Jesus, and who had made the sand and her, gave him the ability to make the picture out of sand.

"Take my picture, Mommy," the little girl called, all smiles.

"What?" asked the mother, caught in the same heart-warming episode as the other spectators.

"Take my picture *now*, Mommy . . . with Jesus."

Flashes went off from every angle as everyone who had a camera snapped them, trying to capture on film the fascination of the young child with Jesus.

And the real *fascinating aspect here is that she is enamored by Jesus - "the real man" - not this artistic interpretation that the adults are caught up in*, Maggie thought, herself caught up in the mood of the moment. She, too, managed to catch a shot of the artist and child before Joshua carried the little girl back to her mother.

The child happily galloped off with her Easter basket, content that she had seen Jesus, and was now ready to go visit with the Easter Bunny and run and play with the other children.

As she took off through the freshly-mowed grass, that lay like lush green carpet under the child's feet, Maggie thought about the passage she had read the day before. It was relative to what she had observed with every child that had approached the giant portrayal of Christ.

"Let the little children come unto me," Maggie could hear the voice of Jesus say in her mind. How many times had she uttered those words during the course of the past week as she observed all the boys and girls who had given credence to that scripture?

A very important realization struck her as she thought about the little girl and the verse, and stood looking at the image in the sand. She thought of young children in the malls at Christmas who were terrified of Santa Claus. Several of the children had been scared of the Easter Bunny at the egg hunt. But not one child had been afraid of Jesus this week as they came with parents to see the picture of the man.

No, he isn't real. But as she imagined hearing his gentle voice calling to children in her mind, Jesus would not have been at all frightening, even to the youngest child. There was an endearing trait in his nature, his speech, his eyes, and his entire appearance that was evoked by his parables and teachings. A trait that drew young ones to him.

Ones young in age, and *young ones in the faith*, she reasoned, cognizant of the scribes and Pharisees who felt threatened by the man's presence. She recalled the stories she had read during the past few days of the ones who considered Jesus a friend.

While Maggie sat contemplating the centuries of children who had shown love for Christ, another child, this time a boy with curly red locks, came bounding from around the back corner of the sculpture. He had jerked loose from his mother's hold. While his father called for him to come back, making threats of what would happen if he didn't, the boy ran even harder.

"Another one on the loose," laughed a man who sat behind Maggie.

Other bystanders commented on the intrigue that the sculpture held for the children.

"Why shouldn't it?" asked a woman in the crowd. "Look at all of us who have congregated here to see Christ, like he were one of the wonders of the world."

"He *is* one of the wonders of the world," added another woman who stood nearby.

Maggie listened as small groups began to talk about the wonder of Christ, sharing stories of his miracles in their own lives, or the lives of their friends or family members.

As she listened to the various conversations and watched the families come and go, her eyes were drawn to an Oriental family with two beautiful girls who looked to be about one and three. They were extremely playful and interactive with each other and their parents. Maggie watched the parents as they talked to the girls and rolled the stroller towards the playground. *What a perfect family,* she thought as she noted the happy faces of the children and parents alike.

"Ask, seek, knock." There goes that verse again. God, what am *I supposed to see here? I'm looking. I'm* truly *looking, and all I see is a park, these beautiful Oriental children and seventy-five tons of sand. I'd be glad to ask . . . or seek . . . or knock . . . if only I had an idea for what.*

She was beginning to feel most frustrated at her loss for an explanation of the words. But then she heard the voice of her grandfather, whose words always sounded like a melody with their tone and rhythm. Maggie began to faintly remember once when she had heard him speak to her father. She couldn't re-member the subject of the conversation at all, and why these words came to her, she had no idea.

Wrong, Maggie! You know exactly why they came to you now.

"When God wants you to know, you'll know," she could hear in her grandfather's lyrical voice. "Think of him as the bridge-builder. He lays the planks out in front of you one at a time as you need to step forward. You can't go any faster than He wants you to go, and He will get you to your destination safely."

Okay, Maggie. Let's see if you've got this straight. You have no clue what you're going to do when you get back to Ann Arbor. You have no clue where you'll go from there. You don't have an inkling of where to begin looking for a job. But you're going to get in your silver Honda, drive off into the sunset and know that there will be a plank out there for each step you take.

Uh-huh! Now you've really *lost your mind.*

"I heard that," she heard Ebony say.

And there goes that sisterly conscience again.

Maggie couldn't resist chuckling as she looked again behind the Oriental family who had reached the swings.

Okay, God. And *Grandfather. I'll try to be patient and watch for the planks before I step.*

Listening again to the small groups around her, she laid her head back in the chair and closed her eyes, letting her ears soak in the stories like a sponge, allowing the words of the speakers to become a part of her being, her thinking.

It wasn't long before Maggie had fallen asleep, dreaming of Christ seated on the picnic table and sharing parables with the adults and stories with the children. Families were perched all around him on the ground, taking in every word.

She looked at his clothes. They were not the long robes that she had seen in the pictures from parochial school or church as a child. Rather, Jesus was dressed in worn jeans, an old shirt and Birkenstocks. The people around him were dressed in modern clothing.

And others were coming in from faraway lands to see and hear this man who had been prophesied in the Old Testament's scriptures.

Maggie's dream was interrupted when she heard a woman's voice querying persons within the crowd.

"Who is the man that made the sculpture?" she asked, her anxious voice totally awaking Maggie.

"He's the one under the tent with the crowd around him," a man pointed. "His name is . . ."

"I know," she interrupted. "I read all about him in the newspaper."

The woman took off toward the tent. "Joshua? Mr. Redford?" She didn't even give the artist time to reply. "I had to come and see you and see your work. Your story was in the newspaper in Fort Wayne this morning. I was so intrigued that I jumped in my car, coffee cup and newspaper in hand, and started driving. And here I am."

She stopped only long enough to catch a breath and keep going. "I had no idea where the park was, or how to get here." You could hear her tired voice running out of steam. "But I knew that once I got to Findlay, I could find you. This is the most exciting way of witnessing to others that I've ever seen."

The woman, who had made such a concentrated effort to meet Joshua, turned and walked toward the sculptural mural, the artist following on her heels. "And I knew that at seventy years old, I might never get the opportunity to see anything like this ever again in my lifetime."

She took a long sigh, caused from her shortness of breath, as she reached in her purse and pulled out a camera. "Do you mind if I take your picture with the sculpture to show all the girls back home?"

"No, not at all," Joshua replied, walking toward the sand.

The artist made small talk with the woman as Maggie watched the two of them.

Taking a picture to show the girls back home. Hmmm. The same thing I've been doing all week. She leaned her head back against the canvas chair. *I guess I'm not the only person in the world looking for the perfect man, am I?* Maggie muttered, her words directed toward the sky.

Chapter 30
Late afternoon, Holy Saturday

The afternoon faded into a perfectly breathtaking sunset. Pastel-colored clouds dotted the sky in so many odd shapes that it literally looked as if each of the children who had visited the park during the day had taken their crayons and smudged them across the sky, leaving traces of their artwork alongside that of the master in the park.

As Maggie sat enthralled by the picturesque scene that was sprawled above her, as well as the one lying at her feet, she thought about all the great masters who had lived before Joshua Redford. She wondered what the sky would look like if they could take their oils and pastels and leave their impressions in the sky like a giant scrim.

Perhaps that's why each day's sunset looks like a different work of art. Maggie smirked at her vision. *It certainly gives a whole new meaning to the Masters Tournament!*

Amateur and professional photographers alike had strategically lined up their cameras and equipment in an effort to capture the phenomenal emotion of the precise moment when the sun's last rays would fall over the thorn-crowned brow of the man in the sand. Some of them stooped, while a few were on their knees. One was even lying on the sand, carefully adjusting his lens' settings for an unparalleled shot.

Maggie felt like all that was missing was an announcer to call out, "And now, the moment you've all been waiting for . . ."

She watched as flashes began to go off, multiple auto-advances were reeling forward, and the photographers were moving their bodies quickly to catch every possible angle of the combination of God's and man's handiwork.

When the last glimmer of light dropped behind the horizon, the patient picture-takers packed up their belongings, some of them comparing notes, and left the mural to those spectators who wanted to remember the scene solely in their minds.

Chapter 31
Evening, Holy Saturday

Individuals were not the only ones who came in search of the overwhelming internal awe created by the sculpture. Carloads appeared, filled with families and friends, who had decided to make this a weekend outing. Some brought hot dogs and actually had a weiner roast, while others took out baskets of sandwiches. To Maggie, the scene was akin to the tailgate parties of the major sporting events at U-M. *Although this crowd is much less rowdy!* Buses from churches and vans from group homes also began to dot the parking lot.

It was obvious that the newspaper, radio and television interviews had captured the attention of the people of not only Findlay, but communities in Michigan and Indiana as well. Maggie could not believe the interest, shown by so many people, in a pile of sand.

Whoa, there, Maggie. It did keep you here all week didn't it? She suddenly realized the miraculous impact this work of art had on people. Hurting people. Healing people. Lonely people.

Happy people. Believers. Non-believers. *All* people.

While she contemplated on the people - all sinners - who had made their way to the park during the week, a man took his guitar from its case and began to strum folksy-sounding music. The people around him began to sing songs Maggie had only heard on "archaic" record albums from her parents' adolescent years. She recognized *Michael, Row the Boat Ashore* and *If I Had a Hammer*. It seemed strange to hear those old folk songs.

Songs that have been around longer than I've been alive, she mused, taking in every word of the lyrics.

Maggie took a scrutinizing look at the small group of singers. Had she not known better, she would have thought she had slipped through a time warp and was somewhere out in California at a Peter, Paul and Mary concert.

She smiled. *At least if that were the case, chances would be great that I'd be near a sunny coast!*

Her glances turned back to the small group of singers instead of the daydream in her mind. They were approximately the same age as her parents. She could easily imagine them in bell-bottomed jeans, angel-sleeved blouses and shirts that laced up the front, with flowers in their hair, either in a round headband with streamers of thin ribbon hanging down the back, or simply loose flowers stuck behind their ears. *All they need is a green tambourine!*

These were the flower children that had never grown up. She looked at them and listened intently to the words of their songs. When they began *The House of the Rising Sun*, she sang along with them. Then as the guitarist repeated the chord progressions, the small group began to sing the words of *Amazing Grace* to the same tune.

Maggie mouthed the words she remembered from her grandmother's visits, and sat spellbound while she both listened and watched as people throughout the park began to join in the singing of the hymn. How odd it seemed that everyone there knew those words, *no matter how young or old they are*, and that everyone recognized that tune, *no matter how young or old they are*.

What was it about that melody that made it so acceptable? And what was it about those words that made them so loved? She decided that the minute she got back to Rose Gate Cottage, she was going to make that quandary her evening's project.

The visitor imagined the university students who had gone on their mission trip. She wondered whether they had taken guitars and sung the inspirational choruses that sounded like modern-day folk songs. *Only now they're called contemporary praise and worship songs of the twenty-first century.*

Even though she was in a completely opposite area of work, she was housed in the same class building as all the other graduate students at U-M. She had heard the debates between the worshippers with die-hard, high-church backgrounds, and the contemporaries who attended the casual, laid-back services, about what they called the "7-11 hymns."

"Seven hymns at each service with eleven stanzas of the same chorus over and over," she had overheard as one student expressed his opinion.

As she studied the small group a little longer, she realized that she had been wrong in her assessment that they were flower children that had never grown up. Yes, they could very easily pass for flower children, but they had definitely grown up. And even though they had grown up, they had carried their faith with them from their youthful days into their middle age.

All around them sat people who had entered the golden age, people who were the Generation X'ers, and young children. And they were all involved in the music and the spirit it evoked, either from the words, or the melody, or both.

Maggie observed that no one was getting up and leaving because they didn't like the old hymns or the contemporary praise songs. They had come together in a common bond and they were worshipping. Everyone had either joined in, or allowed their own thoughts to form and be, surrounded by the backdrop of soft melodic music.

The sculptor continued to work on the figure of Christ praying beside the empty tomb, completely undaunted by all the commotion around him. It appeared he was in his own world, driven by a force inside him that would not let him rest until this work was finished.

People sensed the depth of his emotion through the work of art as it neared completion. They began to hush their singing and talking, one group at a time, to watch Joshua's final strokes take shape. No one spoke a word or dared to move, anticipating the honor of witnessing the grand finale of such a blessed and sacred event.

Their time of singing, praying and sharing had been a form of worship, for they had "gathered together" to know this Christ through the artistic hands of one mere human being.

∞

As evening fell, so did an eerie, sullen mood that surrounded the park. The moon had begun its descent from its full shape, and one lone, bright star lit the sky.

The same bright star that brought those Wise Men to Jesus all those centuries ago is the same one that is pointing the way to him now.

Maggie watched quietly as one by one, more stars appeared in the sky. It seemed that they were tiny bulbs, automatically set so that one popped on every couple of minutes.

The spectators no longer sang, but came in quietness. They all knew the outcome of the story: that come the morrow, there would be a risen Christ. But the image in front of their eyes for the present held them to the gloom of the crucifixion as it gave them an opportunity to feel a small part of what those disciples and first followers of Jesus had felt.

The woman who was to serve as the greeter for the evening arrived carrying a basket that she placed on the picnic table underneath the large tent - the place that had become the headquarters for this event. Several minutes later, she was joined by Yogi, who came to check in and see how things were going, and make sure their city's source of pride was holding up to the crowds and the weather.

Maggie noticed that although more people arrived, they made nothing more than small talk, sensing the ambience that had enveloped this area of the park. It was clear to tell that they all felt the same mystical presence as she did.

Even though she had lost touch with her spiritual side over the past few years, there was no doubt in her mind what brought this feeling. It was anticipation. The anticipation that when the sun – that giant orb that had earlier brought hordes of photographic sharpshooters on the scene - had made its way around the earth and reappeared the next morning, they would all be rejoicing Christ's victory over his death on that cross.

Churches would be filled with singers, trumpeters, and organs blaring out notes of *Christ the Lord is Risen Today*, and every pew would be filled with individuals who only darkened the sanctuary doors this one Sunday of the year. *Or maybe two, if they get up on Christmas Sunday.* Flowers would line the sidewalks, Easter lilies would be placed throughout the sanctuaries, and crosses would have their purple and black drapes exchanged for white cloths.

How strange it was that this pile of dirt could stir so much in the lives of this town, and could touch hearts around the world by the front pages of the newspapers, and through the airwaves of the radio stations, and via on-the-scene television interviews.

The greeter picked up her basket and began to walk through the few people who were still congregated in the park. She took out a plastic sandwich bag, from which Maggie could see her handing some small object to each person.

When she came to Maggie, the Findlay guest saw that the greeter was giving out tiny glow-in-the-dark angels. People nodded or quietly voiced a "thank you" as she passed. They began to take out their flashlights and illuminate the angels so that they would then shine in the dark. It was amazing that, although so tiny, they gave off such an incredible amount of light when the spectators raised them up in the air at the same time.

"The Light of the world," someone said in the darkness as the tiny angels began to lose their illumination.

"Can you believe that one man made such an impression on the whole world?" another asked.

"It wasn't simply one man. It was the Father, Son and Holy Spirit – three in One," offered a teenager.

"Yeah, and all things are possible through the Father. Isn't that the Ohio motto, Daddy?" asked a younger child.

೨ಞ

Joshua stood back to look at his work. Still there was not a sound as people watched for his reaction. He stepped forward, made a slight adjustment in the details of the hands and feet, brushed across the ribs, and then stepped back once again to observe his finished product.

As he fell to his knees in a prayerful pose, the same pose as the image of Christ that he had sculpted outside the empty tomb, you could hear his non-verbal expression yelling to the heavens, "It is finished." The master dropped his head and began to silently pray.

Quiet gasps were heard from various sections of the crowd.

Maggie herself stayed seated, too stunned to move or make a sound. The week of vacation that had been intended solely for the purpose of spending her time in the sun and sand and finding a man had accomplished exactly that.

She finally knelt and began to pray, something she had not done regularly, since she was a little girl. Maggie had no idea where to start, but she did know that God was listening to her. All her years as the daughter of a devout Catholic father had taught her that much.

Throughout the crowd, people began to follow the lead of the artist as they prayed, some falling to their knees where they stood or sat, others moving forward as if the sculpture was a shrine to the majesty and power of the Lord.

Maggie noticed Lynn Redford as she made her way through the throng of people and knelt beside her husband, placing her arm around his shoulder. The two of them prayed together for a couple of minutes, then they stood and walked very quietly to the landscaping truck.

His face held no expression except for one of total awe, as if he had seen the face of God in his work. It was clear that he was just as mesmerized by this sculpture as those around him.

They drove away slowly, turning away from town and leaving the crowd to be inspired, each in their individually private way, by the cross of Christ.

After their taillights were out of view, and a few spectators dispersed to their own homes, Maggie stepped forward to get a closer glimpse of the sculpture. It was most striking, for the moon and stars had come out and were so vibrant that the work of art was clearly visible in the light of nature. Sure that God was shining that light down on His Son, she was moved beyond measure.

Maggie fell to her hands and knees, this time at Jesus' feet. She felt tears from the inside rushing to get on the outside. Her prayer began with the words that she had been listening to for the past three days on her personal CD player while she had read her Bible and watched the sculptor at work.

Kneel at the cross, Christ will meet you there. Come while he waits for you . . .

The prayer stopped. Maggie looked up at the lone bright star and proclaimed, "And Jesus loves me, too!" recalling the giant-of-a-man who had taught *her* a lesson. Suddenly, that man became as a disciple to her – Peter, *the rock*, she had read this week.

That man, he really was *my disciple.* Maggie clasped her hands together. *Dear God, You sent him to me. When I was here all alone, when I had nowhere else for my thoughts to be, when there were no distractions, you sent that man to show me that Jesus can love me again, too.*

જી⁊૦

People began to light the angels again, watching them brighten the way to the parking lot as they walked.

Maggie held up her tiny plastic angel. A man in the distance saw her and came with his flashlight to ignite the glowing power of the object. The humility that came over her was nearly unbearable. She felt the urge to cover her head, drop to her knees and hide from her Father's presence.

But she knew none of that would have mattered. Even though she had strayed horribly from the path that her grandmother had illuminated for her, she had now been given an opportunity to light the way for others. And although the amount of her light was small in comparison, even to the dim lights of the Northern Exposure, its brightness was incomparable by the glow it sent out into the world.

A song she had learned as a child went through her mind as she looked at her own angel shining forth. *"Brighten the corner where you are,"* she heard in her head. She suppressed the urge to sing the words aloud, deciding that they were meant only for her at this point. There would come a chance to share them with others at another time, she felt sure.

Maggie loved the fact that the spectators had verbalized questions created by the mystique of the surroundings – questions about Christ, questions about God, questions about the cross, questions about the tomb, questions about the resurrection, questions about how one human could make such a powerful sculpture - all kinds of questions . . . *and no one is answering them.* It was as if the query was for all, and all were left to contemplate on the answers.

Seeing the crowd begin to scatter and head for their cars, she, too, began to pack up her belongings. The hour had come that she'd planned to head back to Ann Arbor, but after experiencing the overbearing sense of anticipation along with all the other onlookers during the day and evening, Maggie decided there was no way she could head back before rushing here in the morning to see the empty tomb.

She had no clue as to what would be different about it, but she knew, given all the events of the week at the park, that there would be something special here on Easter Sunday morning at daybreak.

Maggie had heard one photographer mention a sunrise service to be held at his Lutheran church on the next morning. He was the man who had been so dedicated to his art and his Master that he slithered on the ground to capture the perfect image of Christ. *Anyone who is that intense has to be at a "what's happenin'" kind of place.*

The thought of sunrise prompted her that she needed some sleep in order to be up in time to visit the park before the service. Then she planned to eat at the community Easter breakfast she had seen advertised at the downtown Methodist church. That would give her enough time to go back to the Rose Gate Cottage, change clothes, and get to the musical presentation at Beth's church. *Then in honor of my father and grandparents, I'll go back to Saint Michael's.*

She laughed that she would then have to go back to her room and take a nap. *Oh well, maybe I can at least make up for some of the lost time when I've neglected to walk with Christ.*

As she put the beach chair and blanket in her Honda, Maggie knew there was no way she would spend the next afternoon napping. She knew exactly where she would be.

Right beside my "perfect man." I expect I'll have to share him with lots of sinners tomorrow.

Sinners! That's what I missed this morning when I was thinking about all the park's visitors. Young, old, rich, poor, married, single – they are all sinners. She looked up at the sky with its stars shining amidst puffs of clouds. *No! We are all sinners.*

Maggie walked back and hugged the woman who had given her the angel. Now, like the stairs of the Rose Gate Cottage, she could have her very own "guardian angel."

Yogi came back to check on the evening's greeter. "Are you sure you'll be alright out here by yourself?" he asked, full of genuine concern, sounding like the man who, the night before, had asked Maggie the same question.

"Are you kidding?" she laughed. "Look who I'm out here with." And with that explanation she pointed to the sculpture.

You had to admire the woman for she had a valid point. But at the same time, Maggie thought of the two men who had stood guard on the Saturday night before Easter morning. They certainly weren't expecting to awake to an empty tomb.

At least she's prepared for the outcome, Maggie reasoned, walking back to her car. She left the centurion, as Yogi appeared to her, and the woman, who had become Jesus' mother in her mind, to keep watch.

CR80

"June?" Maggie asked when she heard the familiar voice pick up the phone.

"Yes." The hostess of Rose Gate Cottage winked and nodded at her husband, letting him know that they were right about who the caller might be.

"This is Maggie . . . correction, Mary Magdalena," she proudly exclaimed, remembering she had shared the story of her grandmother's note and gift with her "adopted" parents. "Is my room still vacant?"

"As a matter of fact, it is. We saved it for you, thinking you might feel the urge to stay through tomorrow."

"Oh, you two are jewels," she blurted, thinking of the word she had used for Ebony. "I'll be right there." The realization hit her that she *had* met a King, and that she was returning to Northern Exposure . . . *Wrong! Ann Arbor* . . . with a crown of her own.

As Maggie drove the few blocks to the bed-and-breakfast cottage, she speculated about how many players God had actually put in place for this week, all for one person . . . *me*.

It crossed her mind that if this many people had been a part of the plan to get God in touch with her, she had to be worthy. She had to have a gift also. A gift to share. The traveler began to wonder what that gift would be, but she was sure, after all the other events of the week, that she would know the answer in time.

In God's time, she smiled.

⚬⚭⚬

Maggie felt the cleansing water warm her skin and leave her refreshed. She looked around the room at the mirrors. This room was the paradigm model for a romantic getaway. She imagined how exhilarating it would have felt to spend her time away this week in the arms of a man, someone who knew her, who knew *all* about her and cared for her anyway. Who cared solely and completely about her.

She got out of the tub and wrapped up in the thick robe, feeling like a new person. Maggie had never spent a relaxing evening like tonight, where she was able to lay back in a huge tub, sip on hot tea, and think of pleasurable memories of her past, *long past*, and hopeful dreams of the times to come.

Watching television was *not* how she wanted to spend the rest of the evening. She reached on the nightstand and picked up the Bible she had bought earlier in the week, the one like she had bought for her friends.

Maggie turned the pages, not sure what she wanted to read, but knowing she longed to read more about the man she had come to know more intimately this week. For whatever reason, her eyes stopped on one of the pages as words jumped up at her.

She looked at the verse. *II Corinthians 5:17*, Maggie said aloud. "Therefore, if any man be in Christ, he is a new creature: old things are passed away; behold, all things are become anew."

Her lips mouthed the words a second time, and then a third. Maggie had felt a change in herself during the week. She definitely did not feel like the person who drove off exit 159 six days ago.

Six days. The world was created in six days. And on the seventh day, God rested.

Maggie read the verse again. "Old things are passed away; all things are become anew." *And on the seventh day, God rested.*

She sat there, in a plush, spotless, white robe, bathed, cleansed . . . *a new person.* Maggie began to see the full impact of the past week.

Before her trip, she had secretly longed to leave her job, find her man, settle down, have kids, and do something of value for others so that she could leave a legacy behind like her grandmother.

Had those longings been interpreted as prayers by God? Had He recreated her in the past six days, and tomorrow, on Easter Sunday, He was going to rest while the rest of the world celebrated Christ's victory over death?

Dear God. Maggie paused. She felt at a loss, not knowing where to begin.

"Just let the words go, Maggie. He'll know what you mean." The words she heard inside were not of her voice, but of her grandmother's.

She knelt down beside the lavish tapestry covers of the Victorian bed, her clasped hands resting against the edge of the mattress with her head bowed on them, and began to speak . . slowly . . . very slowly . . . .

Dear God, I left last Sunday on a mission – a mission of spending the week in sun and sand, and finding myself a man – a perfect man. During these past six days, it seems I have been on a mission, not mine, but Yours. My mission, or rather, Your mission has been accomplished. I've spent the week in the sun and the sand, (along with a little rain and cold!) and now I realize that I have indeed found "the perfect man."

My wrong turn really did turn out to be a right turn. I know, God, that you, or you and Grandmother together, put me here. I know why you put me here. And now here I am, bowed down before You, in a robe of white, Your child.

Tomorrow, I will celebrate the day of resurrection with other believers from around the world. And you won't care whether I've been absent from my faith and church in the past several years, or what my thoughts and actions have been. You will smile and rejoice at seeing me "anew."

Oh God, I hope my grandmother can see me. I want her to be proud of me. If it is possible, please let her see this change in me.

The words stopped. *"There now, my child, that wasn't so bad."* Once again, the words were of her grandmother's voice.

Maggie smiled. *Amen.*

ଓଞ୍ଚ

As Maggie lay down, she made an executive decision. *Just like all the other ones this week!* she chuckled. Her original intention, *wrong — second intention, the one after you realized you weren't going to make it to the sunny coast of Florida*, had been to leave this morning to go back to Ann Arbor.

Then she had felt the urge to stay for church in Findlay. Somehow she sensed that it would be all wrong to leave without paying her respect to the Father, the Son, and the Holy Spirit since they had all been working so hard in her life during the past week.

Now she had decided, in the aftermath of the events of today and this evening, that she wanted to stay until Monday to say good-bye to Joni, to Charlie and June, to Chic, and to Joshua and Lynn. They had been more than passing acquaintances in her life, and she now knew for certain that when she pulled out of Findlay on Monday morning, it would definitely *not* be the last time that she would see them.

She also had an idea that she would see the angel, the centurion, and the man with the piercings again at some point in her life.

Maggie closed her eyes, like a child going to bed on Christmas Eve, trying hard to go to sleep in anticipation of what awaited her on the coming morning.

Kneel at the cross, Christ will meet you there . . . she hummed.

The visitor sat straight up in bed. She knew she had just been told where she would go after she took the girls' presents to Northern Exposure.

Thank you, Grandmother. Thank you, Grandfather. She fell back on the pillow. *And thank you, Jesus.*

She closed her eyes again, turned on her side and whispered, *Come while he waits for you . . . yes, there's room at the cross for you.*

Chapter 32
Dawn, Easter Sunday

Maggie rushed out the door, not waiting for break-fast. She had informed Charlie and June of her plans to eat after the sunrise service, so she hurriedly drove to the park to see the sculpture before her morning of services and meals.

"Good morning," she called to Yogi as she scurried across the grass to the sandy area.

"Happy Easter," he greeted her.

She hugged him, feeling a sense of love for her new brother. "How was last night's vigil?"

"More active than one would have suspected, I'm afraid. There was some woman running around over there," he offered, pointing to the section of Riverside Park on the opposite side of the street, "through the trees. I went over to see what was going on, only to find out that she was running around looking for her-self."

Funny, Maggie inwardly smiled, *I don't remember be-ing here last night*. She thought of all the ways people actually did go in search of themselves. Suddenly, she felt sorry for the woman who had obviously not had the same wonderful experience that she had over the past seven days.

The impact of Yogi's statement combined with her own realization left her feeling a sorrow. Christ's love was out there for everyone, but everyone did not recognize or accept it.

Sadness must have been written on her face for Yogi apologized, "I hope I didn't say anything to upset you."

"Oh, no. Nothing like that. I just felt sorry for all the people of the world who couldn't experience the gift of love that was so prevalent this week here at the park. Like the woman from last night."

"Yeah, I felt that way, too, after I had to pull over a carload of young guys who went speeding up and down the street, spinning tires and raising a ruckus in the neighborhood. It's hard to understand how people aren't moved by this sculpture or the event that took place that inspired Joshua to do it."

The two of them stood quietly looking at the mural of pictures in the sand. People, who wished to pay their respects before going to worship the victory of the Risen Lord, slowly entered the park. Some placed Easter lilies at the foot of the sandy tomb. Others left branches of flowers that had just blossomed that morning - like on divine call from the Almighty - at the base of the green, plastic fence that surrounded the sculpture.

"I guess I'd better go take a look around the rest of the park before I'm off duty," Yogi stated. "My wife is waiting for me to come home so we can go to church together this morning."

"Aren't you tired?" Maggie asked, knowing he'd been awake all night.

"Not too tired to go to church. There's no way I would miss today after watching this take place all week," he replied, pointing to the sculpture.

"I heard that," Maggie agreed, unable to stop the words

236

of her "sister-conscience" before they escaped her lips.

"Hope we see you next year," he invited, shaking her hand. Yogi took something from his pocket and gave it to the guest. "Here, why don't you take this small token of Hancock County and Riverside Park home with you to remind you to come back again? Joshua will be here again next year at Holy Week. It's becoming more than a tradition, you know."

She looked down at the shiny object the ranger had placed in her hand. It was a pin with a raccoon on it that held a sign with the park's logo and proudly bore the words, "Hancock Park District."

"Thank you." Maggie looked down at it, glistening in the early morning's sunlight, as she put it on her collar. "Thank you very much."

"You're very welcome. Just be sure to tell everyone you see what a wonderful place this is to visit."

"You can bet on that," she replied, fully aware that she had every intention of doing that just as soon as she returned to Ann Arbor.

Yogi laughed. "It's not such a bad place to live, either," he added, walking toward his patrol car.

"So I've heard," her voice trailed behind him, as she waved good-bye.

Chapter 33
Afternoon, Easter Sunday

After the three services and two meals, Maggie returned to Riverside Park to spend the afternoon. She had not shared the story of the beads and the cross with Joshua or anyone else at the park. A part of her wanted to stand atop the green stand where people had left food and drinks for the sculptor and shout it to the masses. Yet, another part felt like that was her secret, her prize to be enjoyed fully before sharing it with the rest of the world.

She finally decided to wait until she had at least told her parents about the discovery and her desire to be called by her full name before she divulged the decision to the rest of the world. There would be time for that later, and somewhere, deep inside, Maggie sensed that she would meet all of the park's regulars again sometime down the road.

Just as she reached the edge of the grassy path leading to the sculpture, she heard Jewel announce that over a thousand people had signed the guest book for the day. The crowd had been a steady flow the entire day, with people passing through rather than staying for any length of time. Maggie was no different, for this was the first time since Monday morning that she had approached the site without her beach chair. *Or park chair, I should say!*

She recognized several people who had come through earlier in the week, but wanted to get another look at the completed mural of sand. And others came back simply because they felt this was such a significant part of Easter that they wanted to make it a part of their Holiest of Days.

The mood, that had been evident in the visitors since Thursday, changed drastically with the day's onlookers. The somber quiet had, for the most part, grown to a festive vibrancy of chatter and laughter that echoed throughout the crowd.

Joshua greeted every single person who came to the park. He showed no sign of weariness as he handed each guest a photo of the image of Christ and a small plastic bag of sand to remember the event.

Maggie found it interesting that several of the guests were high school classmates of Joshua's who had come back to Findlay to visit family for the holiday and heard about his sculpture.

"I had no idea you had this sort of talent," she overheard one man saying to the artist. "When did you take it up?"

"I've always had a love for art," Joshua answered. "But I was never encouraged to pursue it when I was growing up. You know how some of the older generation of Midwest farmers were. They didn't see art as a *real* job."

"Yeah, I guess I get your drift. My father would have been the same way had I wanted to do something other than drive a tractor. That's why I moved away."

"Don't think I don't still drive a tractor, too," added Joshua. "That's probably the reason I took up landscaping. I can design and draw and be as creative as the customer allows, and still use the tractor and front-end loader to help with my projects."

"Ah, the best of both worlds."

"You could say that."

"If I could have come up with a way to do my job *and* play around on the farm, I'd still be here, too," the classmate admitted. "I'm firmly convinced that there's no place on earth like Findlay to live and raise a family."

"I agree," nodded Joshua, reflectively.

A young woman tugged on the arm of the man who was speaking to the sculptor.

"I guess it's time to go. It was a pleasure seeing you, Joshua, and an even greater pleasure seeing your work. I hope you'll do it again next year."

"Oh, I plan to," the artist assured as he waved to his friend. "Thank you for stopping by."

The afternoon was filled with people who recognized friends from various settings. Many of them were old acquaintances that had not seen each other in years.

Maggie loved the sense of unity she felt simply by being among the crowd. It made it extremely difficult for her to pull herself away from the sculpture. However, she was determined to have an opportunity to relax in one of the rockers on the screened porch of the Rose Gate Cottage, and to enjoy a book seated on the wooden arbor chair that was shaded by a pink-saucer magnolia. There was so much to enjoy at the cottage that she had missed by spending all her time at the park.

Another reason to come back.

Maggie retreated to the Honda, her photo and bag of sand in hand, feeling a heartache like she had never known. The pain was worse than what she could have imagined, but she knew it was not from leaving a man behind. It was from leaving a spirit, not *the* Spirit, but the spirit that she had come to know and love the past week. It was a spirit of family, not unlike that she had experienced as a child. It was a spirit that came from a loving relationship. It was a relationship that came from a spiritual source. It was a spirit that the lone traveler had lost over the past six years.

She saw a bumper sticker in the parking lot on the car beside hers. "All who wander are not lost," Maggie read aloud. *All who wander are not lost.* A smile formed on her lips.

"Maggie, my dear child," she could imagine her grandmother saying, *"you have been on a journey. Just because you were wandering in the wrong direction does not mean that you were lost or that it was not a spiritual journey. You have learned many things, some of which* not *to do with your life. But the important thing is that you learned the things that mattered. You earned a graduate degree, but the lesson you learned this week will carry you much farther in life. Combine the education of this week with your schooling and there are no limits to what you can do."*

A couple walked up to the car beside Maggie. Seeing the faraway look in her eyes, the man asked, "Can I help you find something?"

"No, I think you already did. Is this your car?" She pointed to the car beside hers with the bumper sticker.

"Yes, it is." This time it was the man's turn to have a confused look on his face.

Maggie explained. "You see, I wandered upon this town quite by accident this week. My intention was to spend the week in Florida in the sun and the sand." She decided not to mention the manhunt. "Anyway, I read your bumper sticker and couldn't help but think that although my being here was totally by chance, I was not lost."

The man nodded.

"I understand completely," said his wife. "I bought that

sticker one day shortly after my only daughter went away to college. She was a wonderful girl . . . young woman, and we had never had any trouble out of her. But when she moved out of our house, she made some wrong decisions. I knew that she was on a detour and she would one day get back on the right path because she was filled with such goodness. Anyway, I prayed every day, on the hour, about the direction of her life."

The woman was beaming with the knowledge that not only was her purchase being appreciated, but her story was touching the life of another. "One day, while in one of these nifty gift shops of a small town, I saw this bumper sticker. It really spoke to me about my daughter, so I bought it and put it on the car. Then when I went to work, or the grocery store, or anywhere, I'd see the saying when I got in the car. It has been a constant reminder that my daughter was not completely lost, but merely wandering while finding her direction."

Maggie stared at the woman in disbelief, not at the words, but the story. "Do you mind if I ask how your daughter is doing?"

"Oh, she's doing great. She's a psychologist and she works with a drug rehab facility trying to help others who didn't get back on the right course as soon as she did. She loves her job. I think it's because she can relate to the people who live there." The glow on the woman's face brightened. "You know what they say. You can't help someone else until you've walked in their shoes."

The lady prefaced her next statement with a nod of her head. "My daughter walked alright. In her shoes and everyone else's for a while. But thank God, she wandered back onto the right track," the proud mother concluded.

The listener wanted desperately to look up to see if her grandmother was grinning down at her, but she didn't dare for fear of what the couple might think. Rather, she moved over to the woman, hugged her, and said, "Thank you for sharing that story with me. I needed to hear that." Maggie looked down at the asphalt of the parking lot. "You see, I've been a wanderer for the past few years, but I, too, had someone praying for me everyday."

"I take it those prayers have been answered?" the woman said, more in the sound of a question than a statement.

"Yes." Maggie paused for a second and took a deep breath. "Yes, they certainly have." The look of contentment on her face took up where the words left off to tell the rest of the story.

"We'd better be going," offered the man to his wife.

He turned back to Maggie and shook her hand. "It was a pleasure to meet you. Good luck with your future endeavors."

"Thank you. I appreciate that. I'm sure my life will be a lot different from now on."

She watched as the couple drove away, reading the bumper sticker again. *No, I'm not lost!* she declared, opening her car door.

On the seat lay two envelopes with her name on them. Beside them was a brown paper bag. Maggie reached for the top envelope, colored bright yellow, and opened it. She pulled out an Easter card and read the sentiment on the front before opening it to find that it was from the Golden Girls. Tucked inside the card was a small piece of paper with their names and phone number on it.

Her eyes searched the park to see if she saw the two women that she had first encountered at Miller's Luncheonette, but to no avail. They had been in the entourage of people who had come shortly after lunch. *Probably at home enjoying a banana split*, Maggie smiled.

She picked up the brown bag and pulled out a small, thin box. Inside the box was a picture frame. Maggie pulled the frame out to reveal the photograph that had been shot from the ground the evening before at precisely the exact second of the sun's set. The photo had been matted and beneath it was a poem that the photographer had written about the image of Christ in the sand.

She began to read the words slowly, tears forming in her eyes.

Cross in the Sand

With grains of sand,
He made a man,
Fulfilling God's plan,
To be all that we can.

Tempted on desert sand,
God, yet still a man,
Fulfilling God's plan,
With His help we can.

Fishermen left the sand,
To follow this man,
Fulfilling God's plan,
Change them He can.

Cloaks spread upon sand,
A colt carries this man,
Fulfilling God's plan,
Made king if they can.

But blood fills the sand,
From an innocent man,
Fulfilling God's plan,
Redeem us He can.

The stone fell to the sand,
He was more than a man,
Fulfilling God's plan
      And through faith we can.

Instead of his name, the poet closed with a footnote that read, "To Maggie, May you always remember that in your search this week, you found 'more than a man.'"

Waves of emotions flooded over her as she thought of the combined artistry of all who had been a part of this week's event. Joshua, as the sculptor; this man as a poet and photographer; the author who had come to write about the mystical event; Beth, whose expertise in reporting landed Joshua and the sculpture in the Associated Press; Marya, whose talent as an announcer had grabbed the attention of listeners around the country. The list went on and on with television reporters and photographers who had tried in some auspicious manner to capture the emotions of the week for others who had been unable to see it for themselves.

Maggie then thought of all the spectators who had visited the site. Their talent had been to take the word, the news of the event, and spread it to the masses. The masses of Findlay, the masses at work, the masses at school, the masses that would in turn spread the word. Not just of the sand sculpture in Findlay, but the Word . . . *to the world.*

And it all started with this one man, she mused, not sure whether the one man was Jesus or Joshua.

Suddenly, the impact of those two names in the same sentence hit her, as she recalled stories that her grandparents had long ago shared with her. Her thoughts stopped rambling as she made a note to check out those stories in her next reading of the Bible and in the university's library as soon as she returned to Ann Arbor.

246

She opened the second envelope to find a hand-drawn card of a floppy-eared bunny standing beside a huge Easter egg. The initials beside it told her all she needed to know, but she opened the card anyway.

"Sorry you missed your perfect man, but glad you stayed in Findlay. Hope to see you next year – same time, same place, same man." It was signed - Joshua Redford.

Tears moistened her eyes as she thought about these people who had become her friends during the week. They knew nothing about her - whether she was good, whether she was bad. Nothing except the fact that she was God's creation. And that was all they needed to know to love her.

She had left Ann Arbor looking for love and she had found it. Not in the form of a living, breathing person but in the form of *many* living, breathing persons and one living, breathing Spirit.

The urge to call her parents was so strong that she could hardly stand it. But she knew the excitement in her voice was sure to show to these two people who had been so close to her for eighteen years of her life. Maggie wanted them to see the transformation on her face and in her being. She wanted it to be a wonderful surprise for them. They had known about her plan to go to Florida, but she had neglected to call them and tell them about the detour of the week.

Now she would have much more to tell them than had she hit the sunny coast of her original destination. And she couldn't wait to see the Easter print hanging on the wall of her parents' living room beside their other Italian paintings. Maggie had decided to give them her print and that she would wait for the other one to come. Besides, she had a feeling that it would not be too long before she would be packing up to leave Ann Arbor and that would be one less thing to pack.

As much as she wished to thank Joshua, the Golden Girls and the photographer for their thoughtful sentiments, she knew they had not left them for that reason. She also knew that these three items were a part of the perfect ending to her mission of finding the perfect man.

A part of His plan, Maggie thought, feeling the watchful eyes of her grandmother looking over her shoulder as they had done on many occasions when she was a little girl.

Chapter 34
Morning, Easter Monday

After eating a baked, apple puff pancake for the last time, Maggie walked slowly back up the stairs to the Garden Villa Suite. She ran her hand across the "guardian of the stairs," as June had called it, and let her fingers cup around it, as if, by that gesture, some of its protective powers would have a lasting effect on her.

The vacationer knew that in all reality, the guardian *would* have a lasting effect on her. But the "guardian" was of a Superior Power rather than a mere bronze statue, no matter how beautiful the object.

She made the bed carefully, leaving the covers pulled back like June had for her each evening. She reached into a brown paper bag that sat beside her suitcase, pulled out two chocolate bars that she had picked up at Dietsch Brothers, and laid them on the pillow. On each of the bars was molded a special message; one read, "Happy Easter," and the other, "Thank you."

Beside the chocolate bars, she placed an envelope that

contained a note for her host and hostess who had become her surrogate parents for the week. Maggie knew this was not the last time her path would cross that of Charlie's and June's.

As she made her way back down the stairs, suitcase in hand, the host came to meet her. "Here, let me help you with that," he offered, with the same graciousness and warm smile that Maggie had encountered when she first entered Rose Gate Cottage.

June appeared behind Charlie, with Emmy following close on her heels, the dog's tail wagging ferociously in delight at the chance to be petted again by her new friend.

"This is a little going away present," June said, as she handed their guest a purple-flowered gift bag with bright, spring-colored tissue paper sticking out the top.

Maggie took the bag and reached inside. She pulled out a hand-sewn bunny, patterned after the velveteen rabbit upstairs.

"I made it just for you," her hostess said, the same child-like twinkle dancing in her eyes that Maggie had seen when she first walked through the door of Rose Gate Cottage.

The guest knew that she really *had* found family here – not just in Charlie and June, but in all the people she had met during the week's stay.

"Thank you," Maggie said, looking lovingly at the stuffed animal in her hand. It was then that she noticed the eyes were blue buttons with maize thread. "Oh, thank you, thank you both," she exclaimed, hugging the bunny, then the man and woman who had opened their home to her.

Emmy barked, letting Maggie know that she was also a part of this family.

"And thank you, too, Emmy," Maggie added, stooping down to give the white Maltese a big rub.

The surprised guest knew she had to get out before she burst into tears, so she opened the door and led the procession down the front steps and to her Honda. She looked around one last time at the porch and the deck with their rockers, and touched one of the blooms of the pink-saucer magnolia.

"It's been a pleasure, an absolute pleasure," she managed shakily, giving the host and hostess one last hug after her suitcase had been shut away in the car's trunk.

She waved good-bye as she exited the driveway. The sojourner turned toward the Swan House Tea Room so that she could briefly relive her lunch of being a "proper lady."

A proper lady to go with a perfect man.

Maggie smiled. She had learned so much during the course of this week – much more than she had in all her years of cramming for a degree at U-M. She had driven into this town, a degree in hand, but still donning a ball cap, with her hair in a ponytail sticking out the back of it. And she was leaving this town with her hair down, no more double identity, and an education of the things that *really* mattered in life.

Chapter 35
Mid-morning, Easter Monday

It had been exactly one week ago today that Maggie first entered Miller's Luncheonette. She couldn't believe how fast the week had flown by, but at the same time, she was blown away by all that had taken place within that short span, most of it inside her.

Tomorrow is definitely *going to be the start of a diet*!

Maggie wasn't hungry, having just finished breakfast at the Rose Gate Cottage. But somehow it seemed sacrilegious to leave Findlay without first stopping by Miller's to say good-bye to Joni, the woman who had first encouraged her to stay in this small town to search for her man.

Between all that food and being filled by the Holy Spirit, I am definitely full.

A broad smile spread across her face as she thought how the food would be worked off, and the Spirit would continue to grow.

"I came to say goodbye," Maggie said, bouncing in the

back door of the luncheonette and finding an empty seat while adding, "and I don't need a menu. I'll have a Number 1, eggs scrambled . . ."

"And an iced tea, light ice and rye toast," Joni interrupted. "A regular already," she said with a smile, one that matched her customer's, splashed across her face as she yelled the order back to the grill cook.

"Yeah, I kinda hate to leave this place."

"I told you we had a few single men around here. And I'm sure we could find you a job somewhere in town."

"Thanks for the offer," Maggie said appreciatively, genuinely grateful for the waitress' concern. "But I've met the only man I need for a while. I've decided there are a few things in my life I need to get in order before I do anything else, or try to have any kind of a relationship."

The newest regular of Miller's looked around the establishment. *Funny,* she thought as she looked around at the walls, again reading all the articles about the diner and its place in the history and society of Findlay, *this small house of service offers much more, with longer lasting rewards, than the establishment where I work. Correction . . .* worked!

Maggie loved the atmosphere of the slow, relaxed group of customers that had dwindled in between the breakfast and the lunch crowd. They were all lost in their own worlds rather than being a part of the "what's-happenin'-in-Findlay-today" crew that congregated each morning.

One of the yellowed pages that hung on the wall caught her eye as she spied everything she could, wanting to take every piece of this place possible home with her – *wherever that is.* The page had been there the entire week, but it wasn't until now that it screamed at her. Maggie chuckled. *I know why, too,* she mouthed, reading the words of the paper to herself.

It was an advertisement announcing Valentine's Day from

sometime shortly after 1949 when Miller's first opened. *"Sweet-heart Special: Saturday, February 14ᵗʰ. $2.09 – Treat Your Valentine to a Choice T-Bone Steak – 12 oz. Choice of Potato, Salad, Rolls, Coffee."*

She sat there and envisioned her grandparents sitting in this same place, more than fifty years prior, enjoying a candle-light dinner, then driving to Riverside Park and walking beside Blanchard River, holding hands, while her grandfather sang *Down By the Old Mill Stream* to her grandmother. They could have very easily fit in this place. Then she pondered on all the places they had spent Valentine's Day around the world in their lives of mission.

A complacent smile hung on her face as she thought about the Valentine special again. She had come here on her way to find the love of her life. Little did she know that she truly *would* find the greatest love of her entire life. Maggie had no idea what her future would hold, or whether she would ever find a companion. But she did know if that day ever came, it would not have as great an impact on her life as the find of this past week.

Her thoughts were interrupted by Joni's arrival with two plates. One had the traditional No. 1 and the other had a Belgian waffle topped off with fresh berries and whipped cream. "A little going away present."

"Thanks again," Maggie uttered, touched to tears. "You're making it terribly difficult for me to leave, you know."

"I just want to make sure you come back. I've gotten used to you this week. You're not like the usual tourist that comes in for Joshua's sculptures."

"Maybe that's because I didn't come for the sculpture. That seems to have been God's idea."

Joni paused at the table for a moment longer. "That's a beautiful necklace. Did you find it here?"

"No, it's actually an heirloom from my grandmother. I was named after her. The funny thing is that it had gotten shoved under some things in my suitcase almost two years ago, where it remained hidden up under the wheels, and I didn't find it until I was packing to leave here. Isn't that strange?"

"No stranger than anything else that went on around here this week," Joni noted.

Maggie caught herself almost saying, "I heard that." But instead, she rephrased her words. "I guess you're right."

"By the way, what was your grandmother's name?"

"Mary Magdalena. And I'm going to use my full name now in recognition of my love and appreciation of her."

Joni looked at Maggie in disbelief. She had just made the comment that the week had been full of strange surprises, but she appeared rather jolted by the customer's response. When she managed to catch her composure and speak again, she asked, "Did you know that Mary Magdalene was the first person that the risen Christ chose to allow to see him?"

"No, I didn't," Maggie answered, with an expression that spoke of sincere pride that Joni had recognized that fact. "Or shall I say that I had consciously forgotten about that until my trip to the bookstore this week . . . with the help of your directions, I might add," she winked at the waitress.

"That name holds great significance. What an honor," exclaimed Joni.

"I'm glad you said that. I had been a little afraid that people would only remember Mary Magdalene's dark past. I figured I would get lots of sideway glances when I returned home and announced that I was going to be using my full name, then blurted it out."

"You hold your head up high every time you tell someone your name," the waitress encouraged.

"Thanks for the words of wisdom. I will."

Joni left Maggie to eat her breakfast, which seemed even better than usual this morning. *Maybe I've forgotten how good cooked food can be,* wondering if she would return to her steady diet of only fruit and salads. *Maybe I can splurge once in a while if I'm careful,* she decided.

"How is everything?" Joni asked, when she returned with a fresh glass of tea.

"Same as it's been all week. Great!" Maggie decided to really play the part of a regular. "And give my compliments to the chef," she yelled across the room, causing everyone, including the owner, who was cooking this morning, to turn and look at her.

Most of them gave her a nod accompanied by a smile, recognizing her from her visits earlier in the week.

Maggie carefully observed the actions of the employees who made this place "home" for all who entered its doors. She loved the way Joni glared over her glasses and yelled the words of each customer's order, while she stood in place beside the tables, her pad and pen still in her hand. And even better was the way the usual grill cook glared back over her glasses, but never said a word to acknowledge the waitress. The customer began to wonder if they ever messed up an order, but she knew better than to ask.

However, as the waitress made her next round with the coffee pot, there was one question that Maggie felt compelled to ask. "Joni, do you remember what you said about that sand, and people being drawn to it, earlier this week?"

"Yeah. What about it?"

"You were right," the visitor acknowledged. "The sand *did* call my name."

The waitress gazed at Maggie with a look that told her customer something she should have already guessed.

"You knew all along that I'd never leave here, didn't you?"

Maggie asked, beginning to feel like the young boy she had seen at the park with all his "Whys?"

Joni simply nodded to the affirmative, offering no words. "How did you know?"

"Because it was written all over your face from that first morning." Joni put down the coffee pot and took a seat at Maggie's table. "You were in search of something, for sure, but your expression said it all. There was something more than just a man missing in your life. I've seen the influence of that sand before, and I knew you were the honored guest to find meaning in it this year."

Maggie sat there, a lump welling up in her throat, knowing that Joni was yet another of the angels that had been used to answer her grandmother's prayer.

"Easter is the season for miracles," she could remember her grandmother saying, in a voice that was so soft that you had to pay close attention just to hear it, but that was so powerful in its words that you were glad you did. Maggie imagined that was much the way that Jesus spoke. And she wondered if her grandmother purposefully asked for her prayer concerning her granddaughter to be answered during the Easter season.

Knowing her grandmother Mary Magdalena, and the pride with which she bore that name, Maggie didn't waste any more time on that question.

The guest left a generous tip, along with her address and the invitation to write. On top of the money and the note, she left two small chocolate bars; one that had the words, "Happy Easter," and another that read, "Thank you." After giving Joni a huge hug, she left Miller's Luncheonette for the last time - at least until next year when she planned to bring her friends to find the "Man" of their lives.

She stood outside under the antique neon sign that had first drawn her into this restaurant with its red letters that said simply, "E-A-T." Taking her camera from her purse, Maggie decided she had to have a picture of this place. The visitor aimed the lens at the front of the building so she could capture the customers and workers inside. Then she looked straight up at the sign to catch its letters. As she snapped the shot, she muttered, with a smirk, "They should have named it 'Miller's Good Time Kitchen.'"

Maggie took one long, last look down Main Street at the row of family-owned and operated businesses that had not only stood the test of time, but had run many corporate businesses out of town. Findlay was hometown. It was the kind of place you wanted to live and raise your kids. It was family.

She got in her Honda, folded up the map that never got used, and put it back in the glove compartment. Before hitting the interstate, Maggie drove by the sculpture, where she had to stop for one last look. She wanted to take out her camera for a lasting photo, but she knew that the picture would never hold the awe and magnitude that would be forever etched in her mind. A few minutes passed while she stood at the base of the cross looking up into the face of Christ. It seemed impossible that a human could have captured the details of that face and body.

But he was truly inspired by God, she thought, recapturing the vision of the artist at work. *I guess there's no limit to what one can do when it is of God*, Maggie reasoned as she turned toward her car, recalling the state's motto.

And the elements of nature did *seem to add a dimension that Joshua couldn't.* She pursed her lips, realizing that the Master's Hand had picked up where the master's hand left off. *The realistic features truly* are *of God!*

Something inside her pulled her back to the temporary fence that had been placed around the sculpture. She stood with her fingers grasping the top edge of it while she gazed again at the mural of sand that lay in front of her. Tears began to move down Maggie's cheek, slowly at first, and then rushing down the curve of her face.

The spectator didn't reach up to wipe them away, but let them run down her face, some hitting her shirt, some hitting the ground. Each tear was like a seed of love that had been planted inside her by the events of the week – *Holy Week*.

The seeds were far more reaching than simply the sculpture she now stared at – albeit that was enough. But they were planted by Joni, the Golden Girls, the man at Dietsch Brothers, the saleswoman in the Maranatha Bookstore, Charlie and June (and Emmy), Jewel, Chic, Beth, Mayor and Mrs. Anderson, the giant, the pierced man, the woman who kept watch, Yogi . . . *and Joshua and his helpmate, Lynn.*

There's more than just that woman behind the power of Joshua, Maggie reasoned as she thought about the artist.

There was the power of the man depicted in the sculpture, and that power was the same Power that was behind each of the individuals who had planted a seed of love inside her during the week. It was the Power of the man who lay portrayed on the cross.

And it was the same Power that was behind all her tears. Tears of guilt that had vanished during the course of the week, tears of joy at her discovery of the "perfect man."

Maggie remembered the humbleness she had felt only four evenings ago at the Holy Thursday service when the priest had washed others' feet in recognition of that act of service Christ had bestowed upon his own disciples.

Her tears now felt like a washing of her entire being – her heart, her soul, her body . . . *her thoughts.*

Maggie's thoughts turned to her past, her present, and her future. There were many things that she had anticipated would be changed by this week's happenings. And there were many things that now *were* indeed changed. In fact, she felt that this week had been an answer to a prayer – *not mine, but my grandmother's.* She thought how proud her grandmother would have been that her prayer of many years had been heard and truly answered, even after her death.

"It is finished," she whispered, her eyes still full of tears. Her statement spoke both of the words she had read over and over during the past few days, and her vacation. Her "mission" had been accomplished. She had not only *found* the "perfect man," but she was taking him home with her, and she was sharing him with all her friends.

Candice had been right in her warning, "Be careful what you ask for. You may get more than you bargained for."

Maggie originally had no intention of sharing her man with anyone, especially the beautiful girls with whom she worked. But now, she couldn't wait for that golden opportunity to present itself. And just as she had met *her* "perfect" man, she knew God would provide that "perfect" moment for their introduction to that man.

As for now, though, walking across the parking lot for the last time, Maggie found herself at a loss for words concerning anything that had happened during the past week. *How will I ever explain to the girls what took place?* Even with all the communication skills she had learned in her college classes, nothing had prepared her for what she had experienced during her spring break.

Her mind recalled a favorite quote by Marcel Marceau. "Do not the most moving moments of our lives find us all without words?" She thought of Marceau's successful and famously noted career of expressing himself without ever verbalizing his thoughts.

And that's how I'll leave the girls. The gift I leave behind will tell them all they need to know. There's nothing I could possibly say that would equal those words.

Maggie's mind was made up. She would say good-bye, bid them blessings, and walk out the door – *forever*.

Knowing her boss, she would probably lose her final check, but that was okay. She had only worked two days on the week of the next paycheck, and as far as she was concerned, she didn't want to see that money anyway. There was something disgusting and "unclean" about the way she had earned it, and Maggie knew, given all the other unexplainable events of the week, that somehow the money would never be missed.

ೞೞ

She looked across the sky and examined the clouds as she got back on the interstate, northbound for Ann Arbor. They seemed to march across the light blue backdrop, parading for all the interested onlookers, proudly displaying their shapes to arouse the viewers' minds and spark their imaginations.

There was a playful spunk in Maggie's own spirit. She felt like a child again, having attended a *real* tea party this week, having gone down the slide board, having swung as high as the park's swings would allow, having played in the sand, and having enjoyed chocolates and ice cream almost every day.

Her childlike faith was bouncing through her, causing a giddiness she had not known in years, and releasing a joyful calm that had been absent since her childhood.

ೞೞ

The drive home gave Maggie time to contemplate what was going to happen next. Looking out over the acres that rambled for miles, revealing nothing but flatland and farms, she chided herself for trying to escape all this exactly a week ago.

She noticed that every farm had a resting tree - the one tree left standing out in the middle of a field where the farmers and the livestock could rest under the shade. Maggie found herself looking for these signs of comfort as she passed each farm.

It seemed strange that all the things she had taken for granted, or tried to leave behind, were the very things that were speaking to her on the way back to Ann Arbor. She slowly thought back through the events of the past seven days.

During that week, she had learned more than she had her entire college career, and she reveled in the fact that she had come to see and accept the beauty in everything around her.

She knew she could never return to the same line of work. Her present thought was to find an area of expertise that would allow her to follow in her grandmother's footsteps of helping others. Her degree of Public Policy held the possibility of many open doors for her. And she knew she would approach those doors one step, *or one plank*, at a time.

Maggie knew that if she prayed as diligently as her grandmother, using the beads and the cross as a daily reminder, she would find which direction to take. Aware that she could be recognized from her past identities, and the taunting she might endure because of the name, she had first feared a crucifixion of her own. But she decided to be proud and hold her head high, satisfied that she was forgiven by the One that mattered.

Others would never understand the change that had transpired in her during the past week. And more than that, there was no way she could explain it. She made up her mind not to worry needlessly, and let time, *and God*, take care of whatever problems arose from her past, if any.

The traffic already backing up on the interstate was no surprise for Maggie, for she had expected all the Easter vacationers to be rushing back to their homes before a new week of the stresses of work and the rat race called "life."

And after all the incidents of the week, the truck in front of her also came as no surprise, but was rather expected. On its bumper were proudly displayed the words, "Real men love Jesus."

Maggie could not resist the urge to roll down her window as she sped up to make her way around the truck. She pulled up beside it, waved at the driver and yelled, "Cool bumper sticker. Real women love Jesus, too!"

The guy in the truck waved back and shot her a thumbs-up sign as she passed.

Chapter 36
Mid-afternoon, Easter Monday

"So, Maggie, how were the sun and the sand?" shot Kara, the minute her co-worker walked in the door.

"Absolutely breathtaking. The weather was perfect. The food was delicious. There were people there from everywhere enjoying the view and the magical, mystical aura it created. I made lots of new friends and got some really cool souvenirs to remember my most memorable, and I must add, *most successful*, search for the perfect man."

"Tell us about the men, Maggie," urged Sabrina.

"You mean you didn't have enough here of your own?" Maggie chided.

"C'mon," coaxed Valerie. "We all know about these men. Tell us about the 'real' men."

"Well, on the first morning I was there, I met the cutest guy I've ever seen," she offered, thinking of the fire hydrant. "He was absolutely adorable, although he was quite short and didn't have anything to say. I really wish I could have brought him home with me, though."

"Did you get to use the blanket?" asked Ebony.

"Every single night," Maggie answered, with a smug, secretive glimmer in her eye.

The women reeled off question after question trying to pry every detail out of the one who had the spunk to do what all of them wished they could have done. As quickly as they rattled off their inquiries, she popped off answers, never giving away what really happened.

Candice noticed the beads around Maggie's neck. "Did he give you this?" she asked, reaching up and carefully sliding her fingers under the cross and admiring its beauty.

"You could say that," Maggie replied, still not giving away too much information while enjoying the curious interest she was building in all her co-workers.

"Woo," all the women joined in, lightly ribbing Maggie, yet congratulating her with pats on the back, thumbs-up signs and high-fives.

Each of the women noticed the difference in the returning vacationer's demeanor as they looked from one another, making sure the others also saw the change in their friend.

"That's enough rambling," said Kara.

"Yeah, tell us all about your perfect man," begged Ebony.

Maggie sat down, the other women following her lead. "To tell the truth, he really *is* the perfect man. He's the most gentle, compassionate man I've ever met. Yet, at the same time, he possesses strength like I've never seen.

"And he listens so intently to every word I say to him." The gaze in her eyes indicated that this was more than the mere dreaminess of infatuation or a new fling. It was clearly obvious that Maggie had found a true love during the days she had been gone.

"When are you going to meet his family?" Valerie asked,

wanting to see exactly how serious her friend really was about this man.

"I've already met his Father. And I feel that I know his closest friends just from spending the week with him."

"So what's the father like?"

"Well, you could put it this way. They most definitely fit the saying, "Like Father, like Son.""

"Does he feel the same about you as you do about him?"

"I think I can safely say that he loves me more than anyone else ever could. And I know that we are going to be inseparable for the rest of my life. I intend to spend every single day and night with him. And he's taking me out of here immediately. No more working in this type of job for Miss Maggie Matelli."

The women that had worked so closely with this transformed lady in front of them stood amazed. There was no jealousy among them, for Maggie was not bragging in her sharing of the facts about this strange, yet glorious, man she had encountered during the past week. The sincerity of her love and devotion for him was evident in her speech, so clearly that they felt a pride for her rather than a covetous attitude.

"Maggie," stated Valerie, "I really didn't put too much stock in this idea of yours about spending a week in the sun and the sand looking for a man. You fully expected to find just the right man, and from the sound of it, you have found exactly what you need for life." The motherly figure of the group was carrying out her typical role.

"I heard that," Ebony smiled, trying to lighten the mood. She gave Maggie a huge hug. "Girl, it really does sound like you found the perfect man."

"Yeah, that's most definitely the kind of man I want to meet," Sabrina said, dreamily.

"I heard that," laughed Kara, poking Ebony in the ribs with her elbow.

"Here, let me introduce you," Maggie offered, as she reached into the shopping bag and pulled out wrapped packages for each of the girls.

They looked at her spellbound as they began to unwrap the boxes to display their carefully chosen contents.

"Are you crazy?" asked Kara, looking around at the other girls to see if they were as puzzled as she was.

"Yes, crazy in love," Maggie answered simply.

She reached in another small tote and pulled out plastic bags of sand from the sculpture for each girl, along with a chocolate bar that read, "Best wishes to you."

After giving each of the women a long hug, she started toward the door, but stopped just before she got there. "Oh, and I did find out one other thing," Maggie added. "Real men love Jesus." Then she headed for the old silver Honda.

The girls noticed the light step in her walk that spoke of a confidence about who she was and where she was going.

"Boy, I don't know where she's been, but I sure wish I had been there with her," Sabrina said, still watching Maggie.

"I heard that," added Ebony.

"And I know who's going to be the first one in the car next year," pronounced Candice, with a longing in her eyes.

"We'll have to draw straws for that honor, I'm afraid," Valerie stated, settling the case.

Each of the girls went back to their own lives, with a Bible, a bag of sand, a chocolate bar, and a whole new world of thoughts.

Thoughts of a wondrous attraction . . . a wondrous beauty . . . on a far away hill.

CB80

Mary Magdalena turned out of the parking lot of Northern Exposure. Her mind gave little thought to the fact that this would be the last time she would ever leave this establishment. Rather, her mind was too busy as it leapt forward to her next stop. She was headed to Cleveland, to the crypt where her grandmother, her namesake, had been laid to rest in the Lake View Cemetery next to Little Italy where she had grown up.

The granddaughter knew that her grandmother was no longer at the burial site, but it was the nearest thing to both a closure and a new beginning that she could make, in her mind's way of thinking. After that, she had no idea where she would go, but she felt sure that when the time came, her beloved Raboni, her new teacher would give her that direction, *and he'll take every step with me.*

What she did know was that she wanted to follow in the footsteps of her grandmother, always wearing the beads and cross that had served as a symbol of love, from both her great-grandfather and her Heavenly Father, to the namesake who had preceded her. During the week, Mary Magdalena had learned that there was a purpose for her life, a very special purpose, and that she wanted to be known, to go down in history, for her love for Christ Jesus.

It had been a long time since she had visited her hometown, and its neighboring cemetery. In fact, it had been on the occasion of her grandfather's burial. Just as her grandmother, Mary Magdalena, had found a man to share in a wonderful life of believing and serving, Maggie felt confident that her "perfect man" would lead her to do the same . . . *in the right time.*

She began to sing, "Down by the old mill stream, where I first met you . . ."

Sun, sand, a waterfront . . . and a perfect man. Yes, Miss Mary Magdalena Matelli had accomplished everything she had set out to do on her trip. A large smile swept across her face, expressing her sheer excitement, that through the master's hands, the Master's Plan was fulfilled, as were her plans.

The master's plan via the Master's Plan! She laughed aloud. *Wouldn't Grandmother be proud that I remembered her words?*

Her words suddenly changed as she added them to music, "*I will cling to the old rugged cross, and exchange it some day for a crown.*"

The Old Rugged Cross

On a hill far away stood an old rugged cross,
the emblem of suff'ring and shame;
and I love that old cross where the dearest and best
for a world of lost sinners was slain.

O that old rugged cross, so despised by the world,
has a wondrous attraction for me;
for the dear Lamb of God left his glory above
to bear it to dark Calvary.

In the old rugged cross, stained with blood so divine,
a wondrous beauty I see,
for 'twas on that old cross Jesus suffered and died,
to pardon and sanctify me.

To the old rugged cross I will ever be true,
its shame and reproach gladly bear;
then he'll call me some day to my home far away,
where his glory forever I'll share.

So I'll cherish the old rugged cross,
till my trophies at last I lay down;
I will cling to the old rugged cross,
and exchange it some day for a crown.

~ George Bennard ~

Most people experience personal tragedy at some point in life and Maggie Matelli - although fictional - is no exception. We choose the wrong path or wander too close to the edge of the right one, and the threads of decency that are woven into our moral fibers become stretched and misaligned. It is at these times the dreaded wolf of despair stalks us at close range, waiting for the first opportunity to ravage our last remaining seeds of hope.

Hope is that which pushes us forward when all else threatens to immobilize our progress, and in the worst of times, drags us backwards. In teaching Bible studies, we often liken hope to hunger pangs; although both are absolutely intangible, you know when you've encountered one of them.

Hope is evidenced in the twinkling eyes of the dying. It's the quickened pace in the step of the weary. And it's the only remedy for despair. There is no more pitiful state than that of hopelessness.

There was One who came to abolish the eternal state of hopelessness and it is the author's sole desire that you found Him in the pages of this book. Catherine Ritch Guess is no stranger to the taunts of despair. We have watched her overcome personal tragedy and been amazed at her resolve to conquer her fears, and the looming despair that accompanies devastating adversity. Catherine's focus on her Father's will for her life is steadfast, and continually enables her to resurrect from near defeat. Her talent and skill for writing, combined with her passion for serving others, bears the proof of her calling.

As we are generally our own worst critics, it is most difficult to forgive ourselves. Life's struggles are often worse in our thoughts, due to our personal fear, than they are in real life. For once we reach out, Christ is always there to give us a hand. The study questions that follow are to help direct and focus your thoughts in the areas of atonement and forgiveness of yourself, as well as others.

We join Catherine in encouraging you to pursue hope and the One who offers it freely to all. And it is our hope at CRM BOOKS that through our line of Reality Fiction, you will find strength and comfort for your own experiences of life.

~~ *C.J. Didymus - Cheryl Karst & Jackie Dasher* ~~

Whether you are reading these questions individually, or as part of a Bible study or reading group, you are encouraged to let the words and ideas flow freely as you reflect on your own life and situation. In fact, I recommend that you write your answers on a piece of paper and place them inside the back cover of this book. Come back to them - a day later, a week later, a month later, or even years laters - as Maggie came back to the note and gift from her grandmother. Your words will speak to you so loudly that it will seem God ordained them for that very moment.   *-- CR?*

1) Isaiah 53:6 tells us, "All we like sheep have gone astray." Where have you gone astray in your life?

2) Think of all the characters in *Old Rugged Cross* who served others in various ways. How do you serve others?

3) The woman who stayed at the sculpture on Saturday evening gave out tiny angels. Her one small act touched the lives of everyone at Riverside Park. And when the gifts were used together, they gave off light into a night of darkness. What gifts do you leave behind to remind others of Jesus? And what can you do to offer light to someone groping in a world of darkness?

4) We meet people each day - at work, in the mall, on the street - who could easily be someone sent into our lives to help us along our spiritual journey. Who have you run into lately that could have played the role of the Centurion; Mary Magdalene; Mary, mother of Jesus; the angel of the Lord; a disciple; or Christ?

5) Many people have distanced themselves from a loved one - either consciously or unconsciously - at some point in their life. It is never too late to rekindle that relationship, whether the distance has been for a day or many years. Is there someone in your life who needs your love? Or someone from whom you should seek forgiveness?

Reality Fiction

The writing style of Catherine Ritch Guess has become synonymous with the term "Reality Fiction" since she opened her own niche in the inspirational market nearly three years ago.

Her novels, most of which are based in real settings, feature realistic characters and situations of contemporary society, and are spiced with historical facts. Although the stories, characters and locales are used fictitiously, her mission is that readers will find themselves within the pages of her writings.

From the letters she receives, it is obvious that her idea of Reality Fiction is working as it ministers to her readers. She intends her work to plant seeds and meet the needs of individuals who would never venture inside a house of worship or pick up a Bible. And for believers, she strives to help strengthen their spiritual lives by weaving a wealth of theology between the lines.

Her message is "if God can love the characters within my pages, he can love everyone." It is her hope and dream that readers will be uplifted in their own individual lives and situations through her characters and their stories.

About the Artist

Roger Powell, whose sand sculpture of Christ on the cross was the inspiration for *Old Rugged Cross* receives the inspiration for his artwork through his love for Christ. Each year during Holy Week, he completes a sand sculpture for the Easter season in his hometown of Findlay, Ohio, at Riverside Park. In addition, his sculptures have been featured at festivals and children's events, on beaches, and on his front lawn for the general public to enjoy.

The artist, whose subjects vary from religious to surrealistic, enjoys sculpting with various mediums including clay, snow and sand. His greatest creative pleasure comes in the form of ink drawings. Powell's career as a landscape architect allows him to express his artistic talent daily.

His works may be viewed at RogerPowellArt.com

About the Author

Catherine Ritch Guess, also a published composer, served as an Organist/Minister of Music for over three decades before turning to a career of writing, speaking and performing for a variety of venues.

Guess, who holds degrees in Church Music, Music Education and a Master's Degree in Christian Education, is a Diaconal Minister of the United Methodist Church. She is currently appointed as the Circuit Riding Musician, a position which allows her to serve globally through her writing and musical talents.

Her next novels include *There's a Song in the Air*, featuring NASCAR driver Dale Jarrett as the main character; *Let Us Break Bread Together*, the sequel to *Old Rugged Cross*; and *On Eagle's Wings*, the third volume of Eagle's Wings Trilogy.

When Catherine is not "on the circuit," she spends her time in the Blue Ridge Mountains of North Carolina.